Shattered

James Patterson is one of the best-known and biggest-selling writers of all time. His books have sold in excess of 400 million copies worldwide. He is the author of some of the most popular series of the past two decades – the Alex Cross, Women's Murder Club, Detective Michael Bennett and Private novels – and he has written many other number one bestsellers including stand-alone thrillers and non-fiction.

James is passionate about encouraging children to read. Inspired by his own son who was a reluctant reader, he also writes a range of books for young readers including the Middle School, Dog Diaries, Treasure Hunters and Max Einstein series. James has donated millions in grants to independent bookshops and has been the most borrowed author in UK libraries for the past thirteen years in a row. He lives in Florida with his family.

James O. Born is an award-winning crime and science-fiction novelist as well as a career law-enforcement agent. A native Floridian, he still lives across the Indian River from NASA.

PERSONNEL FILE

Req #: 2014-PL-10945
File #:

TO BE FILLED IN BY IMMEDIATE SUPERIOR:

Detective
MICHAEL BENNETT ☑

6 FOOT 3 INCHES (191CM) 200 POUNDS (91KG)
IRISH AMERICAN

EMPLOYMENT

Bennett joined the police force to uncover the truth
at all costs. He started his career in the Bronx's
49th Precinct. He then transferred to the NYPD's
Major Case Squad and remained there until he moved
to the Manhattan North Homicide Squad.

EDUCATION

Bennett graduated from Regis High School and studied
philosophy at Manhattan College.

FAMILY HISTORY

Bennett was previously married to Maeve, who worked as a
nurse on the trauma ward at Jacobi Hospital in the Bronx.
However, Maeve died tragically young after losing a battle
with cancer in December 2007, leaving Bennett to raise
their ten adopted children: Chrissy, Shawna, Trent, Eddie,
twins Fiona and Bridget, Ricky, Brian, Jane and Juliana.

Following Maeve's death, over time Bennett grew closer to
the children's nanny, Mary Catherine. After years of on-
off romance, Bennett and Mary Catherine decided to commit
to one another, and now happily raise the family together.
Also in the Bennett household is his Irish grandfather,
Seamus, who is a Catholic priest.

PROFILE: ☐ AMENDED REPORT

BENNETT IS AN EXPERT IN HOSTAGE NEGOTIATION,
TERRORISM, HOMICIDE AND ORGANIZED CRIME. HE WILL STOP
AT NOTHING TO GET THE JOB DONE AND PROTECT THE CITY
AND THE PEOPLE HE LOVES, EVEN IF THIS MEANS DISOBEYING
ORDERS AND IGNORING PROTOCOL. DESPITE THESE UNORTHODOX
METHODS, HE IS A RELENTLESS, DETERMINED AND IN MANY
WAYS INCOMPARABLE DETECTIVE.

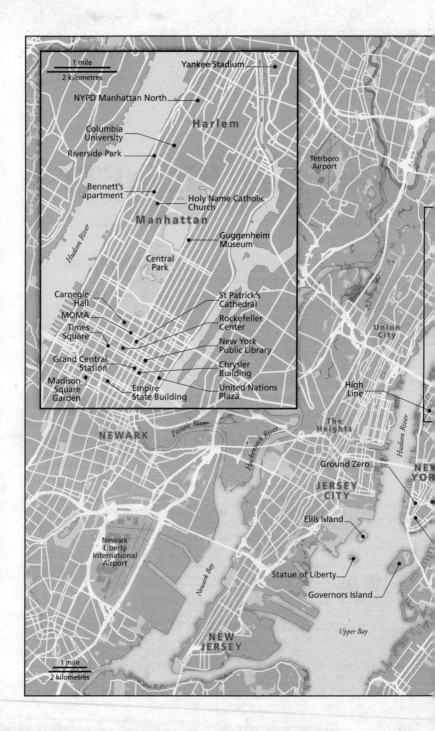

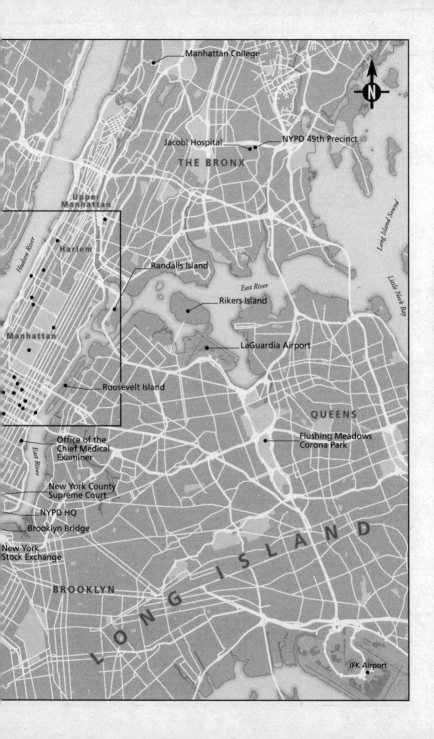

A list of titles by James Patterson appears
at the back of this book

JAMES PATTERSON

& JAMES O. BORN

Shattered

PENGUIN BOOKS

PENGUIN BOOKS

UK | USA | Canada | Ireland | Australia
India | New Zealand | South Africa

Penguin Books is part of the Penguin Random House group of companies
whose addresses can be found at global.penguinrandomhouse.com.

Penguin
Random House
UK

First published in the UK by Century in 2022
Published in Penguin Books 2023
001

Typeset by Jouve (UK), Milton Keynes
Printed and bound in Great Britain by Clays Ltd, Elcograf S.p.A.

The authorised representative in the EEA is Penguin Random House Ireland,
Morrison Chambers, 32 Nassau Street, Dublin D02 YH68

A CIP catalogue record for this book is available from the British Library

ISBN: 978–1–529–15834–2
ISBN: 978–1–529–15835–9 (export edition)

MIX
Paper from
responsible sources
FSC® C018179

Shattered

PROLOGUE

EARLY MORNING WAS one of her favorite times of the day. The sun had just cracked the horizon and traffic was still light. She was in training for the Marine Corps Marathon and intended to put in some decent miles today to make sure she was ready to race in November.

On her way to the Potomac, she would've run in the grass to protect her knees and work a little harder, but an early autumn drizzle had fallen overnight, and the road was as damp as she could manage. She'd already cut through President's Park and was almost halfway through Foggy Bottom.

When she approached the Potomac River Freeway, shit started to get weird.

She wasn't paranoid, but her instinct cued danger. She dismissed the feeling at first and kept her pace. Finally, as she came up on a clump of trees and bushes, she slowed to a jog, backward.

She justified that she was following advice from a series of monthly columnists in *Runner's World*, using all the muscles in her legs from different angles.

She worked her quadriceps as her eyes scanned the road and buildings in every direction. Nothing.

It was just her mind playing tricks. It had been an odd, emotional week. That was half the reason for the long run. To dig her way out of the funk she was in.

She fell back into the rhythm of her run. Her ASICS Gel trainers barely tapped the ground as she mentally prepared to sprint. That's when she felt a cramping sensation in her shoulders. It was the grip of someone's hands.

She involuntarily let out a sound like "Yoww." And just like she'd been trained in countless defensive tactics classes, she swung first her left elbow then her right behind her. The blows didn't seem to make a solid connection.

Now the strong hands were around her throat. She had to break free before the grip managed to cut off her wind. Now she felt the panic shooting through her. Her heart felt like it was racing at almost two hundred beats a minute.

She tried to yell for help just as a hand closed on the front of her throat and cut off her breath before it could build into a scream.

That's when the attacker's grip loosened.

The rising sun and the streetlight cast a blurry glare over the attacker's facial features. Both hands turned her around, clamped around her throat, and suddenly restricted airflow to her lungs.

She looked at the attacker in shock. Her vision started to swim. Somehow she managed to croak, "This is a mistake."

CHAPTER 1

DID YOU HEAR that?"

I listened for a moment and said, "What?"

Mary Catherine said, "It sounded like a growl."

I stifled a laugh. "You mean like a wolf or a bear?"

"It certainly wasn't a poodle in a purse like we'd see in Manhattan."

"They haven't had predators like that in Ireland for hundreds of years. Maybe it's the hound of the Baskervilles. Like in the movie where Basil Rathbone played Sherlock Holmes. A Great Dane. Ha."

We were near the top of Howth Head, a short drive from Dublin. My wife of nine days was hearing the calls of imaginary wildlife. Or was she? I froze for a moment and heard the low, guttural growl of a large animal.

As I pulled myself up the last incline, I saw it. I slowly stood up and held both my hands out. I said in a soft voice, "Hey there." I was staring into the eyes of a black Rottweiler that had to be at least 120 pounds. I tried to signal to Mary Catherine to stay on the lower part of the path. I heard her quick intake of air and knew she saw the dog too.

It dipped its head and growled again. The muscles in its shoulders and back popped as it moved slowly from side to side. The hair on its back stiffened. I wanted to tell Mary Catherine to run, but that might attract the dog's attention.

Our eyes met. I assessed the risk of facing down a dangerous animal. Then I noticed something. Just a hint of a movement. In the stub of its tail. On a whim I said, "Who's a good boy?"

The tail started wagging, fast, like a metronome trying to beat out the rhythm to "Flight of the Bumblebee." I stood up straight. The dog waddled toward me, tail still shooting back and forth. The dog's thick fur felt nice between my fingers. The dog rubbed against my leg, looking for more attention.

Mary Catherine climbed the few steps up to me and said, "You make friends wherever you go. You think it's lost?"

I shook my head as I rubbed the dog's back. It was well cared for. I kneeled to get a look at the tag on the collar.

Just then, a boy, about seven, appeared on the path in front of us. He called out, "C'mere, Lulubell." The dog turned and followed the boy. They trotted away together without another look back.

Mary Catherine said, "Lulubell. Of course a female found Michael Bennett charming." She wrapped her arms around me from behind and kissed me on the shoulder in relief. I had to turn around and give her a kiss on the lips.

I couldn't believe how great this trip had been, how different it was from my everyday life. It was the first time we'd ever been able to let go together. No work, no kids, and no responsibilities.

It was the last full day of our honeymoon in Ireland. I couldn't have wanted to accomplish any more. We had connected with some of Mary Catherine's family and even met a few of my grandfather's cousins. Their favorite saying was that everyone in Ireland had a cousin in New York City.

As we were starting our hike back to the car, Mary Catherine said she wanted to play a game. Name one of our children, she said, softening her command with a smile, and their most obvious attribute. Quick as I could.

Mary Catherine started by saying, "Juliana, talented. Jane, smart. Brian, determined. Ricky, funny. Trent, thoughtful."

When she paused for breath, I jumped in. "Eddie, spontaneous. Fiona, clever. Bridget, serene. Shawna, loving. Chrissy, sweet." I took a quick breath and said, "Great game—I win."

Mary Catherine went to give me a playful shove, but I turned so she fell into my embrace. Then we exchanged a long, loving kiss until we found ourselves lying in clover, making out like teenagers.

I had to whisper to her, "I've never been this happy, and you've never looked so beautiful."

CHAPTER 2

MARY CATHERINE GIGGLED when I tried to fit my six-foot-three frame in the bed in our cozy bed-and-breakfast.

She said, "You look like a cartoon giraffe who goes to the veterinarian and can't fit on the table."

"I know this is supposed to be an 'authentic inn,' but this is ridiculous. Ireland is not a land of short people. How is it that they have a bed only big enough for a Hobbit?"

Mary Catherine slid into the bed next to me. Suddenly the length of the bed no longer mattered. And I was glad for the narrow width. I liked Mary Catherine right next to me.

We gazed out the handblown glass window into the starry night over Dublin. Mary Catherine's fingers played with my hair as I gently made circles with my finger along her neck and shoulders. I could listen to her gentle laugh for days.

Suddenly it turned into a wild night. Not exactly what I'd expected but just as much fun.

We lay together in bed, both of us panting from the exertion. My head was still swimming, trying to process everything we'd just done, even wondering if we had broken anything. I halfway anticipated a noise complaint. If this were a drug, I could understand becoming an addict.

Mary Catherine laughed and said, "God, I've never seen you like that before."

"How often are we away from our lives like this, where we can just let go?"

"Michael Bennett, you always amaze me. Just when I think I've seen every side of you, you surprise me. Making love like that was very non-American."

"What's that mean?"

She snuggled up close and wrapped her arm across my chest. "I just like comparing the American ideas of romance with the European ways. But make no mistake, there was no precedent for what we did tonight."

"What's the difference between us?" I was truly interested. Like many American men, I felt a little insecure when compared to the romantic reputations of the French or Italians.

"Europeans are attentive and experienced. Americans are enthusiastic and fun. What we did tonight was just plain wild."

"I know. I think I strained my back."

After she finished laughing, Mary Catherine said, "A woman has different moods. It's good that Europeans and Americans look at romance differently." After a little pause, she added, "It doesn't matter. I still only love you."

"Wait. What does that mean?" I tried not to shout it in surprise.

She kissed me on the forehead and chuckled. This was one of the most interesting and funny women I'd ever met.

I felt something vibrate. Before I could even ask Mary Catherine what it was, she said, "Someone called you. Your phone is on vibrate."

I leaned over and kissed her on the cheek. "Beautiful and smart. You're the total package." Another playful shove from her almost knocked me off the tiny bed. I reached over to the night table and picked up my cell phone.

Mary Catherine said, "Is it one of the kids or your grandfather?"

"No. It looks like Emily Parker tried to call a few different times."

Mary Catherine said, "You can call her back. I don't mind."

I may have been married only nine days, but I knew better than to fall into a trap like that. Besides, it had to be related to a case. I was on vacation. I turned to Mary Catherine and said, "I'll give her a call tomorrow from the airport."

I turned back to look at my beautiful bride. Her hair looked like she'd just ridden on a motorcycle without a helmet. Blond strands darted in every direction. It was a good look.

She lazily stretched in the bed, then turned to me and said, "Have you ever thought about having more babies?"

I let out a laugh. "Of course. Who ever heard of stopping at just ten kids?"

It turned out Mary Catherine's sleepy look was a deception. The night turned wild once again.

CHAPTER 3

THE NEXT DAY we were at Dublin Airport, waiting for our Aer Lingus flight to New York. I flinched slightly as I leaned down to pick up my carry-on bag.

Mary Catherine patted me on the butt. She laughed and said, "Looks like someone suffered some injuries last night."

"Just a sore back. I might be able to attribute it to the small bed."

"Or you might attribute it to a new wife."

"That's more likely, but I was trying to be polite." It was all I could do not to groan. I needed to hang from a chin-up bar for about three hours to decompress my spine.

It was late in the evening and I figured it to be about four o'clock on the East Coast of the US. We called the kids for a quick chat and to tell them we'd be home at midnight. The time change confused everyone. I'd learned, after eighteen years of being a father, it was much better to warn them exactly when we were coming than it was to surprise them.

Each of the kids home at this hour filed past the phone for a quick hello. Trent was the outlier. He was bursting with some big news and couldn't wait to tell us. He wouldn't even give us a hint now. The call eased my back pain and put me in a good mood.

I had made a call that morning to Emily Parker. It had gone straight to voicemail. I didn't think anything of it. I didn't mind calling Emily during my vacation. Even if it was related to a case. She was my friend first. We worked well together. Never mind that the New York FBI assistant special agent in charge, Robert Lincoln, was still pissed off they'd been frozen out of a serial killer case just before I got married.

Mary Catherine had said earlier, "Maybe she's sleeping in."

I knew Emily Parker better than that. The FBI agent rarely sat still, let alone slept in. I tried her once more before our flight took off, but I assumed she would've already reached out again if it was urgent.

Aside from having to put a pillow and a blanket on my seat to ease the aching in my back, the flight was remarkably uneventful. Even the ride from JFK to the Upper West Side was smooth. My excitement was building at seeing the kids. This was by far the longest I had ever been away from them. Even though we had spoken every day, I missed each kid in a different way. I needed a hug from Chrissy, and insight into basketball from Brian, and a decent meal from Ricky.

We were lucky to have my grandfather, Seamus, gladly take time out from his work at the parish and supervise in our absence. The three oldest kids, Juliana, Jane, and Brian, were expected to do their part as well, though Juliana was always excused if she had an audition for an acting role. We'd been gone so long I didn't know exactly what to expect: the city a nuclear wasteland, our building a shell, or a regime change in which my twins, Fiona and Bridget, were now in charge.

As we pulled up to the building on West End Avenue at close to midnight, everything seemed fine. I let out a breath I'd inadvertently been holding. Maybe I was more concerned about Seamus supervising the kids than I should have been. All was normal.

Until I opened the front door of the building and saw a body lying on the floor of the lobby.

CHAPTER 4

MY POLICE TRAINING and instincts told me to jump into action. I fell to the lobby floor next to the body and slid on the waxed faux terrazzo.

It took only a moment for my brain to click into the first-aid course I took as a yearly refresher. CPR had so many acronyms and mnemonic devices that the learning aids seemed to cancel each other out. I started with the most obvious: I checked his pulse at the carotid artery in his neck. He had one. A strong pulse.

He was breathing. And he stank. Of alcohol. So that was why he was passed out on the floor. His gray hair was cut into a flattop. His ruddy face told me he'd spent a lot of time outdoors and drank a little too much.

Where the hell was the doorman, Darnell?

Mary Catherine already had her phone out, about to dial 911, when the elevator door opened. All we could do was stare at the

14

image in front of us. My grandfather, Seamus, and the doorman, Darnell, were supporting another man on either side. The man was semiconscious and trying to sing an old Irish ballad, but I couldn't figure out which one. A blue cap covered his silver, nicely styled hair.

As soon as he noticed us in the lobby, my grandfather blurted out, "Oh, shit."

I stood up from the man on the floor and said, "The only excuse that will keep me from being pissed off is that these are some kind of half-assed elderly home invaders and you fought them off."

My grandfather's frozen expression would have been almost comical if I wasn't worried about the children and what the hell had happened. Seamus and Darnell helped the man out of the elevator and deposited him on one of the decorative, uncomfortable Louis XVI chairs along the wall.

Then my grandfather turned and gave Mary Catherine a hug and a kiss on the cheek. He did the same to me with very little reciprocity. Then he stood right in front of me. I realized, to his credit, he was sober.

Seamus said, "Don't worry about the kids."

Mary Catherine let out an "Oh, thank God."

Seamus smiled and said, "Ricky won a bundle. But you're going to need to buy more of that Villa Wolf Pinot Noir."

"What are we going to do with your two buddies?"

"I've already called a cab for them. I resent that you think I don't know how to deal with people who've had too much to drink. I did own a bar for many years."

"But my children didn't have to deal with your clients from the bar."

"Your children will benefit from meeting a wider cross section of people in the city. I'm just trying to do my part for the family." Somehow he had managed to keep a straight face during that ridiculous statement.

"You were playing poker with my children?"

"Just the ones who had ten dollars for the ante."

"And they spent the evening with your inebriated friends?"

"No, they spent the evening with my very smart friends, who didn't become inebriated until the last hour or so. By then Ricky was the last child standing, so to speak. He finished on a beautiful ace-high flush. Everyone else is upstairs, having finished their homework and all the things they were supposed to, now just determined to wait up for you. They have been fed regularly and didn't miss a single day of school. I count this whole situation as a win."

As I was about to reply, we heard a car horn out front.

Seamus helped his friend off the floor and somehow guided him to the cab he'd called. He waved to the cabbie, and I heard him say, "Hello, Vonnu, how are you this evening?"

I stepped from the door to the street to make sure there were no problems.

The cabbie called out, "See you later, Father," then drove down West End Avenue and turned toward the river.

I faced my grandfather and said, "'Father'? You know that cabbie personally? You don't care if he sees a priest with drunks?"

"They're not drunks. They are fine men who had a little too much Pinot. Vonnu knows them too. You think this is the first time I've ever had to call him?"

With that, Seamus turned and marched back into the building.

CHAPTER 5

IF I WAS annoyed at my grandfather, the feeling evaporated the instant I opened the door to our apartment. Across the dining room, in full view of the front door, hung a banner that said, "Welcome Home." I could tell by the precision work that it had been supervised heavily by Jane and Juliana. The rhinestones at each corner were Bridget's calling card.

Mary Catherine bumped into me while she stared at the giant banner. Then one of the younger girls—I think it was Shawna—squealed. As if reacting to a starting pistol, we were swarmed with racing children. Twenty arms reaching for us at once. It was the perfect ending to a fabulous honeymoon.

As soon as I saw Trent's giant smile, I remembered he had big news. Once the sleepy-eyed hugs all around were finished, I turned to my quiet teenage son and said, "What's the big news you wanted to tell us?"

Chrissy almost blurted it out, but Eddie managed to get a hand over her mouth before she spilled the beans.

Trent said, "I wrote an essay at school about what it's like living in a multicultural family in a multicultural city and still not knowing exactly where you fit in. It's called 'The Black Face in the Crowd.'"

Mary Catherine said, "I can't wait to read it."

Trent was almost breathless as he said, "That's not the best part. The essay won a contest at school and is now a finalist in a citywide competition. There's a ceremony at City Hall and everything in a couple of weeks."

I grabbed Trent and hugged him. I was so proud I had a tear in my eye, and I didn't trust myself to speak. It was nice to see Trent excelling. He had so many different interests that I wondered what he might focus on as he got older. I looked over and noticed his sister Jane was the only one not beaming. Jane had quietly kept a journal her whole life. I hoped there wouldn't be any jealousy about her brother's quick success with writing.

I was so excited about the news and seeing the kids, I almost forgot that at some point in the coming weeks I'd probably have to go back to work. It was like waking up from a dream I never wanted to end. I could unpack tomorrow.

When I woke up the next morning, I immediately slipped out of bed so I wouldn't wake Mary Catherine. I texted Emily Parker because she had not returned my calls from Ireland. She had to have been trying to reach me about a case, and I wanted to get back to her.

I managed to whip together a pancake breakfast with scrambled eggs on the side. It may not sound like much, but when you're doing it for ten kids and a grandfather who decided to spend the night, it can be quite the task.

Everything went smoothly, and I let Seamus use our van to drive the kids to school. I told him I'd walk down in the afternoon and pick it up. It was an odd feeling to be at the house alone with Mary Catherine at eight fifteen in the morning. Even if I was the only one awake.

When my phone rang, I jumped to answer it, thinking it would be Emily. Instead, I saw it was my boss, Lieutenant Harry Grissom.

As soon as I answered, Harry said, "So you made it back safely. Are you at home? I need to come by and talk to you about something." Harry was my friend, but he'd been to the apartment only once or twice in all the years we'd lived here.

As soon as I opened the door and greeted Harry, the anxiety I'd been holding back flooded in with full force. Harry refused coffee and led me to the couch. He didn't have good news.

When we were sitting, Harry said, "I wanted you to hear it before it was on the news."

"What?" I said, my voice cracking like a schoolboy's.

"Emily Parker has gone missing in Washington, DC."

"What do you mean, 'missing'?"

"No one has seen or heard from her since the day before yesterday. The Bureau is taking it very seriously. They found her car in a grocery store parking lot. Someone from the FBI or DC police blabbed to a reporter, and news coverage is starting."

I didn't say a word. All I could think about was her last call in Ireland. The one I didn't answer.

Harry said, "The only reason the FBI ASAC even called me was because it was on the news. He knows you're tight with her, and he wanted to make sure I'd tell him if you knew anything about her disappearance."

"Knew anything? Like he thinks I'm a suspect?"

"No, nothing like that. More like if she ran off with someone—or from the federal bureaucracy. Mainly they want to make sure she's safe."

"What was she doing in DC?" Bad news seems to provoke meaningless questions. I guess it's a way to avoid fear and grief.

Harry said, "She's been back and forth between LA, New York, and DC. Apparently, she was working on some kind of anarchist group. You know the type, deface signs, toilet paper houses, and do the occasional violent crime."

"Where is her daughter, Olivia?"

Harry said, "She's with Emily's ex-husband."

"She said he was a deadbeat."

"Apparently he got his act together."

"Is anyone looking at him as a suspect?"

"The first thing they checked. He's in Connecticut with Olivia. The FBI verified he hadn't traveled in weeks."

I was glad Harry had made me sit on the couch while we talked. A host of horrible scenarios rushed through my head, hitting hard. Drug kingpins she had taken down, nuts like this anarchist group, or even a stalker. Emily was a beautiful woman. She never wanted for attention from men.

Then something clicked in my head. An idea. A proposal I really needed to run past Mary Catherine. Instead, I looked at Harry and just blurted out, "I'm going to stay on vacation a while longer."

Harry looked at me closely. "You've got plenty of vacation time built up and you've earned every minute of it. Tell me you won't spend your free time doing the kind of thing you shouldn't tell me about."

"You mean like a hobby or exercise?"

"You know exactly what I mean. But I respect your loyalty to a friend."

CHAPTER 6

I NEEDED MORE information. The NYPD trains people who get jobs all over the country. I knew exactly who to call to get the full scoop on Emily Parker's disappearance: Roberta Herring. I couldn't help but smile whenever I thought of my colleague at my first precinct in the Bronx, now a supervisor with the Department of Justice Office of the Inspector General.

The DOJ OIG had oversight of the FBI and several other agencies. The ranks of the OIG were filled with former cops and federal agents. I knew all Roberta's secrets from her rough-and-tumble life as a uniformed patrol officer in the Bronx—more than enough to know that she wasn't really an Internal Affairs type, and also that she excelled in this job.

I preferred to think of her as my friend whom I could trust with my life. And I was pretty sure she felt the same about me.

All I had to do was say, "How would you handle a domestic

violence situation?" Usually, she'd just give me a look that told me to shut up. Once she even shoved me out of a restaurant so I wouldn't keep talking. It was a great game in which I held all the cards. The best way to play any game. I knew she had once told an abusive husband she'd cut off his balls if he ever hit his wife again. Say what you want, it worked.

On the second ring, I heard, "Roberta Herring, may I help you?"

I chuckled out loud and said, "That's very professional. You must've learned that *after* you left the Bronx."

She answered with her own chuckle. "Detective Michael Bennett. I knew my day was running too smoothly. How's that new wife and platoon of children?"

We got through the chitchat and caught up with each other's lives. I told her about my connection to Emily Parker and the cases we had worked. I said, "She personally kept me and my entire family safe when we were in witness protection. I'm just worried about what's being done to find her."

"Same old Bennett. Doesn't believe anyone else can do the job as well as he can. I've seen too many times where you step in and figure things out when no one else can." There was a pause. I heard footsteps and then the sound of an office door closing. "The FBI is taking Emily's disappearance seriously," Roberta said, now that she could speak freely. "The DC police are also taking leads."

If you're in real trouble in a big city, you're better off with a city detective than the FBI. That was our favorite saying when we first made detective about the same time. She didn't say it out loud, but I knew we were both thinking it. I wasn't an idiot.

Roberta said, "I don't know Emily Parker personally, but since she disappeared there have been quite a few rumors. People believe that she's dated a number of very powerful people in DC. The rumors all indicate that she has a real wild side."

"I've known her for years, and I've never had any hint she had a wild side. Are you sure we're talking about the same person? Emily is as dedicated as any cop I've ever met. I didn't realize she made time for much of a social life."

Roberta said, "My concern is not whether the FBI can find her but whether the FBI *wants* to find her. Who knows what happened to her or if someone wants to keep her quiet. These are all questions a lot of us are taking very seriously."

"Who's spreading these stupid rumors?"

Roberta said, "A couple of the local rags ran stories about her personal life. Politicians and judges, none of them named, are said to be part of her social circle. Again, these are the local, fringe newspapers. Nothing the *Post* would ever touch."

"Do you think the local papers have a reliable source?"

"I doubt it. I could quiz the editor. But they usually don't say shit." Roberta laughed and said, "Unless you're holding them by their balls."

"You mean figuratively."

"Yeah, sure, whatever."

CHAPTER 7

MY CALL WITH Roberta Herring convinced me. I couldn't ignore a friend like Emily when she was in trouble. I felt like I needed to go to DC and look for her myself. Not that I doubted the FBI would be able to handle it. But if *I* was in DC, I might do things the FBI couldn't.

The kids were at school, Brian at work, Juliana out with some friends. Mary Catherine and I were alone in the kitchen. She had shuffled in to grab a cup of coffee, still in her bathrobe. Even in terry cloth printed with a family photograph and a message from the kids—WE LOVE YOU, MARY CATHERINE—she looked like a model of beauty and grace.

Her blond hair hung loose down her back and created a halo effect around the top of her head. She had to be on board with this plan because there was no way I could go against her wishes.

We sat on the couch together. Then she realized something was up.

I reached across and held both of her hands.

"What's wrong, Michael?"

"Emily Parker has disappeared in Washington, DC."

"Oh, my Lord, that's terrible. Do the police have any leads?"

I told her everything I had learned so far. Then I leaned in and said, "I feel like I should go down there and help look for her. I have no idea if the FBI will even talk to me. But Roberta Herring said she'd find me a liaison if I wanted to try."

Then I waited. All I really wanted was to hear how Mary Catherine felt about the idea. She took longer than I thought. I felt surprisingly anxious, but then I remembered the depth of Mary Catherine's compassion. She could no more ignore a friend in need than she could ignore one of the kids. She might have had reservations about my getting involved, but she knew I had to do something.

Then Mary Catherine looked me in the eyes and said, "If you really think you can help, you have to go to Washington. Emily's an effective FBI agent, and she's been too much help to this family for us to ignore her when she's in trouble."

There it was. One of the reasons I'd married her. Support. She didn't hesitate to highlight that we were in this together. As a family. Helping people who needed help.

Emily and I definitely had a history, and Mary Catherine knew every detail, including that we almost took a shot at romance years before. Plus, she had eyes. She could see Emily was beautiful.

Even though I considered Mary Catherine in a class by herself, I couldn't testify to her own insecurities. But that was one of the reasons I loved her. She didn't believe in running away from problems.

All Mary Catherine asked was "How long will you be gone?"

I shrugged. I had no idea.

She said, "Please try to be home for Trent's ceremony. I've never seen that boy so excited."

I leaned across and kissed her on the lips. This was a woman who got me. Who could ask for anything more out of life?

CHAPTER 8

I TALKED TO the kids as soon as they were all home. It was harder telling them than it had been talking to Mary Catherine about leaving. All I told them was that I had to help a friend in Washington, DC, for a few days.

Trent immediately said, "Don't forget the ceremony at City Hall."

"There is no way I would miss it, buddy. I guarantee I'll be back for that." Out of the corner of my eye I noticed Jane. She didn't look happy about the ceremony. I didn't want to get into it just now. Jealousy between siblings could get ugly.

I wasn't the kind of guy who was going to shoo away his children, so it was hard having a proper good-bye with my new wife. I had to settle for a hug and a quick kiss.

I whispered in her ear, "I'll make this up to you."

"You already have."

The ride down the elevator was one of the toughest I'd ever taken.

Hopping Amtrak to DC was an easy choice. At Penn Station, there would be no waiting around for two hours, like at an airport terminal. And I could bring my gun without anyone asking questions. I didn't think I'd need it, but I like to be prepared. I grabbed a cab.

On the ride from New York to DC, I looked out at the dreary autumn afternoon and thought about my life and the odd turns it had taken, grateful for what felt like a second chance. I was pretty sure leaving town less than two weeks after marrying Mary Catherine made me a complete and utter jerk. I missed her even before the train had left Penn Station.

As guilty as I felt about leaving Mary Catherine with all the kids, I was also envious. One by one, the kids would be heading off to college. The idea that my time with my family was finite made me miss them even more.

All that reinforced how important it was that I go to DC. I was going to find Emily Parker. Or, at the very least, find out what happened to her.

It was after seven by the time the train rolled through Pennsylvania. There wasn't much to work out in my head about what I was going to do once I got to DC. I needed more information. In short, I needed a lead.

Once I arrived in DC, I felt like I'd overcome a major obstacle. At a car rental kiosk, I immediately discovered another one. The only vehicle available was a purple Toyota Prius.

I looked to the upbeat and friendly young guy behind the counter in his white shirt and polyester red company logo tie and said, "Do you really expect me to fit in that?".

He took a moment to look me up and down before answering, "I know for a fact you'll fit. I will make no comment on how comfortable you will be. You don't have to take it. But good luck finding any other options around here."

A few minutes later, I had the seat of my purple Prius as far back as it would go and still felt like I was driving a golf cart.

Thank God all I had was my small bag and a coat. Now I just had to find Emily Parker.

I called Roberta Herring, who proposed we meet at some swanky Mediterranean restaurant in the city center that was one of her regular hangouts.

She laughed and said, "It's funny. I haven't worked with you in at least twenty years, and we're in entirely different cities, but you never change. You say you're going to do something and there's no downtime between decision and action."

"That's a good thing, right?"

"Clearly you've never dealt with anyone in Washington, DC. No one makes a decision, and no one takes much action. You're going to stir up shit whether you mean to or not. And usually you mean to."

She had me there. I did intend to stir up shit if needed.

CHAPTER 9

I GOT SETTLED in the hotel I'd reserved during my train ride and made a quick call home. It didn't seem to have hit Mary Catherine yet that I was going to be gone for a while. I let her stay cheerful, and that put me in a good mood.

Just as we were ending the call, Mary Catherine said, "Michael."

"Yes, dear."

"Please be careful. I know you're not technically on duty, but I worry about you every day. Not just the days you go to a job where people want to kill you."

"I'm in the new DC," I told Mary Catherine. Like most big cities, DC had its clearly delineated neighborhoods. The Capitol Hill area was next to up-and-coming Eastern Market and one of the ritziest areas in the city. "It's like the new Times Square. Much more family friendly."

What I didn't mention was that the people who lived here rarely acknowledged disadvantaged neighborhoods like Brentwood or Anacostia. No one wanted visitors from the outside.

After riding in the cramped Prius, I didn't mind waiting at the front of a Mediterranean restaurant on Eighth Street named Cava Mezze.

Roberta swept into the place like a tropical storm in a patterned pantsuit and pumps that drew her five-foot-ten, broad-shouldered frame to a commanding presence that topped six feet. A couple of people greeted her in the entryway and led us to our table.

Once seated, Roberta ordered a bottle of Montes Folly Syrah. I looked around the crowded restaurant and said, "This is a notch or two above the places I eat when I'm traveling solo."

"Don't sweat it. Dinner's on me tonight."

"I can't let you treat. You're doing me a favor."

"Actually, you're doing me a favor. As soon as I heard about a missing female FBI agent, I worried they wouldn't have the right agent to look for her. You know that at any agency there's always that one right investigator who can get shit done. Now, instead of me worrying, you show up. And I know you're the right investigator."

I was speechless at what had to be the biggest compliment she had ever given me. Maybe the biggest compliment she had ever given anyone.

Then Roberta said, "Besides, after my last divorce, and being at the top of the federal pay scale, I don't even look at prices anymore. If I'd been smarter when I was younger, I would've married a plumber the first time instead of a mail carrier."

We both laughed.

Roberta leaned in and said, "It's a shame our jobs take such a toll on our families. Everyone talks about the divorce rate among cops, but they never look at why. Maybe because we spend so much time protecting everyone else's family, it's hard to focus on our own."

"You may have been married a few times, but Joey is doing well at Howard, isn't he?"

"He's doing fine, and I'm happy he's studying here in DC, though unless he's got laundry or needs money, I don't count on many visits."

We caught up with family news for a few more minutes, then I had to get serious. "Have you been able to follow up on any of the rumors you've heard about Emily? I'm looking for any available leads."

"According to my casual inquiries, she was definitely involved with the newest Supreme Court justice, Robert Steinberg. He's only a little older than Emily. It looks like he might have known her since she started at the FBI. There's just one problem."

"What's that?"

"He's married." She paused for effect. "To the daughter of Lom Wellmy."

"The senator from New York?" I almost shouted in surprise.

"The very same. And it looks like Emily's had some other high-profile lovers over the past couple of years."

Emily and I were friends, but once it was clear we weren't going to be romantically involved, I didn't think it right to ask her any questions about her romantic life.

Roberta said, "The most important thing I was able to work out was finding you a decent FBI contact. He's the lead agent on Emily's disappearance, and he's worked with her for the past year. His name is Bobby Patel. The only problem is, it might be a day or so before he can sit down with you. You'll have a couple of thick files to occupy yourself. I know how antsy you get."

"He's okay being a liaison with someone not officially on the case?"

"I spoke to him face-to-face. He'll benefit from experience like yours. But remember, this is a completely unofficial association. I said you wouldn't cause too much trouble or talk to the media. I even told him there was a slight chance you might be helpful."

That sounded more like the Roberta I knew. It also put me at ease.

CHAPTER 10

IT TOOK A day for everything to line up so I could sit down with the FBI agent Roberta Herring had arranged for me to meet. I used the time to read the case file Roberta had given me. It had the FBI reports along with the DC police reports on Emily's disappearance. I also used the time to catch up on the DC gossip surrounding Emily. Every story and internet post I read led me to another five. Then I started learning a little more about the new Supreme Court justice, Robert Steinberg. By the time the FBI agent was ready to meet me, my head felt crammed with conspiracy theories as well as a few facts.

It was no surprise that my FBI contact, Bobby Patel, didn't want to meet me anywhere we might be seen by FBI people, but I picked him out as soon as I walked through the door of Baked and Wired, a coffeehouse on Thomas Jefferson Street, not far from the Potomac.

The basic color scheme and unfinished ceiling were trying a little too hard to be trendy. Bobby was a tall, fit guy in his early to mid thirties with a dark complexion and black hair. In a dark suit with a yellow tie, he wasn't trying too hard to blend in among similarly dressed federal workers occupying chairs and stools at a long communal table.

His expression made him look like he was brooding. Maybe he was. The dark stubble on his cheeks and bags under his brown eyes made it clear he was driven and stressed. His thin lips spread into a brief smile as he recognized me too and stood from the long table to greet me.

He turned his head in either direction. "I picked this place because I figured we could talk in private. In the ten minutes I've been sitting here, a couple of guys from my unit have already come and gone. There're another two FBI agents sitting in the mock living room in the back, reading the paper like they're at home on their own couches. I feel like I'm a target of surveillance."

"We can go somewhere else."

He declined the offer. Bobby Patel had a certain childlike energy and antsiness I found endearing. I knew that look. It was the same one I got when I had leads on a major case.

Bobby said, "I'm exhausted from going out on useless leads. I hope you have some ideas. I've read about some of your cases and wish I worked with a guy like you."

I'll confess, working with a smart, young FBI agent wasn't the worst idea. I doubted I'd ever have the trust I'd built with Emily Parker, but it was always good to have a contact with the Bureau.

The two FBI agents sitting in the back corner of the coffeehouse got ready to leave. I noticed Bobby tense slightly as they passed our table. The shorter of the two agents had a military-style haircut. His thick arms made me think he was compensating for his height. He said, "See you in the office, B."

I asked, "Is that short for Bobby?"

Bobby Patel shook his head. "Somehow someone in my office discovered I won a spelling bee when I was twelve. I'm a black belt in judo too. No one ever brings that up."

"Sorry, just naturally curious."

Bobby shook his head and looked at the floor. "No, *I'm* sorry. I'm a little sensitive. People wrongly assume everyone of Indian descent studies hard, has strict parents and a crazy work ethic."

"None of those sound like a negative."

Bobby said, "I do work hard, but I never hear anyone say, 'I want to party with the Indian guy.' And everyone calls me Bobby, like I'm still a little kid."

"What would you prefer to be called?"

Bobby stayed silent for a moment. When he looked up at me, his face was hard to read. Finally, he sighed and said, "Okay, I prefer Bobby. But you're the only white guy who's ever asked what I prefer."

As we laughed together in the coffeehouse, I thought that of all the FBI agents in Washington, Bobby Patel seemed like the best one I could be teamed with. I made a quick assessment that this guy was all right.

CHAPTER 11

THEN WE GOT down to business. I asked Bobby about the rumors I'd heard of Emily Parker dating powerful men in Washington.

Bobby shook his head. "Everyone hears rumors. Emily can't defend herself, so I ignore them. She's a very effective agent, and we're work friends. More like buddies. You know what I mean?"

I just nodded, but I knew exactly what he meant. I had a number of female buddies. Emily was my best female bud. And I intended to find her.

Bobby kept going. "I'm looking at the actual information I have to go on. Not rumors that could be spread by anyone for any reason. Emily's car was found in the lot of a Whole Foods on I Street."

"Any idea how it ended up in that lot?"

"We're pretty sure she left it there. She parks there and a half dozen other lots in the city when she does her marathon training runs. Always runs the same courses to compare her time. Very specific in her schedule." Bobby looked down at some notes and said, "We couldn't locate her purse, FBI credentials, phone, or gun."

I said, "Did you find anything on security video from the Whole Foods or anywhere else on the street?"

Bobby shook his head. "We checked with everyone. We even created a website that aggregated security footage from a number of stores. Nothing. One of the problems at the Whole Foods was that their main system was broken. They were using a backup DVR system with little storage capacity, so the staff downloaded to DVD daily, then wiped the DVR for the next day. But the DVD that would've had the files showing Emily pulling into the lot was missing. Just a simple screwup that's causing me a lot more hassle."

"You have any leads or suspects at all?"

Bobby shook his head. "Nothing that's panned out. We searched for a square mile around where we found her car. The DC police have had an extra boat patrolling the Potomac and looking for any sign of her. Still nothing."

"What about her FBI investigations? Would one of her targets be a viable suspect?"

He shook his head. "She's been tracking an anarchist group known as The Burning Land. Mostly younger men who like to stir up trouble by pretending to resist authority. In reality, they're thugs looking for chaos. They've been linked to half a dozen fires, looting, and some of them are suspects in two separate murders of former members. We talked to a few of them. They didn't realize anyone has been looking at them. I guess you can beat up people and riot and expect no one to pay attention."

Then Bobby passed a folder across to me. He said, "Everyone we've talked to with a quick summary of what they said is in this folder. So are the principals in The Burning Land." He looked me in the eye and took a beat. "I'd like to set up a few ground rules for our investigation."

"Anything you want."

"First and most important, no one at the FBI can know I'm feeding you tips. I know your friend from the OIG called me personally, but my bosses won't cut me much slack if they hear I've been farming out leads."

"I understand completely. It's generally my goal not to have contact with the FBI."

Bobby let out a laugh and said, "I get the feeling that's most cops' attitude." He looked down at his notes again. "You need to tell me everything you find out related to Emily's disappearance. And I mean everything. Even suspicions."

I just nodded at that one. My experience with the FBI had not made me particularly open to sharing everything with them. This was a unique situation.

Finally, Bobby said, "I'll feed you some interviews, but you can't tell anyone you're working the case."

"I'll just say I'm looking for my friend. Which is true." Somehow I had the distinct impression that a lot of the interviews would fall into one of two categories: people who had no useful information and people who were powerful enough to ruin an FBI agent's career.

CHAPTER 12

BEFORE I RAN out to stir up shit, I made a quick stop at my hotel's cramped business center. One of the first steps in any investigation, after gathering information, is research.

An internet search told me that, as a group, The Burning Land was suspected in several deaths, fires, and a whole host of crimes related to riots they helped start. I was shocked they hadn't been designated domestic terrorists.

The FBI may have spoken to a couple of the group's members, but that didn't mean much to me. I wasn't restricted by the rules of the FBI. I didn't have to be polite or courteous. And I could spot a liar.

Everyone in the damn group had some kind of arrest record. One member, a guy named Jeremy Pugh, stood out. He was a little older, about thirty-seven, and was listed as a direct suspect in two fires. I was able to track down public records of his arrests for stalking, aggravated stalking, and assault with a deadly weapon. That gave me the impression of a dangerous man backed by the encouragement of a dangerous group. A note on a booking photo listed Pugh as six foot four and 250 pounds.

It didn't take me long to find the warehouse where The Burning Land might ostensibly be headquartered. At any rate, one person in a web forum had listed this address as a meeting place in the past few months. I drove past slowly and looked through the open bay doors, any identifying signs missing above the patchwork of asphalt. A few young people in an unmarked bay sat talking on crates or on the concrete floor. My guess was they used this place because the rent was cheap, or maybe it was the base of some other activity that helped fund the group.

Since no one ever would make a small purple Prius for a police car, I drove past several times. Nothing changed. Then I started looking through the rest of the neighborhood. A block away stood a diner-coffeehouse with a sign that spelled out in familiar greenish lettering BARBUCKS. Clearly ripping off a well-known coffee chain, this place also sold beer. Something told me this was where members of The Burning Land would come for their caffeine fix. Besides, I could've used a shot of some about now.

The atmosphere was a step down from Starbucks. Plastic wrappers littered the floor, and the garbage can near the back door was barely visible under a hill of trash dotted with plain disposable cups. Sitting at a high top were two young men and a young woman who had to be part of The Burning Land. Between them I estimated they had fifty visible tattoos.

I ordered a cup of coffee at the counter, then took the high top right next to them, saying hello as I slid onto my stool.

A skinny man in his twenties with long, greasy hair scowled at me. He said, "Do you mind? This is a private conference. Go sit over there." He used his bottle of Budweiser to point across the empty room to a sketchy table with empty cups on it. The other young man had gauges in his ears big enough to pass a finger through.

I kept my voice calm. "No, thanks. I'm fine here." I wanted to be unobtrusive, but you can't give bullies too much room or they never stop.

The man stood up. So did I. He was of average height, so he came up to my chin. I kept hold of my hot coffee. It would slow him down if he lunged for me.

The young woman at the table reached up to touch the young man's arm. "Let it go, Tyler. He's not worth the effort."

I let Tyler see a hint of a smile. Just to see if that might set him off. Instead, he huddled with his friends. I kept my stool facing them so I wouldn't be surprised.

This was a golden opportunity to pick up information. A smart cop will always talk to people before taking action. But we'd gotten off on the wrong foot. Now I worried about explaining to the local cops why I tore up a coffee shop mixing with these thugs.

Tyler glared at me again. "You have no idea how lucky you are, mister."

"You mean because I have a job and live in an apartment?" This was fun. I might have to try unofficial investigations more often. All three of the young people just stared at me.

Then the front door opened. The cheap bell above the door tinkled. I looked up to see the man I'd read about. Jeremy Pugh stood in all his glory, though his thinning hair and body odor probably didn't attract many prospective mates in The Burning Land. At thirty-seven, he wasn't a kid. And it was hard to settle my concern about whether his 250 pounds were mostly muscle or mostly fat. He was just big. Like a linebacker five years after college. A gut hung over his belt, and he wore a TIJUANA FLATS TACO TUESDAZE shirt that was a size too small. His grungy, three-day stubble didn't improve my first impression.

As soon as Pugh plopped onto a stool, the guy I'd confronted leaned in and whispered something to him. Then the big man turned to face me.

He said, "Who the hell are you, causing shit in here? This place is ours."

"I don't think that's how the DC police would see it."

He let out a laugh. "You really think those pussies would even come down here?" Then he scowled as he said, "How do we know *you're* not a cop? Or worse, a reporter." He had a hint of a Virginia drawl.

"Why would a reporter be so bad?"

That seemed to enrage the big man. "Are you kidding me? The way they cover us? They make us look like terrorists. Nothing but lies." Spittle sprayed his table as he started to shout. He stood up and took a step toward me.

I kept quiet and tried to stay calm.

Pugh said, "This is our turf. We got a right to know who's trespassin' and why they're asking questions." Then he reached into my sport coat like he was looking for my wallet. I slapped his hand away out of instinct. It felt like an invasive, childish move. That's why I treated him like a brat.

That might've been my mistake.

CHAPTER 13

THE BIG ANARCHIST pulled the most basic move known by every kid who's ever been in a fight: he wrapped his arms around me in a giant bear hug. Holy shit was he strong. He squeezed the breath out of me instantly. The sound I made when the air rushed out of me was not particularly dignified. I was immediately immobilized in a cocoon of muscle and fat. He lifted me off my stool like I was a child. As he walked toward the back door, the others just followed his lead. The young woman even opened the door for us.

Pugh called over his shoulder to the barista. "Just taking out the trash, Cheyenne. Nothing to worry about."

I decided to go with it until we got all the way outside. I was lucky he hadn't noticed my gun on my hip. He was too intent on crushing me. There was no reason to expose who I really was yet. If things got much worse, I wouldn't have a choice.

Even though I was being physically carried by a remarkably strong giant, I kept my head. I thought out a few different scenarios. None of them involved pulling my duty pistol. The barista clearly hadn't called the police and didn't seem to care that that might work in my favor. Then again, she didn't care what happened to me.

When we were out of view of the parking lot, things got worse. Quickly.

Jeremy Pugh released his arms from my ribs and dropped me roughly on my feet. My right ankle twisted on the loose gravel scattered along the walkway. The pain felt like an electric shock as it worked up my leg to my brain. My teeth clattered so hard I was afraid I chipped one. I gulped some air quickly.

I was about to say something witty when Pugh hit me with a hammering blow. His forearm connected with my back, snapping my head back and forth like whiplash and knocking me to one knee. Semiconscious, I realized that these guys were serious. And certainly Jeremy Pugh could be a good suspect in the disappearance of Emily Parker.

My worry turned to embarrassment that these morons had escalated this to a level I hadn't anticipated. I stayed on one knee, motionless, trying to clear my head before I stood up again. I did flinch at a kick that wasn't thrown. Then I felt something else. First on my leg and then on my back. Then I realized with a sickening feeling what it was. Piss. Jeremy Pugh was peeing on me.

I'd like to say it was the first time I'd encountered the use of urine as a weapon. But as a uniformed patrolman in the Bronx, my team had all been showered with jars of urine from the upper floors of apartments. This just seemed so much more personal and disgusting.

By the time I was upright, Pugh had zipped up his fly and his friends were all laughing. Then they just wandered away like I wasn't worth another thought.

I watched them. I knew we'd see each other again. Maybe soon.

CHAPTER 14

I MADE IT back to my hotel room, holding my jacket at arm's length as if it had been sprayed with a biological weapon. I cared nothing about the view from my seventh-floor window. I didn't care that I could see the Library of Congress clearly. Instead, I jumped into the shower, still wearing my pants and shirt. Eventually I stripped down and threw the clothing into a laundry bag. I'd spring for the hotel dry cleaning before I ever wore that jacket again.

I try to never let emotions dictate my actions. I was thinking this might be an exception. I needed a little time to cool down. And to pick my time and place to remind Jeremy Pugh that I would not forget what he'd done to me. Now I had Pugh on my list of suspects.

That brought up a lot of questions. How did he find Emily? Did he know she ran most mornings? Where did he take her?

As soon as I was cleaned up, I called home. Trent answered with such enthusiasm it made me smile.

He said, "I knew it would be you calling the house number. That's why I raced from the living room to answer it. I got my official letter from the mayor's office. And guess what?"

"What?"

"The mayor signed the letter himself."

I let out a laugh and told him how great that was. I could be a pretty good actor when I had to be. If my kids were excited about someone, I could be too. At least on the outside. Most people understood the relationship between cops and the mayor of New York. But I couldn't deny that he made my son happy with the signature. That was good enough for today.

Trent said, "In the letter, he called me a 'national scholar.'"

"That's big-time, Trent. I'm very impressed. I'm also proud of you. But I'm always proud of you. You don't have to see the mayor to make me proud."

"Thanks, Dad."

I said, "You're in the fast lane now. Don't do anything too idiotic and get knocked onto a side street."

Trent laughed, then said, "C'mon, Dad. I'm fourteen. You want me to use good judgment. Isn't that asking a lot?"

He waited while I paused. Then all Trent said was "Love ya. Gotta go." He handed the phone to one of his sisters.

The nature-versus-nurture debate has extra meaning in my house because all ten children are adopted. But I realized nurture was winning out because Trent had my sense of humor.

After I'd talked to a couple of the younger kids who still liked chatting with their dad, Mary Catherine came on the line.

I needed this kind of distraction. I wasn't thinking about Jeremy Pugh or what I wanted to do to him.

I filled Mary Catherine in on most of my trip, leaving out a key detail of what had happened to me in the last hour. I also told her about the rumors I'd heard concerning Emily Parker. I don't like to gossip, but I wanted a female perspective.

I said, "I know Emily really well, and I never would've suspected she had a thing for powerful men. Or that she would possibly date someone who was married."

As usual, Mary Catherine could set me straight quickly. "Usually I'd make some joke about your age and how you're out of date. But truthfully, the way I see couples today, I think we're *both* a little old-fashioned."

"You think I need to update my thinking?"

"Of course I don't. At least not about romance. It wouldn't hurt you to update your ideas about fashion. Or maybe even sports. It wouldn't kill you to watch more soccer or cricket. But I think you and I are on the same page as far as romance goes. We're old-fashioned, and that's the way I like it. You're the only one I want, and I want to be the only one you want."

I was pretty sure I agreed with her, although the way she had said it sounded like a trap. After a few moments of silence, she said, "Isn't that right, Michael?"

For a moment, I had a flashback of my days at Holy Name School. Mary Catherine's question sounded like a comment one of the nuns would've made during geography class. I knew to say, "Yes, right." I was just having a little fun. She was right. She was the only woman for me.

Mary Catherine was quick to add, "I'm not judging Emily. I'm just saying, that kind of love life is not for me."

"So you're happy with just boring old me."

"Don't say that, Michael. You're not that old yet. We've got at least three more years before that happens."

Sharing a laugh together was exactly what I needed to set my head straight and get back to work.

CHAPTER 15

AN HOUR LATER, dressed in very casual clothes, I stood in the lobby of my hotel, waiting for Bobby Patel. He'd called me and wanted to drop something off. He said he didn't care if other federal workers saw us together. They couldn't be any more inquisitive than his friends from the FBI who had seen us at the coffee shop.

We grabbed a sofa in a corner where we could speak privately. I felt underdressed compared to the younger FBI man. It wasn't just his tailored suit but his precise hair, perfect tie, and polished shoes.

When I told Bobby about my day, I left out the assault. I didn't know how he'd react. He might want to take official action. Now was not the time. I just told him The Burning Land people seemed to be assholes. He agreed.

I told him I'd read an article in *Rolling Stone* magazine

about the group's formation and its early members. One of the founders had dropped out of Harvard, and his mother was the representative from his district in Massachusetts.

Bobby laughed at that. He said, "I wouldn't have survived telling my parents I was dropping out of Harvard. My mom almost killed me when I didn't go to med school."

Bobby handed me a thick file folder. He said, "Here's some background our analysts did on the people we talked to."

I took the folder and judged its weight in my left hand. The extra information almost felt like a distraction.

I said, "I'm going to do a little research on my own. Starting with Justice Steinberg."

The look Bobby gave me when he heard the Supreme Court justice's name gave me pause. He asked, "How are you going to do something like that without drawing attention to yourself?"

"This evening there's an author signing a new book at the Barnes & Noble about a mile from here. I figured I'd go for a nice stroll and listen to what the author had to say. The book's about the history of the Supreme Court and how it affects decisions today."

"Sounds thrilling."

"It might not be a Tom Clancy novel, but I expect it will have some good information. Maybe the author will be inclined to give me a little inside scoop."

Bobby just shrugged. It was his way of telling me I was wasting my time. But that was why I was in DC, wasn't it? To do the odd things the FBI and the DC police weren't going to waste time on. You never know what will turn an investigation.

Bobby said, "Along with the analyst's background info there's a 302 on my interview of Emily's mother." He stopped short.

I knew a 302 was just FBI jargon for an interview report. "Did Emily's mom say anything worthwhile?" I noticed Bobby's hesitation. I was patient. I waited for him to decide what he was going to say.

Finally, Bobby said, "Mrs. Parker didn't go into much detail. At least with me. I think my dark complexion threw her off."

"Are you saying she's racist?" I couldn't imagine anyone who raised Emily being a racist.

Bobby said, "Maybe not in the specific sense of thinking less of people of color. I can't put my finger on it. I got the idea she didn't like me working so closely with Emily. It was clear she didn't even want me using Emily's name."

"How many FBI agents went to see her?"

"I went alone. I didn't want to intimidate her. Plus, we've got so many leads—all useless so far—each agent has to cover as many as possible so we don't cut into our resources."

As I opened the folder and paged through for the report, Bobby said, "She lives in Bowie. That's about forty-five minutes away, depending on traffic. It's a typical DC suburb."

I already knew where I'd head tomorrow. I might be able to speak with Emily's sister as well. I worried that Bobby was too by the book to stir things up. Sometimes an investigator needs a fire to get moving.

I tried something. I said, "You gotta be done for the night."

That drew a quick laugh. "Are you kidding me? I have three stops to make before I even think about heading home to Alexandria. My longest stop will be at local corporate security for Whole Foods to see if anyone found the missing DVD of the security footage of when Emily drove into the lot." He sighed and rubbed both his eyes with the palms of his hands.

That response satisfied me for now. He had a good attitude and was a hard worker. Maybe it would be good to work something with him if he ever transferred to New York City.

Bobby looked at his watch, and I noticed a woman in an oversize chair in the lobby pretending to watch TV. She had long dark hair and wore a baseball cap that made her look like a teenager. On closer inspection, she appeared to be around thirty. And she was watching Bobby and me, not the TV.

I let Bobby go on his way to see how the woman would react.

She stayed with me.

I decided to act.

CHAPTER 16

I STOOD RIGHT where I had been talking to Bobby. I pretended to look at different reports from the folder while I gathered information about the woman watching me. She looked over her shoulder twice. I followed her gaze to two other men. A tall black man and a shorter heavyset white dude wearing a shirt and tie. The tie was way too short. It only accentuated his gut. At least now I knew there were three people I had to deal with.

After acting like I dropped a page from the folder, I used a decorative column to block the woman's view. It was only a couple steps to get me into a hallway. Then I did a quick jog through the hallway in a giant loop around to the other side of the lobby. By the time I came out the other end of the hallway, the woman was with her two male companions. They weren't even trying to conceal the fact that they were looking for me.

I'll confess that I had no clue who they might be. They looked too old and well dressed to be members of The Burning Land. Maybe Bobby hadn't been honest with me and felt like he needed an FBI surveillance team to keep track of me. A lot of thoughts ran through my head. I decided the best course of action was just to ask them.

I waited till the three of them were deep in discussion and stepped up almost behind them. I couldn't hide my smile when all three of them jumped as I said, "Are you guys looking for me?"

Now I could see the black guy was in really good shape. About my age and almost as tall as me. The woman was also very fit. It was only the older white guy who clearly didn't care anything about physical fitness. As I looked a little closer at him, I realized he didn't care much about fashion either. His windbreaker had a mustard stain on it, and his tie looked even more ridiculous up close. It was a circus scene with judges and lawyers in the role of clowns.

They turned to stare at me. Like I was a giraffe at the zoo. I realized they were some kind of law enforcement. I said, "Is this like a surveillance practical from the academy? Do you guys want my notes on your effectiveness?"

Now the black guy spoke up. "Hello, Detective. I hope you're having fun."

"I am. I appreciate your efforts to make me laugh."

He held up a credential case with a DC police badge on the outside. "I'm Paul Daggett. We're assigned to Special Investigations. Can you guess why Special Investigations is at your hotel to talk to you?"

"Because I'm special?"

This time the woman answered. "We're trying to be polite and show you some professional courtesy. You're not making it easy."

"You know why I'm not making it easy?"

The woman said, "Because your vagina hurts?"

I had to smile. Banter between cops could often be hysterical. I liked her attitude. I took a moment, then said, "If you're serious about showing me courtesy, you would've walked up and introduced yourselves, not followed me around like stalkers."

Daggett said, "You mean like the way you gave us a heads-up you were coming down to DC?"

"I did give a heads-up to the FBI."

"Now I've heard it all. A New York City detective calls the FBI before he calls a DC detective."

"How did you even know I was here? Why do you care?"

Daggett said, "If it goes on in the city, Special Investigations knows about it. Also, we're looking for Emily Parker too. We don't need some hotshot from New York to come down and tell us how to do things."

"Or show you up?"

Daggett didn't answer.

I said, "If you're working so hard to find Emily, why are you here at my hotel hassling me instead of following leads? Maybe you're not as sharp as you think." I felt my face flush with anger. It had been a tough day. "I'm here for one reason and one reason only: to find Emily Parker. You're not the only one who can make vague threats. I won't bother you, and I expect the same." I turned and walked away.

Daggett called after me, "If you interfere with any investigation, in any way, you'll see us again. And you won't be happy about it."

I turned to look back at the three cops. "I'm not happy I saw you this time." Then I looked at the older white cop, who hadn't spoken. "You need to represent law enforcement better. Get your jacket dry-cleaned, lose about forty pounds, and get your head out of your ass."

The fat cop said with a grin, "Your wife said she liked my belly."

I couldn't keep from smiling. That was petty, old-school-cop trash talk.

CHAPTER 17

I'D BEEN TO only three book signings in my life. Two of them were at a bookstore in New York called The Mysterious Bookshop. A buddy of mine who retired from the NYPD wrote a couple of novels. The bookstore was packed with his friends and supporters.

The other signing I went to was at a Barnes & Noble in Manhattan. I went with the kids, who wanted R. L. Stine to sign their Goosebumps books. It was a lot of fun, and the author could not have been more gracious. There were also about three thousand people waiting for him to sign.

That's why when I walked into the quiet Barnes & Noble, I wondered if I'd gotten my days wrong. Then I found the area where author Julia Raz was speaking to six people in the front row of a nearly empty seating area. There were four more rows of ten folding chairs, each empty behind the six fans.

I sat quietly about halfway back. The author was in her mid forties and dressed in a sleek, professional skirt suit that would be a perfect fit for a corporate boardroom. Her dark hair was cut short, and expressive eyebrows flared behind designer glasses.

I listened as she gave a brief review of some of the justices who'd served on the Court over the past one hundred years. Then she started talking about the current Court. Nothing she said was particularly surprising or shocking.

I waited until after she'd finished speaking. Three of the six people brought copies of the book up for her to sign. I hung back until the others finished and then moved forward hesitantly with a copy of her book, *The Best Hundred Years of the Supreme Court*. She smiled warmly and opened the book to its title page, where she signed her name with a flourish.

I said, "I didn't want to cut in front of the other people in the seats."

Ms. Raz laughed. "One of them is my niece, one of them is my publicist, and another is my publicist's sister she brought along to make the crowd look bigger."

I wasn't sure if I was supposed to laugh or if she was making light of a bad situation. I said, "It's the middle of the week. I wouldn't expect many people to be free."

She laughed and placed her hand on my forearm. "You're just being nice. And I absolutely appreciate it. But these are the realities of being an author. It matters a lot more how many books I sell on Amazon than it does how many people come to my book signings. This was fine. I live right in Georgetown so it's not even a long ride home."

"I'm anxious to read your book."

"Is there anything in particular you're interested in? I'm

happy to answer questions for anyone who ventured out for my signing."

"I had a few questions about Justice Robert Steinberg. But I don't want to keep you from your friends."

"Don't worry. They know how to keep themselves occupied for a few minutes. Besides, I could use a cup of coffee. Can we take this to the café?"

A few minutes later, I had learned that Julia Raz had been an attorney for twenty years and appeared in front of the Supreme Court on a regular basis.

I had to ask, "Do you still practice or just write books?"

"I love the law, but lawyers were starting to annoy me. After I was part of a big tobacco settlement, I decided to retire and do exactly what I wanted. This is my second book on the Supreme Court."

I asked about Justice Steinberg, and she told me a lot of what I'd already read. He was considered a great legal mind. He was somewhat nonpartisan, especially considering who his father-in-law was. And he was private. He rarely gave interviews, and when he did, his chief of staff always sat in with him. Blah, blah, blah.

I asked, "Do you know his chief of staff?" I downplayed my knowledge of the justice.

"Everyone knows his sister, Beth."

"His sister is on the payroll?"

"She doesn't take a salary but acts in a purely administrative role. She's very bright. Went to Stanford. But she's not an attorney."

"If she's not an attorney, is she that much help to the justice?"

"She's everything for him. Mostly, she protects his privacy.

She could be a bouncer at a high-end nightclub. Athletic, no-nonsense. I think she's the perfect chief of staff for a town like Washington."

"So Beth is the key to the justice?"

"That's a good way to put it. Why so interested?"

"Just curious. The fact that he's married to my senator's daughter is one thing. We have some other people in common."

"Justice Steinberg's wife is also very bright. She may not be as tough as his sister, but she got her law degree from Columbia."

"Is she going to get one in the US as well?" That made Ms. Raz guffaw, and I had another lead: Justice Steinberg's sister, Beth.

CHAPTER 18

WHEN I CAME to DC to find Emily Parker, I realized that I might run into some roadblocks. I anticipated petty FBI people wanting to keep the investigation to themselves. DC police could do a lot to discourage me. Now I'd been told in no uncertain terms that they didn't want me here.

And I still had no idea what had happened to Emily. I had some background information. I had no real leads. And no matter what Bobby Patel was telling me, the FBI had no decent leads either. I was going to talk to people they had already talked to. Maybe stir things up a little bit.

I endured a snicker from the valet when he brought my little purple Prius around in front of the hotel. Two other valets joined him to watch me get into the tiny car. I took a moment to gather my thoughts before I wedged myself into the driver's seat. I must've looked like one of my kids when they would drive the little electric cars I bought them when they were little.

I took the John Hanson Highway out to Bowie, Maryland. This was one of the nicer suburbs that served DC. Very neat and orderly. I found the subdivision where Emily Parker's mother had a nice three-bedroom, two-bath. It matched virtually every other house on the street. A single tree shed a few leaves in the otherwise tidy front yard.

This was not an interview I was looking forward to. No one wants to bother the mother of a missing person. The FBI report I'd read indicated that she had no usable information but hadn't mentioned anything about her demeanor, so I had no idea what state of mind she was in. I pictured a lot of cats.

When I rang the front doorbell, I realized how wrong I was. It started with one bark. A deeper, resonant bark. Then it was like a floodgate had opened. The cascade of different woofs rushed toward the door. I could hear bodies of various sizes slamming against the door. Mrs. Parker was a dog person.

The door opened, and I was prepared to be mobbed by dogs. Instead, an attractive woman with auburn hair and glasses sitting at the top of her head said, "You must be Michael Bennett. Emily says you're a bulldog. As you can see, I appreciate any kind of dog."

I looked down to see six dogs. Most of them were mixed breeds, but one of them was related to a German shepherd and one to some kind of toy poodle. None of them crossed the threshold of the front door. They all just stared at me silently.

Mrs. Parker smiled. "That's called proper training. While you and I are chatting, they won't make a peep. They'll bark when someone knocks at the door, but they won't run outside unless I give them permission."

"Their training is very impressive."

"Too bad my control over my children isn't as good."

I stepped inside as I said, "You think you could've stopped whatever happened to Emily?"

"I would've stopped her from ever joining the FBI. I would've talked my youngest daughter into going to school closer to home, and I would've tried to convince my middle daughter not to marry that moron. I would've convinced my son that pot affects your life decisions in a bad way."

Mrs. Parker led me to a comfortable couch and offered me some coffee. I had to admit that the dogs were extraordinarily well-behaved and never intruded on me. There was nevertheless a musty funk in the room. I don't know if the smell was just the dogs themselves or if they had newspapers they peed on.

One dog, with a face like a basset hound and the body of a heavy-set Doberman, stood next to my place on the couch and laid a head on the cushion. His giant, brown eyes looked up at me. I knew a command to rub a head when I saw one. I tickled the top of the dog's head. His body remained motionless, but his tail started to wag.

When Mrs. Parker walked back into the room, the dog withdrew. It was like magic. I thought about stealing her training secret. My human kids didn't listen nearly as well as these dogs.

Now that I looked at Emily's mom, after she settled into an easy chair across from the sofa, I could see the strain on her face. Emily had told me years ago how she admired her mother for her toughness. A missing child can break through anyone's tough facade.

I went through all the obvious questions. Last time she had seen Emily. Did Emily talk to her about any concerns? Had Emily talked about any of her cases? The usual. Then I wanted to go a little deeper.

"Does Emily ever talk to you about dating or boyfriends?"

"No, that is something she keeps to herself. If I ever ask, she changes the subject. I understand. I was young once. She had a rough time with her marriage. John has turned himself around, and I'm okay with my granddaughter living with him for now. But since she divorced him, Emily has never told me about any boyfriends."

I said, "Has Emily ever disappeared before?"

Mrs. Parker thought about it for a moment. "No one has asked that yet. And the answer is yes. Several times. She can suffer from depression. And once, while in college, she was gone for almost two weeks. All she ever told me about it was that it was like hunkering down for a hurricane in a hotel room. She called it her own emotional hurricane.

"Then about four years ago she dropped out of touch for five days. At least that time she gave the FBI a heads-up and told them she didn't feel well. But no one could reach her. Her sister Laura figured it out. Emily was staying at a cabin in Virginia owned by a boyfriend. Laura said she was just sitting there by herself and hadn't eaten in two days."

"Did Emily ever tell you if getting away for a few days helped her?"

"I never pressed her for answers. It was important that the girls knew I was here for them no matter what. Emily's father used to press her for answers, and they barely spoke for the last three years of his life."

"I'm sorry. When did your husband die?"

"He's not technically dead. He left me. He said I loved the dogs more than him. Which is probably true. Anyway, he's dead to me. And to my girls. My son, Tom, still has a relationship with him but not so much with me. He calls once a week, but that's it. One day he'll come back into the fold. All I have is my son and three girls. And I need you to find the missing one."

For the first time since I started looking into things here in DC, I had some hope of finding Emily alive.

CHAPTER 19

I MADE THE short trip from Bowie to Springdale, Maryland, again on the John Hanson Highway, back to the I-495 interchange. Emily's sister Laura, whose married name was Nardo, was two years younger, a fourth-grade teacher who lived with her husband and baby in a development that looked almost exactly like her mother's. Even the house was a similar three-bedroom, two-bath one-story. With a single tree in the middle of the trimmed front yard.

When I knocked on her door, I did not hear the sound of dogs.

I should have told myself to beware of memories. The woman standing inside the open door looked exactly like Emily. Laura had the same slender frame and pretty face. Her hair was a little lighter, cut in a similar style as Emily's so that it fell playfully across her face. My heart hurt looking at her.

Laura gave me a weak smile. The first words out of her mouth were "I can see why Emily always talks about you."

She was a little like her mom: direct and to the point. In no time, I found myself on a comfortable sofa in a living room littered with baby toys. A mesh playpen stood in the corner.

Laura noticed me looking around the room and said, "You have good timing. The baby's been down about fifteen minutes and usually sleeps for a good two hours."

It was my hope to get background, so I kept the interview more casual than official. If it felt like we were just chatting, Laura might come up with some morsel of information that would put everything into perspective. Maybe an old cabin the family used to visit. Or an old lover Emily might flee to if she was having problems.

I said, "Your home has a different atmosphere than your mom's."

"You mean the dogs? I had to stop her from calling them my brothers and sisters."

Laura was all movement and nervous drumming of her fingers, more animated and fidgety than Emily.

When I felt like I was starting to gain her confidence, I asked, "Are you and Emily close?"

"You have any brothers or sisters, Michael?"

"Nope, I'm an only child."

Her eyes opened in surprise. "Really? Considering you have ten children, I would've thought you came from a big family."

She read the confusion on my face.

Laura smiled and said, "Relax, I'm not stalking you. Emily really likes you. She respects you. I don't think I've ever heard her talk as well about anyone as she does about you. She even likes your fiancée."

"Wife."

"Really? When did that happen?"

"About two weeks ago."

"I guess I haven't talked to her much in the last few weeks. She's been so busy." Laura took a moment to wipe her red-rimmed eyes with a tissue. And she blew her nose. "Sorry, this has been hard. I took some time off work when Emily went missing. Mom is in denial, and my younger sister, Liza, calls every ten minutes. We told her to stay at Northwestern until we learned more. She's in the audiology program."

"She's in what?"

"Good dad joke," Laura said.

I looked Laura in the eyes and said, "Can I ask some personal questions about Emily? Embarrassingly personal."

That made Laura smile. "Anything you want."

"I didn't see Emily judge people and I'm not going to do it to her. I just want to find my friend. And I don't know what will help me."

Laura solemnly nodded her assent.

"I'm hearing rumors that she's dated powerful people. Like it's a regular occurrence. Does she talk to you about that kind of stuff?"

Laura nodded again. "Emily was very quiet growing up. I'm sure my mom told you my dad could be tough. It wasn't till Emily enrolled at the University of Virginia that she came out of her shell. She told me about dating a philosophy professor. She said knowing influential people made her feel like a star. She was giddy telling me about it.

71

"In the last year, since she's been in DC quite a bit, she's started to see a few different people. She's told me about some, and others she says she can't talk about."

"Did she give you any names?"

"She dated some congressman from Delaware. I think his last name is Bryant. That's all she really told me. She was a little secretive about him. I don't know if he's married or something else." Laura looked off toward the corner of the room.

I could tell she was hesitating. I tried not to rush her.

Eventually she focused back on me. "I think there have been a few other politicians. And of course Justice Steinberg."

"You say 'of course.' Why is that?"

"She talked to me about it like everyone knew. Everyone on the inside."

"Do you think Steinberg's wife knew? Did being married mean anything?"

"Not to him or Emily. I think his wife was even okay with it."

I made a few notes on a pad mainly to cover my shock.

Laura said, "Not everyone is into traditional relationships. Like a man with ten kids."

I held up my hands in surrender. "You're right. But I'm not judging. Just surprised. I've spent a lot of time with Emily and never had any idea this was one of her interests."

Laura shrugged. "You get used to it. Emily's other qualities are more important. She's bright, loyal, and caring."

"And apparently secretive."

Laura nodded. "And secretive."

Secrets tended to make any investigation more difficult.

CHAPTER 20

SAUNDRA HYLAND LIKED taking her gifted third-grade class outdoors to discover the "hidden nature" in the DC area. She'd already taken the kids to two parks near the private school where she'd taught for almost six years.

Now they were in the southernmost area of Rock Creek Park. The green space was named after the Rock Creek tributary that joined with the nearby Potomac, but at this end of the meandering greenway, extending from the larger park farther north, it wasn't particularly natural given the nearby connection between Interstate 66 and K Street.

While Saundra could hardly keep up with some of the children's grasp of advanced mathematics, this was an activity in which she flourished. Her youth in Florida had trained her to appreciate nature. Her days at the University of Florida had taught her how to teach. That, and how to haggle for the cheapest bag of pot.

Now she stopped next to the smartest boy in the class—maybe the whole school. "What have you got, Jake?"

The boy held up a small plastic bottle with a spider inside.

Saundra fought the urge to jump when she saw the spider.

Jake said, "It's a banded garden spider. *Argiope trifasciata*. They build their nests close to the ground to catch tiny pests. They're vital in controlling insect populations." Then he looked at his teacher with disdain. "Only the ignorant are afraid of spiders."

Saundra made a note not to engage Jake again today. Or possibly tomorrow, if she could get away with it.

Her phone sounded with Ariana Grande's "The Way," the ringtone giving her an excuse to step away from Jake. She looked at the screen and saw it was her on-again, off-again boyfriend, Dave. She let the call go to voicemail. He was literally the only person she wanted to speak to less than Jake.

Saundra's usual response was to deal with each tiny drama as it appeared, but she wasn't getting any help from Donna Andrus, the other teacher on the field trip. True to her slacker reputation, she'd told Saundra to cover for her for a few minutes. That was almost an hour ago.

Having sole responsibility for sixteen kids running around a park near open water was overwhelming. The kids were having a good time learning. But now all Saundra could think about was having a couple of beers tonight.

She occasionally called out, "Don't get too close to the water!" Usually that was directed at Lainey Steele. At this moment, a group of kids clustered right at the shoreline. And of course Lainey was in the middle of them. The small, beautiful girl had the charisma of a cult leader the other students followed blindly.

This time Saundra yelled with some force, "Everyone step away from the water!"

A few of the kids listened. But four or five stayed right where they were. What was so interesting that the kids would risk a letter of discipline to see? Saundra took a few steps closer. Then she saw that little Lainey was poking something with a stick. Four boys watched her intently. Typical.

Then Saundra realized what she was seeing. This time she screamed, "Get back!" She had 911 dialed into her phone before the first kid moved.

CHAPTER 21

THE RIDE FROM Maryland back to DC gave me time to think. I went over my interview with Emily's sister Laura again and again. Her description of Emily's romantic life made me feel like Mary Catherine and I were out of step with the times. I liked romance and the "old-fashioned" love affair I had with my new bride.

Both Mrs. Parker and Laura had said that Emily had withdrawn in the past. That was the shred of hope I was clinging to. I had the feeling Bobby Patel was working under the presumption that Emily was dead. Now, knowing some of her emotional history, I could see where suicide would also be a concern. But I was looking for anything positive. And the fact that she had been known to disappear gave me hope that maybe she'd done it again.

On my way back to my hotel, I decided to take a swing past

The Burning Land's warehouse headquarters. To my surprise, the bay door was down. I drove a few more blocks and stopped at a sports bar.

How long had this place been here? Its ten-car lot was riddled with potholes, and it had been at least a decade since the exterior was painted with a now barely discernible rendition of Redskins great John Riggins as MVP of Super Bowl XVII. Exactly the kind of place I would expect Jeremy Pugh and his other Burning Land members to frequent. Maybe I'd get lucky.

The door creaked against its frame and one of the hinges wiggled. The place was dark and empty. Ten TVs, only three of them flat screens, played reruns of various sporting events. I took a seat at the bar, where the two closest TVs played the same local channel.

A tubby bartender with a four-pack-a-day voice croaked, "What can I get you?"

"Grilled chicken sandwich."

"Don't got no chicken."

"Turkey?"

He shook his wide bald head.

"Maybe you could make a suggestion."

"We got hamburgers and cheeseburgers. Your choice."

"Cheeseburger, please." I glanced at the screens around the bar. I didn't care about a Nationals game from four years ago or a Redskins game when Joe Gibbs was still coaching. I looked over to the TV directly above the bar where I was sitting. A promo said the local news was on next. That sounded good enough for me.

I debated asking the bartender if any of The Burning Land people came in here. If I showed him the printed photographs

Bobby had given me, he'd know I was some kind of cop. That might tip off Jeremy Pugh and his friends that I was looking at them.

A young newscaster with blond hair popped on the screen. She was doing a live remote from a waterside park.

The reporter said, "I'm on the banks of Rock Creek, where about three hours ago students from a local elementary school stumbled on the remains of a human body tangled in the weeds." The station showed file tape of the arrival of emergency personnel.

The reporter continued her story. "We spoke to several officials with knowledge of the discovery who believe the body is that of missing FBI agent Emily Parker. Agent Parker disappeared earlier this week while out for an early morning jog."

I stared at the TV silently as my world crashed down around me. Was this my fault? Had Emily been calling me because she knew she was in danger?

The bartender's voice broke me out of my trance.

"Eat it before it gets cold. No refunds," he said, pointing at the plate I didn't even notice he'd placed in front of me.

I had completely lost my appetite.

CHAPTER 22

I SAT ON the stool in the rundown sports bar and stared at the TV until a follow-up segment came on the news. The bartender never walked by to see if I had eaten my cheeseburger or needed anything. I laid a twenty on the bar and shuffled across the sandy hardwood floor and pushed through the door with the sketchy hinge.

I'm not even sure how I got back to my hotel. All I did was nod at the valet as he took possession of the small purple Prius. I shambled to my room like a zombie. I was numb. And my brain was working no better than that of a mental patient who hasn't received his daily meds.

I've never been a big drinker. Most times that was probably a fortunate decision. Right now I could understand turning to alcohol to numb the pain. I sat on the edge of the bed and let my brain run unfiltered.

I had lost friends before. Cops are murdered on a regular basis. The public doesn't say much about it, but cops mourn together at the loss of every officer. The fact that Emily was also my friend only sharpened the pain. I wasn't ready to accept that interesting, intelligent Emily could just stop being part of my world. Whether it was her choice or not. I already knew how much I'd miss her.

My mind turned to the small gestures that had made Emily dear to me, how she had gone above and beyond the call of duty when my family and I were in witness protection. Or how she would call just to say hello.

I thought about making a call home. Then I decided to not let my mood infect my family.

When my phone rang from across the room, it startled me. It was Bobby Patel calling, and I knew why. Even though I didn't want to talk to him, didn't want to hear confirmation, I answered.

The first thing I said was "I saw it on the news."

Bobby said, "Just making sure. Are you doing all right?"

I mumbled, "Yeah. I think so." I didn't even know what I was saying. Then I remembered to ask, "What about you?"

Bobby groaned, then said, "It's tough, but what are you going to do?" There was silence between us until finally Bobby said, "I'll call you tomorrow after the autopsy."

I had to do something, so I got off the bed and walked with a purpose down to the business center. My favorite computer was free, and I started doing research on the Supreme Court justices. I looked through some websites. There were a lot of them, and much discussion of conspiracy theories about who should or should not be on the Supreme Court.

Then I focused on Justice Robert Steinberg. An article about his sister, Beth Banks, who'd kept her name from a previous marriage, ran with an impressive photograph of an attractive, athletic-looking woman in her early thirties. Her short dark hair and glasses didn't soften her image at all.

I thought again about Emily's calls to me in Ireland. Maybe she had been going to tell me who was trying to kill her. Maybe it had been just to say hello. Either way, it made me realize there was no way I was going back to New York without knowing who murdered my friend.

This was now a homicide investigation. That was my territory.

CHAPTER 23

I WOKE UP with what felt like a hangover. An emotional hangover. It was probably a good thing I hadn't drunk alcohol. I could barely imagine feeling any worse than I already did.

I lay in bed and stared at the ceiling of my standard hotel room. I thought about all the hotels I'd stayed at over the past twenty years. Most were exactly like this. Clean, cold, and dull. White ceiling paint dotted with a sprinkler head and a fire alarm.

I'd slept in fits last night. I had called Mary Catherine a little on the late side. I had to break the news to her before I went to bed. I felt pain as intense as a smack in the face when I had to say out loud that they had found Emily's body. After all the years of seeing bodies, I never get used to the way they seem discarded. Especially a body that's washed up onshore.

They're often mistaken for trash. It's a sad and unthinkable situation.

Mary Catherine cried and, trying to support me, attempted to sound brave. I told her I was fine but tired. She accepted that, and we kept the call unusually short.

I knew the only way to find peace in this situation was to go at it hard. No matter what the DC Metropolitan Police thought. No matter how the FBI might react to me going rogue. I knew my time in DC was limited. Sooner or later the FBI would find out I was here and complain. So the first thing I did was call someone *not* with the FBI. Someone who got me: Roberta Herring.

Roberta agreed to meet me at the entrance to the Smithsonian National Air and Space Museum, a short walk from my hotel. As I made my way through the lobby, a local TV news story caught my attention.

The reporter narrated a montage. Emily as a young agent, walking a crime scene. Cut to the crime scene around her body. Finally, an ambush of Emily's mother. I cringed when I saw the reporter shove a microphone in Mrs. Parker's face and ask how she felt about her daughter's death. I didn't go to Northwestern's Medill School of Journalism, but that seemed like a pretty obvious question.

Mrs. Parker didn't acknowledge the reporter. As he followed her up the porch steps, the reporter yelped. Then the sound dissolved into dogs barking or growling. I don't know which one bit the reporter, but I was definitely a fan.

As soon as the story ended, I walked out the front doors of my hotel. Fresh air and the brief autumn sunshine did me some good. I was wearing my Holy Name basketball windbreaker while my sport coat was still at the hotel dry cleaner. I thought about making them do it a second time just to be on the safe side.

I waited on the museum steps. Looking through the windows, I could see the lunar module LM-2 sitting directly under the *Spirit of St. Louis*. I'd have to check this place out when I had more time.

I could see Roberta strolling toward me from almost a hundred yards away. I felt a little like a spy, checking each way for countersurveillance.

Before she even sat down, Roberta said, "I can tell when you're jumpy. I knew that the news of Emily's death would hit you hard, but I'm sensing something else."

I told her about my visit from the DC police as well as my run-in with The Burning Land.

Roberta smiled and shook her head. "He peed right on your back?"

All I could do was nod.

She chuckled. "I'd hate to be him in the near future." She looked out over the pedestrians walking in front of the museum, which was an hour from opening. "The DC Special Investigations cops who tried to scare you are sharp and hardworking, but they don't play particularly well with others."

I went over a few things I'd figured out. Nothing that was going to help nail Emily's killer.

Roberta said, "I've been listening to gossip. Something I don't normally do. Anytime I hear someone mention Emily Parker, I pay a little extra attention. It looks like she did have a wild side. The three names I hear the most are Justice Steinberg, an oil lobbyist named Minshew, and the congressman from—"

"Delaware. And his name is Marty Bryant."

She looked at me and smiled. "Sometimes I forget you're smart enough to keep your mouth shut and your own ears open. Those seem like three pretty solid leads. I'm confident you can do something with them."

CHAPTER 24

AN HOUR INTO my research on Congressman Marty Bryant, Bobby Patel called me. He filled me in on Emily's autopsy. Her cause of death was strangulation. They figured she'd been in the water more than seventy-two hours. I didn't ask questions or engage him at all. I just couldn't.

I threw myself into researching Congressman Bryant, then decided to take my chances and try to see him at his office on the Capitol campus.

I went through the public entrance to the Longworth House Office Building. I showed my ID to a Capitol Police officer next to the metal detector. We chatted for a few minutes about how police work is similar wherever you go. The young man, freshly out of the army and built like an Olympic swimmer, personally led me to the congressman's office. The helpful officer even introduced me to the congressman's assistant.

I don't know if the assistant was confused by my escort, but I got immediate attention. She hustled into the inner office, then motioned me to come in. I'll admit to being momentarily stunned when I stepped through the doorway.

The office of this second-term congressman was as plush and well decorated as any CEO's office at a major corporation. Dark walnut furniture, bookshelves that lined each wall, two seventy-plus-inch flat-screen TVs built into the wall. I noticed one was playing Fox News and the other was playing CNN.

As I regained my composure, I focused on the six-foot-tall congressman. He strode from behind his desk and had a broad smile on his face. I noticed his World Wildlife Fund tie. I knew exactly what the panda meant. A coalition of my younger kids bought me a different World Wildlife Fund tie each Christmas.

I shook the congressman's hand as he said, "What can I do for one of NYPD's finest? I was in the army, and I know how tough your job can be. Got an idea for a crime bill?"

"No, sir. It's more of a personal matter."

The congressman gave me a closer look and studied my face. "Have we met?"

I shook my head. "I'm looking into Emily Parker's death."

That froze the congressman in place. It also shut down his manufactured friendly facade.

I didn't mind the awkward silence. Sometimes that works in a cop's favor. Make someone uncomfortable and they might blurt out something incriminating. He looked at me with his intelligent brown eyes. He was about my age, but it seemed like the job might be putting unnecessary wear and tear on him.

Congressman Bryant looked over to his assistant, who was

still standing in the doorway. The middle-aged woman didn't say a word.

The congressman managed to say, "I-I don't understand. Why is an NYPD detective involved in a case in Washington, DC? Why would you want to talk to me?" Now his voice sounded more like a little kid's.

I waited a moment before I replied. Then I said, "It's a joint investigation. And I heard you were close with Emily."

Panicked wasn't quite the right word to describe the congressman. I think *stricken* was a better descriptor. He had no idea what to do next. Congressman Bryant gave his assistant another look. She calmly took a step back and closed the double doors to the inner office.

The congressman staggered back and plopped into an overstuffed leather chair that looked like it had come from the White House.

I took an identical chair directly across from him. He still didn't say much. He looked up at me for a moment but couldn't meet my eyes. I was starting to wonder if his relationship with Emily had been serious. Serious enough for him to have done something drastic if it wasn't going his way.

Finally, the congressman took a deep breath and said, "I'm sorry. You caught me a little off guard. I was very upset to hear they found Emily's body. But I really can't add anything to the investigation. We were just friends."

"Nothing more?"

"Friends. That's it. She listened. I liked her."

I noticed the perspiration building around his eyes and forehead. He still fidgeted in the seat. But now he could at least look me in the face. I said, "I'd think a member of Congress could find a lot of women to listen." That gave me the awkward, uncomfortable silence I was shooting for. I wanted to keep this guy off-balance. At least until I could figure out where he fit into this investigation.

Now the congressman looked at me and leveled his brown eyes. "Am I a suspect?"

"Should you be?"

That frustrated the congressman. He said, "I don't think I like your tone."

I gave him my own version of a friendly politician smile. Then I switched directions and said, "I don't really give a damn. You're not my congressman. And I'm trying to figure out who murdered my friend. You're lucky I'm not screaming at you right now. Or maybe, if I used a nicer tone on TV, people might listen to me." That had the effect I wanted.

The congressman rubbed his hands together. He took a long time to gather his thoughts. Finally, he said, "Is this interview confidential?"

"Absolutely."

"How do I know I can trust you?"

"I was in the Boy Scouts for almost four months when I was twelve."

The congressman just stared at me. He didn't find me as amusing as I found myself.

I cleared my throat and used my best solemn voice. "I have never broken my word in twenty years with the New York City Police Department. Never. I'm not about to start now."

He looked convinced. Then he said something I didn't expect. "The first thing you should know is that I'm gay."

CHAPTER 25

THE OLD PHRASE *crime of passion* is one of the most accurate terms in homicide investigations. The congressman knew as well as any investigator that the absence of any romantic relationship greatly reduces the motives for homicide. He needed to show me he had no romantic interest in Emily, and I understood that need.

Now the congressman had regained a little of his composure. He said, "Look, Detective, I don't advertise that I'm gay. I guess you'd say I'm not 'openly gay.' I think it could be hard on my career. But I want you to know that Emily was my friend. And that's it."

"Emily understood you were gay?"

"Yes, of course. I'm not ashamed of it. I just don't think it's anyone's business but my own. I didn't tell anyone when I was in the military, and I would prefer not to do it now."

I said, "Did Emily share any secrets with you?"

"We might have different definitions of *secret*. But she confided in me on several private matters."

"Was she involved with Justice Robert Steinberg?"

He hesitated. "She was cagey about that one. She had a relationship with Steinberg, but she didn't talk about it. I think it was because she promised him not to talk about it. That's how I knew I could trust that she wouldn't tell anyone I was gay."

"Was there anyone else she was involved with?"

"There is an oil lobbyist everyone knows. A guy named Donald Minshew. I met him a few times. It made my skin crawl to think that Emily ever saw anything in him. He's a disgusting loudmouth. He's a bully. Thank God Delaware doesn't have enough oil for me to ever deal with him."

"You think he's capable of strangling Emily?"

"Hell, I have no idea. To be honest, I don't see how he could've ever hurt her. She could've kicked his ass. You know how she was always working out. If nothing else, she could've run away. She was training for a marathon."

"Did she ever talk about work? Any of the investigations she ran?"

He shook his head slowly. "Nothing really. She might've bitched about a particular boss or a bad day, but she never got into the specifics."

"Have you ever heard of the group called The Burning Land?"

"Those assholes? All of us have had to deal with them. Why? Are they suspects?"

"Just being thorough. I'd like to look at them a little closer."

"I have an aide who keeps track of any group that's a threat. The Capitol Police also brief us. They tend to have really good insight into these groups." The congressman turned to his desk and picked up a sheet of paper. "They're protesting on the National Mall today." The congressman handed me the paper.

It was a map of the mall. *X*s marked where groups were protesting or holding rallies. I looked up at the congressman. "Can I keep this?"

He nodded.

"Thank you for the info. I might have a few more questions. But you've been very helpful."

"All I ask is that you find Emily's killer."

He didn't even need to ask that.

CHAPTER 26

I TOOK THE short walk from the Capitol campus, considering what I was hoping to accomplish, as I crossed Union Square past the Ulysses S. Grant Memorial. The Capitol Reflecting Pool spread out behind the bronze and marble statue. I wanted to see these morons with The Burning Land in action. I didn't want to alert them to my investigation. It was a tightrope to walk.

The temperature had dipped, and I zipped up my light windbreaker. I wasn't sure there was a reason to confront Jeremy Pugh or anyone from The Burning Land. I had to keep telling myself I only wanted to help the investigation. No matter how much I'd like to punch Jeremy Pugh right in the face, I'd have to wait.

I had to glance at the map once to see exactly where The Burning Land would be positioned on the wide-open fields. Ten minutes later, I was watching the hulking Jeremy Pugh, surrounded by the group's other members. They looked like children next to him. I could make out a couple of signs among the half dozen protesters. One said, NO POLITICAL PARTIES. The other said, BOTH PARTIES ARE THE SAME. It seemed redundant, but I wasn't going to mention it.

Next to the area where The Burning Land was putting on their show, the Wounded Warrior Project had a couple of information tables. They were collecting money and informing anyone who wanted to listen about the organization. I wanted to listen. As I drew closer, I wondered if anyone from The Burning Land would recognize me out of context. I doubted it.

Before anyone noticed me at the table, I slipped a twenty into the WWP's donation jar. A young man wearing jeans and a long-sleeved T-shirt with a tan leather glove on his left hand stepped up to me. We chatted for a moment, and he told me he was a volunteer who had recently been discharged from the army.

The lean young man, who was a little over six feet tall, still had the short-cropped hair of an Army Ranger. He told me about some of his assignments and training.

I said, "The Wounded Warriors are doing great work."

The young Ranger said, "Thanks. It has a much more personal meaning to me."

I stared at him, but he must've been used to questioning looks. He didn't say a word as he raised his left arm and pulled his sleeve up his forearm. It was a metal prosthetic with pistons in a titanium case.

The young man smiled. "I wear the glove even when it's warm. The prosthetic hasn't been completely tuned to give me function in two fingers. It also tends to freak out kids."

"Can I ask how you lost it?"

"Sniper near Bagram Air Base. Took it off from the elbow

down. My brother calls me the Terminator because I'm learning to use the arm in a hundred different ways." The young man cocked his head and looked at me. "What about you? Were you ever in the service?"

"No. I joined the NYPD more than twenty years ago."

"That's cool. Anyone who's doing something in public service deserves credit. Especially cops."

I enjoyed talking to the young man as people walked past without even glancing at the table. I could also look over at The Burning Land members. There weren't many of them right now.

I took a risk and said to the young Ranger, "Have you talked to any of the people next to you?"

"The Burning Land? Only for a second when we got here. The big asshole in the Tennessee Titans shirt told us we had to move over because they were expecting more than 200 people to protest. We've outnumbered them all day. You looking at them for a crime?"

"Sort of. Really only the big dude. I had a dustup with him, and I don't want any of them to see me."

The Ranger smiled. "The army always helps the police." He turned and walked away from me, grabbing a folding table as he walked. Then he got right next to The Burning Land and started to set up the table.

I couldn't keep from smiling when I realized what he was doing. It was a simple passive-aggressive provocation. And I liked it.

I saw Jeremy Pugh rush over to the young man setting up the table. Pugh shoved him and said, "I told you to stay over there."

The Ranger smiled and said, "You also said you'd have 200 people. I guess I just don't know when to believe you."

"You can believe I'll kick your ass if you don't move that table."

The Ranger said, "I'll move it when your extra 195 people show up."

Pugh stepped toward the table, and the Ranger gave him a halfhearted push. I knew this was his plan. I wanted to see what was going to happen. I was also ready to intervene because I didn't want this Ranger to get in any trouble.

Before I could move, Pugh threw a wild right-handed haymaker.

The Ranger calmly raised his left arm to block it. And he smiled.

Pugh's wrist caught the titanium under the young Ranger's sleeve. It sounded almost like a muted gong. The sound was so unusual that everyone looked in that direction.

Pugh grabbed his wrist and held it to his belly, as if he could squeeze the pain away. It didn't work. Pugh sputtered a few curses before he stared at the Ranger. After a few moments of trying to intimidate him, Pugh stomped away.

The Ranger gave me a broad smile and a wink.

I put my last ten-dollar bill in the jar.

CHAPTER 27

I ENJOYED MY walk back to the hotel to get my rental car. The sky was clear. I felt sunshine on my face. I had leads to follow. And I'd achieved a small measure of revenge. I chuckled every time I thought about Jeremy Pugh's wrist. And the Ranger had been just so casual in the way he'd blocked that punch. Clearly he knew that by never punching Jeremy Pugh himself, he had committed no crime.

By early afternoon, I'd driven past the address for Donald Minshew three times. I hadn't seen any cars in the driveway or anyone in the front yard. This part of the Capitol Hill neighborhood was beautiful, and the Minshew town house was no exception. It was three stories tall, with wide balconies on the second and third floors. The front yard was awash with imported flowers and colorful plants. I noticed tulips and some kind of tall tropical-looking flower. They must have installed a heater system. The flowers looked healthy now, but I didn't think many of them would make it through the winter. That was what I'd call conspicuous consumption. Texas style.

I parked more than a block away. Part of it was stealth, part of it embarrassment at the car I'd rented. After I maneuvered my way out of the car, I took a moment to straighten my shirt and pants.

My research on Donald Minshew was slim. He had no arrests, but the lobbyist had been censured twice for reasons that weren't clear to me. Fat, balding, and a little over fifty, with the red face of a serious drinker, he looked in his pictures like a caricature of an oil lobbyist.

And he was obviously rich. Not just *I have a vacation home* rich, more like *I have a Gulfstream to fly to my private island* rich. I already hated him.

I rang the bell and waited by the wide oak front door with hand-etched frosted glass. One side of the door had an etching of an oil well gushing oil. The other side was a wild horse rearing up.

There were two different security cameras as well as a Ring video doorbell. I knew I was being observed from inside the house. After almost a full minute, I heard several of the locks on the door move.

I was momentarily surprised when a beautiful woman with wild reddish hair opened the door and said, "May I help you?"

"I, um…" Her blue eyes locked onto mine. I guessed she was in her late thirties. She had a slight bump in her nose from a break years ago. It gave her an interesting profile. Finally, I was able to spit out, "I'm looking for Donald Minshew."

The woman didn't say a word. She just stared at me. Eventually, she said, "And you are?"

I fumbled to grab my badge quickly. I pulled it from my rear pocket and showed the badge with the credentials to her. She welcomed me inside. She had the kind of long, droopy robe I'd seen only in movies. It was almost like she was playing a role.

She looked over her shoulder and smiled. "I'm Don's wife, Ellen. Just curious, what's a New York City detective want with my hubby?"

"Just a few quick questions." I didn't want to give away any hints just yet. I changed the subject. "You have a lovely home."

She turned and took my arm. "I'm very proud of this place. My husband won't be home until around eight-ish. Can I give you a quick tour? Of course, this is just our home while Congress is in session. Our main house is about forty minutes outside Dallas. That's where we have a little bit of land and some horses."

"Thank you for the offer, but I do have some questions. You think I could meet your husband at his office?"

"Why would you want to do that? I assume you want to talk about *my* relationship with Emily Parker. Don really doesn't know much about her."

CHAPTER 28

I TRIED TO hide my surprise as I stared at Ellen Minshew. She was clearly a woman used to shocking people. For some reason I didn't want to give her the satisfaction.

She led me onto a patio, where we sat at a round glass table. The backyard was more spectacular than the front. Ferns hung from branches of some tropical tree. I had no clue what they did when the temperatures dropped. I was still trying to get a read on this woman. I wanted to make sure she wasn't playing me. I tried to focus on what she had said. Her "relationship" with Emily was all I could think about.

Without any obvious orders or movement from Mrs. Minshew, a young woman brought out a pitcher of iced tea. My host sat across from me like we were at a garden party.

She said, "When I first met Don, he was an oilman. That was over fifteen years ago. I'd just graduated from Yale with my economics degree. I sensed the change in the oil business and shifted Don into lobbying. You can't believe how much lobbyists get paid."

I glanced around the lush backyard. I thought I could believe how much they were paid.

I said, "Sounds like you're the brains and, forgive me, your husband's just the front man for this band."

"That's a beautiful analogy, Detective. Aren't you as sweet as peach pie? Don's got a few tricks up his sleeve too. We work well together. He knows the right people and I know what to say."

"Obviously you guessed correctly that I want to talk about Emily Parker. How did you meet her?"

"At one of the endless parties here in the district. She struck me as an interesting and intense young woman. We hit it off almost immediately."

"Did your husband have much interaction with her?"

"Don doesn't have much interaction with anyone who's not connected to the House or the Senate. He knew Emily and I were friends, and that's about it."

"If I may be frank, Mrs. Minshew, I heard a rumor that Emily and your husband were an item. Now you're saying that wasn't true. *You* and she were an item. I didn't realize that Emily was interested in women."

"Emily was interested in a lot of things."

"But not your husband."

"I never said our relationship was sexual. We were close friends. We liked the outdoors and marveling at how immature men could be. You know, the usual."

She winked at me like she was making certain I understood she automatically included me in that assessment.

She said, "It was fun to let people think she was sleeping with Don. In fact, she and I had a lot of laughs about it. Emily was a good friend who was smart enough to not care what people thought."

Now she leaned across the table toward me and put her hand on my forearm.

She said, "I have a lot of things I'm interested in too. Tall cops from New York are right at the top of my list."

I pulled my hand from her grip and off the table. I didn't want there to be any confusion about why I was here. I concentrated on pulling my notepad and a pen out of my jacket pocket. Then I said, "Did Emily ever say anything about Robert Steinberg?"

"A little. He's another wild one."

"Is that what Emily said?"

"No. She didn't speak about the justice. She could really keep secrets. But I've known Steinberg for years. I knew him when he was a regular at Jeffrey Epstein parties. He didn't slow down much once he got married."

"You know Justice Steinberg's wife?"

"Of course. Everyone knows Rhea. She's just a slip of a woman with big, fake boobies and a pretty face. That's all some people need. I like a little danger as well. Maybe if she didn't think she was some kind of artist she could focus more energy on her husband."

I didn't really see this interview going anywhere toward establishing who might have had a motive to kill Emily.

Mrs. Minshew said, "You know how some people say they don't like to gossip?"

I nodded.

"I'm not one of them. I can imagine what people say about

102

me, married to a roly-poly old man. They probably say a hair weave would improve his looks. I don't really care. But I get a kick out of hearing comments about everyone else. Would you like to hear some juicy gossip?"

"I would."

She gave a smile that was both dazzling and terrifying. "One of the women associated with the Steinbergs was found dead in Baltimore almost two years ago."

"When you say found dead…"

"Murdered. Strangled in her car. It was all over the news for about five days."

Now I made use of my pen. "Do you know the victim's name?"

Ellen Minshew snapped her fingers. "It was a foreign-sounding name. I saw her photo in the *Post*. She was lovely. I think she was a fitness trainer." Then she snapped her fingers again and said, "Luna. Her last name was Luna. And she was found in her car somewhere in Baltimore."

Finally I had a real lead.

CHAPTER 29

I SPENT TWO minutes on my phone verifying the information Ellen Minshew had given me about the homicide in Baltimore. News articles from twenty-one months ago corroborated her recollection that Michelle Luna was a fitness trainer. Luna's photo looked like a professional model's. Brown hair in a ponytail, dark eyes, and an engaging smile. She radiated health. As I did when I read about any victim of a homicide, I said a little prayer for her and her parents. The families of homicide victims are quickly forgotten, but their pain lasts a lifetime.

I wasted no time in getting on an interstate headed northeast to Baltimore. I called the Baltimore Police Department's homicide unit and spoke to a Detective Stephanie Holly, who met me in the lobby of the department's headquarters. I was surprised at her wholesome, midwestern appearance. I tried to hide it with a cordial greeting.

The detective saw right through it. She smiled. It was an amazing smile. "I know, you never would've guessed I was a homicide detective."

"I'm sorry. You're not my typical image of a tough Baltimore cop."

"I'm older than I look."

A passing uniform sergeant chuckled and said, "She's taller than she looks too."

I tried not to laugh, but I could tell this was a common line of jokes. Detective Holly was probably five foot one and couldn't have weighed more than 110 pounds. Though she wore her hair short in a practical style favored by cops and nurses everywhere, she could almost pass for a University of Maryland student. I noticed scars on the knuckles of her right hand. She had punched a few people over the years. I bet she was tough.

I followed her one flight up a rear, wooden staircase, our footsteps sending echoes up the stairwell. Detective Holly looked over her shoulder and said, "I checked you out through the blue hotline. You've had some pretty decent cases with the NYPD. My friend Chuck, who works at One Police Plaza, says you're a legend in the department."

The blue hotline is a back-channel way for cops to check one another out. Everyone knows someone at a major department. From there it's just a game of six degrees of separation. New York and Baltimore are both on the East Coast. Both right along I-95. And both cities have active underworlds that no one wants to talk about. At least no one other than the cops.

I caught some interaction between Detective Holly and the other detectives on her squad. I was impressed.

A tall, younger black detective, trying to pull off a porkpie hat, stepped right in front of her desk and looked me up and down. He said to Detective Holly, "Why'd you bring your pops into the office today?"

"Because your dad was still getting his toenails done."

When another detective tried to grab a file off her desk, Detective Holly cut her eyes to him and simply said, "If that file is not back on my desk by the time I sign out this afternoon, you're going to have to pee sitting down for the next six months."

I didn't know what that meant and it scared me. I'm sure if I understood the inside joke, I'd be even more terrified.

Then, without missing a beat, the detective unleashed that perfect smile and said, "C'mon, I'll give you a tour and brief you on the entire case." She handed me a copy of her case file on the Michelle Luna homicide.

A few minutes later, we were in her city-issued Crown Victoria. A real police car. I was relieved she hadn't asked me to drive my rental. That would've been humiliating.

My impression of Baltimore was that it was like most cities on the East Coast. To a New Yorker it seemed smaller but rougher. There was little new construction, residential or commercial, in this part of town. Young men lingered on the corners, their eyes following our car.

Detective Holly said, "We don't concede Baltimore to New York as being the toughest police job."

"We have about forty thousand cops."

"I don't think that would be enough to get Baltimore under control. And we only have about twenty-five hundred cops. Between gangs and a DA who's not much interested in prosecuting, crime has spiraled out of control. We've had mayors go to jail, and no one trusts a single council member. We were hoping some of the national attention we've been getting lately might lead to some relief. But the city administrators don't seem to care."

I said, "I think most cops feel that way. Although, I agree: Baltimore does get its share of time in the spotlight on the national news."

We pulled down a street with two abandoned cars on one side and no vehicles at all on the other. It reminded me of a postapocalyptic movie. Or of Newark. Only a few people were on the sidewalk, and more than half the businesses appeared to be closed. A cat sprinted across the street.

Detective Holly said, "I'm a little short on time, so I'm showing you one of our rougher neighborhoods closer to the PD. The Fairfield area, where Michelle Luna was murdered, is closer to the water.

"The body was found in the front seat of a newer Audi the victim had leased in DC."

I tried to visualize exactly how crowded the streets might be on a Saturday night. I had read in the report that the medical examiner put her time of death sometime between 11 p.m. and 2 a.m. Her body wasn't discovered until nine o'clock the next morning.

Detective Holly said, "It's one of the few WWHs in that part of the city."

"WWH?"

"White woman homicide." She did a tactical 360 sweep with her eyes all around the car. "At the time the body was found, the news was calling her a victim of street gang violence. I don't buy that for a minute. Street gangs commit violence to protect their territory or their drug routes. They don't give a shit about a woman from Washington coming up to get her kicks."

"Do you have any suspects?"

"Nothing decent. The killer seemed to know what he was doing. He sprayed the entire interior of her Audi with WD-40 to screw up any forensics. But an industrious forensic scientist checked everything and came up with some DNA on the back of the victim's earring. We believe it's from the killer. He choked Michelle Luna from behind.

I thought about this for a moment. They had DNA evidence. This could get interesting.

CHAPTER 30

I MADE SURE to say good-bye to Detective Holly at the front door of the police department. I wasn't about to risk her seeing my rented purple Prius. I thanked her and made sure she had my contact information.

Sitting in the Prius, I flipped through the file Detective Holly had given me. It was very thorough. Using the victim's cell phone, they'd made lists of everyone Michelle Luna had talked to in the previous month. Just scanning the list, I happened to notice one of the numbers belonged to Justice Steinberg's wife, Rhea Wellmy-Steinberg. That was going to take some following up. And it gave me some ammo for when I actually spoke to the justice.

I drove south, crossing the Patapsco River, then along Chesapeake Avenue, not far from Interstate 895, into what many people considered the toughest neighborhood in Baltimore: Fairfield. I looked at a hand-drawn map I'd taken from the police file and tried to figure out where her Audi would've been parked.

I triangulated my position based on an out-of-business pawn-shop opposite a methadone clinic. There were few pedestrians, few parked cars, and a single bus carrying only two passengers rumbled away from me. I pulled the Prius into the spot where Michelle Luna's was found almost two years ago. I looked up and down the street and saw nothing that was wildly out of place.

The place reminded me of parts of New York in the nineties. Desolate, hopeless, and not interesting enough for investors. But the story of New York was informative. It taught me not to give up on neighborhoods. People were able to turn around New York. I had hope that could happen here as well.

The homicide case file for Michelle Luna was fairly standard. Detective Stephanie Holly had done a good job coordinating forensics and canvassing the neighborhood. No investigative information jumped off the page as pointing to the murderer. But I was confident the clues were in there somewhere.

As I got lost in the case file, I didn't pay careful attention to what was going on around me. In fact, I did exactly what I tell my kids not to do: I was not aware of my surroundings.

The loud rap on my driver's side window startled me. I looked up and to my left to see two young black men staring at me. One of them motioned for me to roll down the window.

They were two strangers approaching me in a strange city. I wrestled with the age-old question that went back and forth in training classes: Do you interact with potentially hostile strangers from the protection of a car or outside where you can move? Exiting the car went against common sense, but I knew I would learn nothing by sitting inside.

I decided to greet my visitors in person. I struggled out of the Prius with as much dignity as I could muster. By the time I was standing up straight, the two men had stepped to either side of me. Was that on purpose? From a tactical standpoint, if they were going to attack me, doing it from two directions was their best bet.

I turned to put my back to the little car. Before I could say or do anything, the man to my right spoke.

"Are you sure you're in the right place?" His Baltimore accent had a touch of Brooklyn. He was a little heavy and wore a light Ravens jacket over a fluorescent Nike T-shirt.

I said, "As a matter of fact, I'm not sure I'm in the right place."

The heavier of the two young men said, "We always try to help lost tourists so if something bad happens they can't blame our neighborhood. It's all about optics."

The thin man on the other side of me, who was maybe twenty-five, said, "What are you looking for?"

I said, "The usual: love, security, and a long-term investment plan."

That earned an odd look from the thin man. The chunky fella on my right laughed out loud.

The chunky young man said to his friend, "This guy has seen some shit if he'll joke with two strangers in the hood." Then he looked at me and said, "What are you really doing here?"

"No bullshit. I'm interested in the murder of a woman who was found in her car just about in this spot almost two years ago."

The thin man said, "The white woman in the Audi?"

"That's exactly it."

"You probably heard it was gang violence."

"I know that's what was on the news. I'm not sure I see it that way."

"That makes you smarter than the average reporter. No one has any idea why someone killed that lady. Technically, we're a gang according to the city. We call ourselves the Fairfield Crusaders."

"You're not acting much like gang members."

"How are gang members supposed to act? Maybe we should sell drugs or rob people. Don't watch so much damn TV. There's all kinds of gangs."

I nodded. "You're right. I'm sorry."

Now the chunky guy said, "Know what our toughest achievement is?"

I shook my head.

"We built a playground in the next block that gives kids under six a place to play safely. When we were done with that, we made sure Meals on Wheels came in to help serve the elderly people. They refused to come out here until we started taking over the routes. Never listen to the news, mister. Reporters don't know shit."

The thin man said, "You want to find out more about the woman in the Audi?"

I nodded.

"Come with us."

CHAPTER 31

I FELT COMFORTABLE with these two. They hadn't bothered to give me any names, and I wasn't going to ask. This wasn't an official investigation. I didn't have to write any reports.

The chunky man and the thin man led me into the next block. A man who could have been anywhere between fifty and seventy-five was balancing on a plastic chair with only three legs. His sparse gray hair circled around a bald crown over one of the darkest complexions I'd ever seen. His right eye was gauzy with cataracts. Half of his teeth were missing. The others were yellowed and jutted out in odd directions. He had that worn look of a man who had lived on the streets a long time.

The chunky man said, "Charles, tell this man about what you saw two years ago when that lady was killed in her car."

I looked again at the old man. He lowered the bent cigarette he was smoking and squinted up at me with his filmy eye. The man said, "I seen two people pull up in that fancy car. About ten minutes after it parked, one person got out and walked away alone." Before I could ask any questions, Charles added, "And no, I couldn't see the person walking away. Not sure if it was a man or a woman. But I could tell they were white. That's about the only thing that stands out in this neighborhood."

My chunky guide prodded the man some more. "Tell him the rest, Charles."

"I tried to tell the cops. They just told me to get lost. Never got to tell no one. No one who matters. Ain't no one ever going to believe a white person murdered someone in this neighborhood, then just walked away. But I swear to Jesus, it happened."

The thin man looked down and said, "You get your water for the day, Charles?"

The homeless man held up two bottles in one hand.

To me, the thin man said, "Some of the people who live on the streets forget about the basics. We make sure they have water and arrange for them to wash up at the community center down the street."

I asked a few more questions but quickly realized the only firm detail was that someone had walked away from the car. That reinforced my theory that the homicide had had nothing to do with anyone local.

My two guides led me back to my car. As we walked, I said, "This neighborhood might be in bad shape without you guys."

The chunky guy said, "The neighborhood *is* in bad shape. No one gives a shit about these people. None of the city resources come to us—except to arrest someone or put out a fire.

The entire country has the wrong idea about neighborhoods like this."

"Is there anything I can do to help? Sort of a thank-you for your guidance."

"You can pray for us. And if you go by the community center at the end of the block, they take donations."

"I'm headed there right now." I shook hands with both men. They had reinforced my belief that most people are basically good.

CHAPTER 32

I'D RECEIVED A lot of information in a short amount of time. My head was spinning as I tried to figure out how the murder of Michelle Luna might be even remotely related to Emily Parker's death. And I had no idea how I'd explain to Bobby Patel my theory that the two murders might be connected, that I'd gone to Baltimore and looked into Michelle Luna's death.

Then I thought ahead. What if I came up with information the FBI didn't want to hear? What if they focused on me for some kind of obstruction charge? Bobby Patel didn't impress me as that kind of petty prick. But I'd dealt with enough FBI supervisors to know that many wouldn't think twice about sacrificing a city detective.

My other concern was, if Emily really had been interested in "powerful men," what would those individuals do to limit this investigation?

I went ahead and called Bobby. I told him all about my trip to Baltimore.

Bobby said, "I knew about the Luna homicide. It was news in both Baltimore and DC. She may have known some of the same people as Emily, but we can't find any connection between the two. That's a dead end."

"How can you call the strangulation of two women in the same social circle a dead end?"

"Because Michelle Luna never met Emily Parker. They had a few friends in common, but everyone in DC does. You make it sound like the FBI ignored this. I was giving you the shorthand." He paused, sighed, and said, "I get the feeling that you think you're the only one trying to find Emily's killer. I'm busting my ass on it too. I'm doing it officially. Making notes, writing reports. Not roaming round talking to people who *might* know something."

"Sorry, Bobby, you're right. You've done a good job. I'm not disparaging it in any way."

He mumbled an acceptance of my apology.

We ended the call on that awkward note. After I drove back to my DC hotel, I was still unsettled as I handed my Prius off to yet another snickering valet. Though maybe not as tall as me, he was on the heavy side. All I could think was *Good luck squeezing in there, pal.*

I was tired. I did another zombie shuffle through the lobby. The typical chain-hotel happy hour—business travelers downing cheap vodka tonics as fast as the elderly bartender could pour them—was in full swing.

I took the elevator up to the seventh floor, the Baltimore PD case file in hand. All I could think about was lying down for a few minutes. Maybe an hour. Maybe until tomorrow morning. Just as I was about to put my plastic key card into the sensor, I thought I heard someone inside my room.

I paused and listened. I definitely heard something. I took a second to scan the hallway while I reviewed the list of possible suspects. Members of The Burning Land, the DC cops who'd harassed me at the hotel, the FBI, or maybe someone else I hadn't thought of.

I put my ear to the door, trying to figure out how many people were inside. There was no way to tell. And I didn't have the patience to wait it out. I swept back my windbreaker, wedged the Baltimore case file into the back of my waistband, and put my hand on the butt of my pistol. In one quick motion, I swiped the card and turned the handle.

It's fair to say I burst into the room. I was prepared to draw my pistol in an instant. Instead, I froze when I heard "Michael!"

I just stared. Mary Catherine stood in the middle of the room. She looked spectacular in jeans and a button-down shirt. Maybe it was the unexpected and sudden shift of blood that made me dizzy.

I took my hand off the pistol and stood up straight. Mary Catherine didn't say anything. She just rushed to me.

Between kisses, I blurted out, "What? How?"

All I heard was "Shhhhh. It's all right. I'm here now."

We kissed. Gently at first, then our lips seemed to lock together. Mary Catherine eased me onto the bed. She moved as carefully as a nurse. I tossed aside the case file and fumbled with my jacket, feeling as nervous as a teenage boy. My heart raced. I could feel the beats in my ears. I started to pant, a little breathless with excitement.

This was heaven, with Mary Catherine as my guide. I went with it.

We made love on the bed like it was our wedding night. Then we made love in the shower like it was our honeymoon. Then we were back under the covers of the king-size bed.

CHAPTER 33

I PUT MY arm around Mary Catherine, and she snuggled up next to me. Our hotel room had the vague air of a crime scene, with our clothes scattered around. Mary Catherine's jeans were nowhere in sight.

Mary Catherine gazed out the window at the early night sky typical of mid-Atlantic autumn. It was weird to think how many parts of the country were still light and sunny.

Just having Mary Catherine near had energized me. We hadn't said much other than "I love you" since I'd burst into the room. We'd been too busy concentrating on other things.

I said, "Ready for a little dinner?"

Mary Catherine sat up in bed and faced me. "Oh God, I wish I could. I've got to make the 8:30 train."

"What? Why? You're not staying the night?"

"I'd love to, sweetheart. But this was all I could work out. I missed you so badly, I just needed to see you for a few hours. I'm volunteering in Chrissy's class tomorrow. Seamus is spending the night, but I told him I'd be back at the apartment." She caressed my cheek with her hand. "I hope you're not sorry about the short visit."

I didn't answer. I kissed her. What a woman. I doubted I had another round of lovemaking in me. At least not for a couple of hours. But I was ready to give it a try.

We ended up snuggling for half an hour until my fantastic dream came to an end.

As we got dressed, Mary Catherine asked me if I'd found out anything new about Emily Parker's murder.

All I could do was shrug. I told her about some of the interviews and about Michelle Luna's murder, that I felt useless for not connecting any of it to Emily.

Mary Catherine said, "I never would've guessed about Emily's personal life. She was always so proper. Goes to show how little anyone knows about other people."

"I've been surprised by some of the revelations. It doesn't change the fact that she was murdered. Or the fact that I desperately want to find out who killed her. I'm still not sure how the FBI would react if their management knew I was here and working on the case."

"I thought you said your FBI contact seems like a decent guy."

"Bobby is working hard and hasn't really disappointed me yet. I just wonder if he has the backbone to stand up to his bosses if they disapprove of me helping."

Mary Catherine hugged me and said, "Whatever happens, I hope you can find peace. The kids and I just want you back home. As soon as you can make it."

"No one seems to want me here. It's nice to know I'm wanted somewhere."

"Don't get me wrong. I want you to find Emily's killer first. I know you will. You always do. Then you can come home to an epic feast and party."

I chuckled. "It sounds like you've been reading more of those historical novels about Rome. You sounded like Caesar just then."

After another passionate kiss, I had to introduce her to the ugliest rental car of all time. She made her train with less than three minutes to spare.

CHAPTER 34

I HAD CONTEMPLATED getting on the train with Mary Catherine, but in the end, I let her go home to our family. It was after nine by the time I dropped my car back at the hotel. I was a little down. Seeing Mary Catherine for a few hours was wonderful, but it also reminded me of what I was missing while I was here.

Even though the kids didn't make as much of a fuss over their father as they got older, I knew they missed me. I got texts from them all through each day. Just little notes to make me smile. But it also made me miss them. Trent kept me abreast of his plans to attend the ceremony meant to recognize his writing achievement. Juliana said she loved me. Shawna sent me a string of emojis that I think said she missed me and loved me. I thought civilization had moved on from hieroglyphics.

As soon as I stepped into the lobby, I noticed a couple in

123

their thirties, wearing business attire. They seemed out of place as they tried to lean casually on the vacant concierge desk. Their glances at the face of each person who walked through the lobby left little doubt they were looking for someone, and even less that I was the one they were looking for.

Then they noticed me and seemed to take turns watching. I decided to have a little fun and take my time in the lobby. At the very least I'd be wasting someone else's time. Maybe some FBI agents or more DC cops.

I took a long moment to select a chocolate chip cookie from a tray. I enjoyed stoking my observers' anxiety as I prolonged my gaze at the cookies. It gave me a second wind for the night.

I guess I took too long because the couple started marching across the lobby directly to me. Based on how they were dressed, I wasn't too worried about some kind of armed ambush. Although, in all honesty, I had sort of let my imagination run wild with conspiracy theories. There was no telling what someone might do to get me out of town.

I turned to face them. I stood tall and placed my right hand on my hip as a signal that I was willing to draw a gun in self-defense. It was a quiet threat understood by most people in the parallel universes of crime and punishment.

The man, in a blue sport coat, hung back. The woman walked to about ten feet in front of me and stopped. She turned to one side and nodded. I wondered if that meant *Grab him.*

But it didn't. Then I saw why they were being so cautious. A shorter, older man dressed in a very nice designer suit and flashy blue tie strolled toward me. He had a slight limp. I recognized him immediately.

The man called out, "Hello, Detective Bennett."

I said, "Senator Wellmy, nice to meet you." It wasn't really nice to meet him, but when I was younger, Seamus taught me how to be polite. Some of it had latched onto me over the long years.

"Always nice to see a constituent down here in Washington."

"I didn't vote for you."

The senator was clearly used to being disparaged. He didn't miss a beat. "You're still of value to the constituency."

The two security people had moved to within earshot. Maybe the senator wanted witnesses in case I went off on him. I broke the strained silence with "What can I do for you, Senator?"

"I'd be happy if you went back to New York. Maybe help the citizens who pay your salary."

"I don't understand. I'm on vacation."

From everything I had heard about the senior senator from New York, his way was the only way, and he clearly wasn't expecting any pushback. He stared at me as if to get a better look. Then I realized he was trying to intimidate me. I'd been threatened by drug dealers with knives to my throat. His idea of a threat was damn near pleasant.

The senator decided to take a different tack. He said, "You ever thought about what you're going to do after the NYPD?"

I didn't answer. I knew it would drive him crazy.

The senator was undaunted. "I could use a law-enforcement liaison on my staff. A lot more money. You could move your family to someplace more livable, like Albany."

I had to concentrate not to make the face I usually make at the sound of the three syllables in New York's state capital. Then I looked at the senator and said, "You're worried I'm poking around your son-in-law."

"When he did nothing wrong."

"Then he's got nothing to worry about."

The senator glared at me.

Then I said, "Your son-in-law is an interesting guy. With an interesting family. It's funny, it feels like his whole family works for the government."

"You mean his sister, Beth?" Now the senator gave me a crooked grin. "I'm pretty sure she's a woman. Tough as nails but odd. As my mom would say, 'as odd as a kid raised in a remote Adirondack farm.' You should thank me for steering you away from her. Probably just another reason to leave. If you got on her wrong side, she might twist your head right off your body."

I couldn't control myself any longer. "What do you have against finding justice for a murder victim?"

"That's not what you're doing. You're simply trying to ruin the reputation of a good man."

"I don't know what you're talking about. I'm not even in Washington officially. Like I said, I'm on vacation."

The senator stepped closer to me. He lowered his voice so his two security people wouldn't hear. "And I'm not speaking to you officially. That's why I can say, go home or hold on tight. You have no idea what's coming your way if you don't stop."

Then I laughed out loud. If the senator thought it was uncontrollable nervous laughter, he was mistaken.

The senator almost shouted, "What's so damn funny?"

"You sound like the blowhards who tell cops 'I pay your salary' when they're being arrested. You're not even any more polished than those assholes. You're just an obnoxious, entitled politician. Good day, Senator." I spun in place and marched away like I'd just dropped the mic. It felt glorious.

CHAPTER 35

THE NEXT MORNING, I had an appointment with Emily's psychiatrist. She knew, thanks to calls from both Emily's mother and Bobby Patel, that I was involved with the case.

Her office was two rooms in a professional building occupied by a few lawyers and a plastics company and located in Columbia Heights near the Smithsonian National Zoological Park. With no receptionist monitoring the waiting room, she opened the door to her office almost immediately.

I introduced myself and shook hands with the sixty-year-old Elizabeth Zeta. Her long dark hair had dignified streaks of gray. Her brown eyes were clear as she gave me a quick once-over. She had nice laugh lines around her eyes. I like that in people. I noted diplomas from Notre Dame. As Seamus would call it, the Holy Grail of the Catholic community.

She offered me a chair in front of her desk, but my eye was

drawn to the green leather couch. In movies, psychiatrists always have similar couches. I really wanted to ask if I could lie on it while we spoke. I realized that would be unprofessional, so I sat in the offered chair. She sat in a second chair across from it.

Dr. Zeta explained to me that although she was trying to help the criminal investigation, she was required to follow certain parameters so that she didn't expose any of Emily's personal issues. I commended her professional attitude toward my dead friend.

After a few questions, Dr. Zeta said, "I'm sure you understand, Detective, that we all make choices. Some choices turn out well, and some don't. Some people might agree with those choices, while others don't." She leveled those intelligent brown eyes at me and added, "I'm sure you've made choices others might disagree with during your career."

I withheld a smile as I said, "You have no idea."

She paused as she assessed my answer. Clearly she was sharp enough to pick up on body language and read into comments like that.

She made me consider my choices during this visit in DC. For the first time I wondered if insulting a US senator was helpful. Would it lead to finding Emily Parker's killer? Or did I just throw up another roadblock to my investigation? To be fair, I've resisted my entire life being told what to do. Listening to that pudgy politician as he basically ordered me to return home had made something inside me snap. I wouldn't have left if he had been holding a gun to me.

Dr. Zeta said, "Emily was a little withdrawn. I will say she really respected you. She spoke about you several times. That's one of the reasons I agreed to meet with you."

"I'm not questioning your assessment of Emily, but I knew her, and I never would've considered her 'withdrawn.'"

"I'm using that term in the clinical sense. She did find some solace in certain social interactions. But on a day-to-day basis she could feel overwhelmed with the number of people she had to meet and talk to."

I thought about that and said, "Doesn't that run counter to her social life? She seemed to go to a lot of parties and meet a lot of people."

The psychiatrist thought about it for a moment. "Those were the kinds of social interactions she appreciated."

"Dr. Zeta, all I really want to do is find her killer. I think her death might have had some connection with her romantic relationships. Is there anything you could tell me that might be useful? Was she having a rough time in a relationship? Did she feel threatened?"

"Emily was relatively private. She liked strong, ambitious, and motivated people. She enjoyed their company."

"Did she talk about any of her relationships specifically?"

"Now I have to use a little more caution. I don't want to drag anyone into your investigation who might be mourning her death. She never gave me any indication she was in danger from a relationship. She didn't care about rumors, so she didn't care that people gossiped that she slept around. I can tell you she didn't. She had romantic relationships, but they were private. I really can't name names."

"So you couldn't talk about Supreme Court justice Robert Steinberg?"

The psychiatrist's startled pause told me she knew about the relationship between the justice and Emily.

I realized, talking to the doctor, that every interview I did wasn't attacking the primary problem. I needed to go to the source. I knew exactly what my next move would be. If I was going to insult powerful people, then I'd do it to the people who might know something about Emily's death. That did not include Senator Wellmy, no matter how much I wished he was involved.

CHAPTER 36

DR. ZETA HAD inspired me. At least that was the excuse I was using the next day for doing something potentially stupid. I was on my way to the Supreme Court's administrative offices. I counted on the same ploy I'd used at the Capitol when I'd gotten in to see Congressman Bryant from Delaware.

At the entrance, I waited until there was no one at the magnetometer. I used the southwest door to the administrative offices. I strolled in casually and quickly.

I waved to the General Services security guard manning the metal detector. I smiled and badged him.

The tubby guard looked at my badge and volunteered that he was a retired Virginia state trooper. "What's a New York City detective doing here?" he asked.

"I don't know if you know Beth Banks, the chief of staff for Justice Steinberg."

"Oh, sure, I know her. See her every day. She just went upstairs about ten minutes ago."

"She has some DVDs on her workout routine she said she'd give me if I came by." I didn't like to mislead a retired cop. But this was about the only way I figured I could get up to the office.

The security guard couldn't have been more accommodating. He said, "She loves her workouts. Won't even use the gym in the building. Every lunch hour, 12:30 on the dot, she heads over to Gold's Gym on D Street. It's a little more hard-core. I can escort you to her office."

"I don't want to waste your time."

He shook his head. "It's nice to get away from the magne-tometer once in a while. Overall this is a pretty good gig. Low stress and a good retirement supplement. But it can get a little dull at this post."

The simple comment made me wonder. This guy wasn't much older than me. Would I end up on a metal detector at some federal building in New York? The fact that I had ten kids made it obvious I wouldn't be retiring anytime soon. After speaking to this security guard, I realized that might not be such a bad thing.

I let him tell me about a couple of his big cases. Then he asked a younger man to stand his post as he personally walked me up to the office. He even asked for Justice Steinberg's sister by name at the door.

A moment later, a woman in her early thirties with short dark hair and wearing a professional skirt and blouse stepped out. Even behind a pair of glasses, the confused, annoyed expression on her face told me she didn't want to talk to anyone. My guess was she was going to reprimand the security guard.

I felt bad about my deception as I looked and watched him realize he'd screwed up by bringing me to the office. I blurted out, "It's my fault he brought me up here, Ms. Banks. I insisted and I misled him. Please don't punish him for my ruse."

Now her face turned red. She looked toward a receptionist who was clearly worried about what was going to happen next.

She took a couple of deep breaths. She dismissed the security guard with a nod of her head. When she turned to face me, I realized her broad-shouldered swimmer's build had to stand at least five foot nine. My abrupt arrival had disrupted her day. She looked frustrated, frazzled.

Exactly how I wanted her to feel.

CHAPTER 37

BETH BANKS LED me into a conference room. Clearly someone walking in off the street had no place in her own office. She didn't offer me a seat at the long hardwood table. Instead, she turned and faced me.

Ms. Banks said, "I'm confused. Who are you?"

"Michael Bennett."

"I've heard your name. You were listed in some briefing. I'm not sure why you're here. I'll give you twenty seconds to say what you have to say."

She stepped to the end of the table and leaned on it. I realized from experience some sort of emergency alert button was installed at that end of the table. The moment she determined I was a threat, she could summon help. By the looks of her, I doubted she ever needed much help with personal security. Even in those business clothes, I could tell she was in fantastic shape.

I had to start out with a little smart-ass comment. "Is that twenty seconds from now or twenty seconds from when I start talking?"

She kept her poker face. "Fifteen seconds."

I started to talk fast. Like a real New Yorker. "I'm a detective with the NYPD. I'm looking into Emily Parker's murder." I looked down at my nonexistent wristwatch. Then I said, "I think I have eleven seconds left. Is there anything you'd like to say?"

I felt a good deal of satisfaction looking at her stunned expression.

Ms. Banks said, "You're the guy who's been bothering everyone in DC."

"To be fair, I bother a lot of people in New York too."

"You have no jurisdiction here. What gives you the right to barge into my office?"

"First of all, if I were to be technical, I'm a US citizen and you work for the US government. You should be embarrassed at restricting access to a government office. Second, I'm not going to stop until I find Emily Parker's killer."

"You say this like anyone would have an objection to you finding a killer. I knew Emily. I'd love for someone to find her killer."

"The only way that happens is by asking questions. By gathering information."

"You can't do anything with the information you gather. In DC, you're just an observer. You're wasting everyone's time."

"Really? You don't think the DC Metropolitan Police Department would want to hear about my findings?" That brought her up short.

"Mr. Bennett, I run the office here. That's clerical staff, more than thirty law clerks, as well as managing the justice's schedule. What makes you think I have time to chat with you about this foolishness?"

"Because I'm trying to handle this quietly without any media coverage. I don't know how long that can last."

Beth Banks just stared at me. Was she calculating what kind of trouble she'd be in if she murdered me? Was she thinking of talking to her brother?

Then she seemed to regain her senses and said, "I think we're done here." She turned toward the door and started to open it.

As I walked out, I said, "I'm just getting started. I've heard from a number of sources that your brother and Emily had a relationship."

Ms. Banks cut me off. "We all did. She was our friend. I don't like the idea that you think you can walk in here and bully your way into a meeting. My brother and I want nothing more than to see Emily's killer caught."

"Great. Then you won't mind if I get more specific in my questions."

"Get out, Mr. Bennett." She didn't need to raise her voice to make her point. She definitely fell at the upper end of the scary scale.

When I paused for a moment before leaving, Ms. Banks said, "Do you want to explain to your tough NYPD friends how a woman broke your nose before she tossed you out of an office?"

I smiled and slowly started to step through the door. She wasn't all that smart. She should've let me ask my questions.

That way she'd know what I knew. She'd also know where the investigation was heading.

As I walked through the front office to the main door, I said, "I'm sure we'll see each other again."

"For your sake, Mr. Bennett, I hope not."

That seemed like classic Beth Banks.

CHAPTER 38

I'D MADE MY voice heard. I felt good, satisfied, that I'd upset another bureaucrat so badly. But to what end? I hadn't learned anything of value. The only thing I'd really done was go completely overt. There would be no hiding anymore.

When I was trying to do things quietly, I still got harassed by the DC police and my own senator from New York. I didn't see any reason not to go full speed with my sirens blaring, so to speak.

I still couldn't get over the fact that Senator Wellmy had tried to buy me with a job in Albany. That was insulting. What happened to the good old days of bribery? Something simple like a suitcase full of cash. Instead, he'd offered me a job I didn't want in a place I didn't like. How'd that bozo ever succeed in politics?

I intended to sequester myself in my room and sort through

the information I'd picked up. I sure could've used an intelligence analyst to help me organize everything. But I was on my own. I wasn't even sure the FBI would help me if I got in trouble.

I figured Bobby Patel would hear about my attempt to interview Beth Banks. Who knows? That may have been my one step over the line. I still needed Bobby. I counted on information from him. I might even need him to make an arrest, God willing. But I wasn't on board completely with trusting the FBI.

I handed my rental car off to a valet and started to march toward the hotel lobby. I'll admit my concentration wasn't where it should've been. Instead of keeping my eyes on my surroundings, I was thinking about Emily Parker and who could've done something like that to her. That was my error.

Before I even made it to the front door, someone shoved me hard from behind. I stumbled forward and caught myself before my head crashed into a set of four tall valet lockers.

Before I could recover, a strong forearm across my back pinned me to the lockers. The clang echoed. Maybe it was only in my head. I managed to look from the empty valet stand toward the entrance to the hotel. No one was around. What kind of hotel was this?

Then someone spun me around. I should've guessed. It was Jeremy Pugh.

He had a buddy with him. A wiry guy about thirty with thinning hair. The kind of balding that drives young guys crazy.

Now Pugh had his forearm firmly across my chest. An ACE bandage was wrapped around his wrist where the Army Ranger had blocked his punch. I turned my head quickly but still didn't see anyone around.

Pugh said, "You think you're smart, huh?"

I said, "Not to brag, but I did graduate from Manhattan College with a degree in philosophy." I shifted my eyes back and forth between my assailants. "Sorry, you two know what *graduate* means, right?"

Pugh pushed a little harder on my chest. I think I felt my internal organs shift. "Hey, asshole, I went to USC."

"No shit? You went to the University of South Carolina?" I was shocked.

"No, University of Southern California."

"Wait. What?" I wondered if the shove into the lockers had scrambled my brains. "You went to Southern Cal?"

"We don't ever call it that. Just SC or USC. And I did three years there studying marketing."

I just stared at him. I had so many questions.

Pugh said, "Don't look at me like a monkey in a zoo. Accents don't indicate intelligence, no matter what you might think."

"Why'd you leave school?"

"I learned the truth."

"What truth?"

"Unless we hold shiftless politicians accountable, we'll never make progress. We fight oppression wherever we see it."

"By oppressing people?" I was pinned. I couldn't do too much except play for time.

Pugh said, "We know who you are. You paid for your coffee at Barbucks with a credit card. We got your name. We got eyes everywhere. We figured out where you were staying."

I smirked. It was hard with this gorilla holding me. "You mean you called every hotel in DC until someone put you through to a room. I'll admit that's smart. It's not as scary as having eyes everywhere, but it's smart."

Now the little guy said, "You're a New York cop. You've been following us."

"I think you've got it backward. This is *my* hotel. You're following me."

The little guy said, "You were at the National Mall when that cyborg came after us."

I had to chuckle at that one. I also subtly moved into a bent-leg stance. I didn't want to break this up yet. Not while Pugh thought he had the upper hand.

I looked at the little guy and said, "C'mon, Rogaine, you're not that stupid, are you? He wasn't any kind of cyborg."

That was just to get a rise out of him. In fact, I now realized Jeremy Pugh had been playing a role. He was much smarter than I'd realized. He'd misled me like a Texas Hold'em poker player. That also made him much more dangerous in my eyes.

Now Pugh said, "I even know why you're here in DC."

This was a surprise. I stifled my smart-ass replies. I swallowed and said in a calm voice, "Why do you think I'm here?" I really wanted to hear this. For some reason, Jeremy Pugh decided to take a dramatic pause and glance around for witnesses.

CHAPTER 39

WHEN PUGH REFOCUSED his attention on me, I managed to keep my mouth shut. That was no small accomplishment. Not considering I was raised by Seamus Bennett.

Then Pugh said, "It's about that *New York Times* asswipe we got into a scuffle with in Manhattan. It was nothing. I don't care what he said."

I didn't remember hearing about a *Times* reporter getting into a fight. What the hell was he talking about?

Pugh said, "We were just having some fun. Maybe it got a little out of hand. Why aren't you trying to arrest real criminals?"

I stared at him. Son of a gun, he was right. I needed to be more active on Emily's case. If Pugh was a suspect, I needed to deal with him. Not let him think he could assault a cop without me doing anything about it.

Pugh said, "You got no authority here. In DC, you're just another jerk."

The little guy said, "And we know how to deal with jerks."

Before I could contemplate exactly what Jeremy Pugh meant, the big asshole decided to demonstrate.

Pugh drew back his forearm for a massive blow across my face.

I ducked the forearm. His forearm struck the locker with a boom. The locker popped open.

The little guy threw a punch.

I passed it with my hand. The little guy's momentum carried him toward the locker, and I pushed him into it. I kicked Pugh and forced him back a few feet.

Quickly, I spun the lock on the locker with the little guy crammed in it. Then I faced Pugh. Now it was time to deal with this asshole. I owed him.

Jeremy Pugh and I squared off in front of the locker. I barely noticed the guy I'd stuffed into it as he yelled for help from inside. Now a couple of people glanced our way as they hurried toward the hotel entrance. I'm sure they didn't realize exactly what was happening.

I savored what I was going to do with Jeremy Pugh.

Then a car pulled through. At this point, I didn't care who saw this. I'd been patient long enough.

Then I saw it was a DC police car.

We both froze in place.

The young female cop looked into the lobby. Maybe someone had called in a disturbance, maybe not. She idled in front of the entrance, then slowly gave us a good look. She must have been satisfied because she parked the cruiser and walked into the lobby.

Pugh backed away.

The guy in the locker banged on the door and screamed, "I think there's a spider in here. Let me the hell out."

Pugh barked to his friend, "Shut up, Kyle. We got a cop close by." Then he looked at me. "If you were here on official business, a cop pulling in here wouldn't stop you. You're full of shit."

He was right for now. But I wasn't going to give up. Until I found Emily's killer, I guess I *was* full of shit.

I said, "See you around."

"You bet you will."

I turned and headed into the lobby.

Content for now.

CHAPTER 40

IN THE LATE afternoon, a call from Bobby Patel sent me over to the Vietnam Veterans Memorial. He thought we could talk in private there. I'd always felt the memorial to the fallen soldiers of the Vietnam era was particularly powerful. I had been there four times previously. Each time I was moved by a family tracing a pencil across white paper to capture their lost loved one's name exactly as it is etched into the black granite. Somehow seeing the creation of these poignant mementos seemed to personalize the tragedy of war, bringing the soldiers from statistics spewed out on the nightly news to figures of despair.

As the sun coasted to the west, only a small crowd was gathered at the memorial. Bobby Patel stood out, not only because of his gray business suit but also because of his urgent pacing. Clearly no history buff or mourner, he barely glanced at the black, polished walls.

Before I even reached him, Bobby blurted out, "You went to the office of a Supreme Court justice?" Then he almost shouted, "Are you crazy?"

"Not according to my last checkup. But that was last year, so…" I shrugged.

"Joke all you want, but barging into Justice Steinberg's office is not normal behavior. And that useless and stupid gesture won't help the investigation."

Now I lost all good humor. "Has 'normal behavior' gotten us any closer to Emily's killer?"

That shut up the FBI agent. He stood, silently fuming. Occasionally he glared at me.

I softened my tone. "Seriously, Bobby, do you have any decent leads?"

His hesitation was all the answer I needed. Bobby said, "We're looking at a few things."

"Why isn't anyone from the FBI taking The Burning Land seriously?"

"Who says we're not?"

"I know they're not under surveillance."

"How the hell would you know something like that?"

"Because a couple of them paid me a visit at my hotel this afternoon. I would hope the FBI wouldn't stand by while they pinned me against the valets' lockers and grilled me about what I was doing in DC."

Before Bobby got too outraged, I gave him a little backstory. Enough to shut him up. I left out the part where they had confessed to assaulting a *New York Times* reporter. I had already called our Special Investigations unit in New York to learn exactly what was going on.

Bobby started to calm down. He ran a hand over his perfectly combed hair. Then he scanned the area like he was looking for surveillance. He turned to me and lowered his voice. "Did Steinberg's sister, Beth, tell you anything of importance?"

"She made it pretty clear she didn't want to see me again."

"I've wondered about Steinberg's wife, Rhea. She goes by Rhea Wellmy-Steinberg."

"I know what she goes by. And I know Beth's last name is Banks from a previous marriage. Now tell me what suspicions you have about Rhea."

Bobby shrugged. "Just a hunch. She's pretty odd. But you probably figured that out from the reports."

"Odd enough to commit murder?"

"Who knows? You're the homicide detective. You tell me. How often do people you'd never suspect actually kill someone?"

I thought about that. He was right. I just nodded.

Bobby said, "Be careful. But most importantly, don't tell me what you're doing. I have a feeling I'll need to deny any knowledge of you at some point." He turned and walked away with purpose.

I had just been scolded.

CHAPTER 41

AFTER A COUPLE of hours in my hotel room to clear my head, I started to think about dinner. Dinner alone. I was tired of talking to people. Very few people had been particularly nice to me today. That made me miss Mary Catherine. The nicest person I knew. With just a look, she made me feel like I could conquer the world. But she was so much more. She got me. She got the kids. She'd found a way to integrate her life with ours and make all of our lives better. It made my heart hurt to think about her and my kids in New York City. And me stuck in DC.

Then my phone rang. At least I'd get to talk to them. I sprang up from the bed and jumped for my iPhone on the cramped hotel desk. When I looked at the screen, I felt a wave of disappointment. It was Harry Grissom. He knew I was officially on vacation. This wasn't a call from a friend.

As soon as I picked up, all I heard was "Mike, what the fuck!"

"Hey, boss, nice to hear from you too."

"Cut the shit."

This was un-Harry-like. He rarely got rattled. It made me pause and just listen for a change.

"I've gotten calls from our captain all the way up to the commissioner. Who'd you piss off in DC?"

"Actually, Harry, there's a whole list of them."

"Come home. Now."

"Harry, I have a gut feeling on this. My gut tells me no one's going to solve this if I don't stay here."

Harry's voice was even but scary. "I have a gut feeling you're going to be fired. Let the goddamn FBI handle this."

"C'mon, Harry. If it was someone close to you, would you let the FBI handle it?"

There was just silence. Finally, Harry said, "Sometimes it's tough being your friend. That doesn't compare to being your boss."

A smile crept across my face. I said, "If it means anything, you're a good boss and a better friend."

Harry said, "When you get to be my age, you realize that's really all there is. Friendship. That's also why I'll try to buy you some time."

"I won't forget this, Harry."

"When we're working together at McDonald's, I'll remind you of that."

It was good to have friends like Harry.

CHAPTER 42

GENERALLY, I LISTENED to Harry Grissom. Why not? He was a smart guy. You didn't get to be where he was in life without making good decisions. As a lieutenant with the NYPD, a friend, and one of the people I would trust with my life, I listened to him. Except when I couldn't.

He'd told me to let this go. He wanted me to come home. But I couldn't. Seamus was big on going with your feelings. Usually he'd apply that by saying, "Trust in faith." It was a Catholic way of saying, "Don't overthink things." That's why I was trying to figure out why I felt this need, this compulsion, to find Emily Parker's killer.

It made me remember an incident from my childhood. Something I hadn't thought about in years. I got a nice Spalding basketball for my twelfth birthday. At least it was nice for me. It was one of my most treasured possessions.

One day I decided not to use the courts at Holy Name, where I knew everyone and they knew me. I made the perilous journey across West 97th to the courts at PS 163. I knew a bunch of kids from the neighborhood who went there. It just felt a little cooler to be playing with my new ball at a public school instead of a private, Catholic school.

A few minutes into a three-on-three pickup game I made a beautiful pass to a kid a little older than me. Maybe thirteen or fourteen. He tried to look like a surfer with long blond hair that hung in his face. He caught the pass, smiled at me, turned, and ran away with my ball.

He was fast. I chased him. I guess it was my first foot pursuit of a criminal. After a few blocks, I lost sight of him and lost my ball. I was heartbroken. I remember sitting on the steps of Holy Name and crying uncontrollably.

Later, at home, Seamus told me to let it go. Just like Harry had done. The next day he bought me another ball and told me not even to think about the last one. In his own odd way he could be quite comforting. He explained that not everyone had the same sense of right and wrong. He even said maybe the boy couldn't afford his own ball. We should consider it a good deed that he'd ended up with mine.

But it still bugged me. Enough that even Sister Sheilah—a much younger version of the one who has guided my ten kids through Holy Name—sensed something was wrong. When I told her what had happened, she simply said, "You're a good boy, Michael. I've never seen you show malice toward anyone. The boy who took your ball had a lapse of judgment. Perhaps one day he'll see his error. Either way, God will work it out in the end." She suggested I pray for the boy's soul.

I should've listened. Of course I didn't. I haunted the courts around PS 163. Not playing. Just watching.

Eight days later, I saw him. The same kid, playing with *my* ball. His hair still flopping in his face. I thought about what Sheilah had said. Looking at him, I realized he wasn't poor. He was wearing new Nike Air Maxes. He was just a jerk.

I marched up to him. When someone passed him the ball, I intercepted it. Then I ran. What I hadn't considered was that if the boy could run away from me, he could also catch me. And he did.

He was at least a year older than me and a fair amount bigger. He punched me in the arm, then punched me in the face. The second blow knocked me off my feet. Then he calmly picked up the ball and stared me down.

I sprang to my feet. I got in one good lick. Straight jab right to his face. He stumbled a step backward. Then he smiled. A trickle of blood ran from his nose. I waited for the thrashing, but it turned out to be worse. He just looked at me and snickered. Then he walked away with my ball.

I remember the feeling of satisfaction that I'd at least done something. It hadn't helped the situation, but I'd felt better.

Maybe I hadn't changed. Because right now I drove past Supreme Court justice Robert Steinberg's beautiful house in Georgetown. It was a freestanding three-story with a brick facade. The lights were off, but at least I felt like I was doing police work. I was seeing where a potential suspect lived. There was something comforting in the action. I felt like it was exactly what I was supposed to be doing.

Then a car pulled up behind me.

CHAPTER 43

I STAYED IN the driver's seat of my rented purple Prius. Headlights flooded inside and reflected off the rearview mirror into my eyes. I didn't think a Supreme Court justice had twenty-four-hour security, so I felt myself tense at the direct approach.

Whoever was in the car was in no rush. That's when I started to think it might be the Metropolitan Police. Someone was running my tag. When both people in the car got out at the same time and one hung by the trunk of my car while the other approached me, I figured they had to be cops.

A plainclothes African American female officer had her badge out and stayed about three feet away. She said, "My name is Officer Lila Barrett of the DC police. Leave your hands on the steering wheel, sir."

Officer Barrett was very professional and smart. I did exactly what she said.

Her partner stayed in my blind spot on the passenger side of the car. Good tactics. She continued. "Do you have a reason for being parked here, sir?"

I knew what she really wanted. I said, "I have ID in my sport coat pocket. I'm a detective with the NYPD, and I also have a pistol in a holster on my right hip."

That brought her partner a step closer on the passenger side. Now his flashlight cut through the dirty rear passenger window. At about the same time, Officer Barrett opened my door. Her hand was behind her back. I figured she was at least touching her own duty weapon.

They were both polite and courteous, as well as tactically sound, as she invited me out of the car. Less than a minute later, they'd checked out my credentials and felt satisfied I wasn't an immediate threat. We all chatted at the rear of my car.

I said, "I'm sorry. I was just looking at where some potential witnesses live. I didn't mean to attract any attention or bother anyone." Now I could see that Officer Barrett was about thirty with short hair and a little scar above her right eyebrow. She'd seen some action at some point. She also had a big, pleasant smile.

The other cop, a tall white guy, was a little younger than Officer Barrett. He never said a word. He looked like he wanted to be in a car chase or a fight. Anywhere but talking to a New York detective in a quiet upper-class neighborhood.

As Officer Barrett smiled, she said, "You're almost in front of Justice Robert Steinberg's house. His wife doesn't like the idea of marked police cars going up and down the street. Our chief doesn't like the idea of a public figure like the justice being open to potential threats. So we get to patrol the whole neighborhood in an unmarked car in civilian clothing. Not a bad gig."

I said, "Actually, it's Steinberg's wife I need to talk to." I got a chuckle from both the cops.

"She calls in about once a week with some story about people following her. She's paranoid as shit. We call her the Supreme Nut Job."

"Doesn't sound like I'm going to have an easy time of it. I hope she doesn't try to duck me."

Officer Barrett said, "I'll let you in on a little secret, but you can't tell anyone I said it."

I raised my hand and said, "Scout's honor."

"She eats lunch at a little place called Rose's Down-Home Diner a few blocks away. It's right next to some New Age art studio she goes to almost every morning. The Supreme Court Police brief us every couple of weeks about what's going on with the Steinbergs. That's her latest passion."

I thanked them and was on my way a minute later. You've got to love the brotherhood of cops.

CHAPTER 44

I WAS STARTLED awake by my phone at about seven. Immediately I realized it was the first full night's sleep I'd gotten since coming to DC. I grabbed the iPhone, cleared my throat, and tried to say, "Hello," without sounding like a pirate.

The cheerful voice on the other end of the line made me smile immediately. It was my son Trent. I could picture the broad smile on his cute face as he said, "Rise and shine, Dad. God's giving us another chance to achieve our dreams."

"What if my dream was to sleep until ten?"

"Then I gave you a chance to follow your dream tomorrow. That's what it's all about, looking forward to things."

I had to smile. This young man had been paying attention during the sermons at Holy Name. Trent seemed to be getting sharper by the day. I managed to grunt, "What's up?"

"Nothin'. Just wanted to talk to you."

"That's nice. I like talking to you too. What's going on around the homestead?"

"Not much. Commandant Mary Catherine has everyone in line. That's why I'm already up and packed for school an hour early."

"Don't call her 'commandant.' That's disrespectful."

"Juliana called her that to her face. Mary Catherine likes it so much she's faking a German accent when she gives orders. She's kind of nailed it. Even Chrissy's cleaning up after herself."

"Well, if Chrissy is pitching in, maybe there's something to it. What do you hear about your big date with the mayor?"

"Everything's still a go. You'll be here for the ceremony, right?"

"Wouldn't miss it for the world." I could picture the ear-to-ear grin on his face.

Trent said, "Cool. I guess I should let some of my siblings talk to you now. They're lining up like they want to talk to Don Corleone on the day of his daughter's wedding."

"You and Ricky watching seventies movies again?"

"*The Godfather* and *The Outlaw Josey Wales*."

"What do you think?"

"Just like you say, they don't make them like that anymore. Did you know the guy who starred as Josey Wales made a bunch of great movies?"

"Clint Eastwood? I knew."

"Have you ever seen *Dirty Harry*?"

"Every cop has many, many times."

We finished up our dive into great movies, then Trent handed off the phone.

Each of the kids took the phone for about ten seconds to

say, "Hey, Dad." I knew Mary Catherine was behind the efficient tactic. Only Fiona hung on at the end for an extra minute.

She said, "Sister Lora asked if I would play on the basketball team. I'm not sure what to do. I've never played sports before."

"How does she know you'll be a good player? Were you shooting around in class?"

"Nope. She just walked up to me in the hallway and asked if I was interested. I wasn't at first, but the more I think about it, the more I want to try it. Is it okay with you?"

"Of course it is, sweetheart. I'll support any activity you want to try." I paused and thought about that for a moment. "I'm going to walk that last statement back. I know how you guys pride yourselves on trying to outdo one another in tricking me. I support any activity that's within the structure of civilized society and doesn't involve violence or any sort of crime." I paused for a moment to be sure I had included outlawed behavior. "And nothing to do with human sacrifice."

Fiona said, "Wow, Dad. It's not like I'm one of the boys. They're the ones who do all the stupid things."

"I have to set the same guidelines for everyone. Even if you do have exceptional judgment."

"Sister Lora also asked if you would be available to coach the team."

I'd say this for her. Lora was a subtle one. Sister Sheilah, whom I'd done battle with my entire life, would've just told me to be the coach. I thought I liked Sheilah's approach better.

All I could say was "Of course I'll coach. It'll be fun. We'll work on your shots as soon as I'm back permanently." Fiona giggled, and I knew I'd made the right choice.

A few seconds later, Mary Catherine came on the line. Her

voice soothed me, set everything right. I smiled just hearing her warm greeting.

I said, "How's it going? Everything good with the kids?"

"The kids have been great. I've been tough on them too." Her voice sounded scratchy, like she was starting to get a cold.

I let out a laugh, but I didn't say anything about what Trent had called her. I didn't have to.

Mary Catherine laughed and said, "The kids have taken to calling me 'the commandant.'"

"I'll put a stop to that in a heartbeat."

"I kinda like it. I'm not used to people being afraid of me. I don't know what I did, but no one's questioning my authority in any area. Usually one of the older kids will give me some pushback."

"Fiona told me her news."

"Somehow I don't see her running up and down the basketball court. But I think it'll be good for her."

"Sounds like you're against the idea."

Mary Catherine hesitated. "No, it's not that. I'm just tired. Bone weary."

"I'm sorry. Can I help?"

"Not for this. I just need a little rest."

We chatted for a few more minutes. I'll admit it may be hokey, but just a call with my wife and kids puts me in a good mood first thing in the morning. That's rare, especially when I'm traveling.

CHAPTER 45

I FOUND ROSE'S Down-Home Diner easily enough. It was less than half a mile from the Steinberg residence in Georgetown. A tiny place with a brick facade covered with creeping vines. Near the entrance, more than a dozen decorative ferns hung from the ceiling.

An older woman worked behind a bay window open to the kitchen. I wondered if it was Rose. A solitary waitress with two nose studs and a tattoo of a knife on her left hand made no effort to greet me. I took a far booth. Two other customers sat sipping coffee at a booth at the other end of the restaurant.

The daily menu was a card about six inches long by five inches wide. Today's specials were an organic turkey and kale salad or a meat-free meatball over whole-grain pasta. How could they call this place a diner? Let alone a "down-home" diner?

I didn't want to miss Rhea Wellmy-Steinberg, so I had come

in at 11:30 for an early lunch. The waitress definitely didn't fit the decor. She reeked of cigarettes when she came to the table and plopped down a glass of water. Her lank hair popped out of a black hairnet.

"Know what you want yet?" She didn't have a "down-home" accent. She sounded like she was from Jersey City. She was starting to act like it too.

"Not quite yet," I said.

Just then, Rhea Wellmy-Steinberg walked through the front door, carrying a copy of the *Washington Post* under her arm. The waitress at least smiled for Rhea. She was a regular, just like Officer Barrett had said.

My first look at Justice Steinberg's wife got me thinking that Ellen Minshew's description of her as a pretty face with big, fake boobies wasn't particularly fair. Rhea was pretty, but there was no way to tell what was or was not real.

A slight streak of dark green on her cheek gave her a rough-and-tumble look, and below the goggles that hung loose on a strap around her neck, her smock was smeared with different colors like she was part of a kids' finger-painting class.

I sat for a minute, sipping my water.

Rhea took a corner booth and ordered lentil soup and a sparkling water.

As the waitress turned to fill Rhea's order, I knew I had to move quickly. If I could get to Rhea before she started reading the paper, our encounter would seem like a complete surprise. I stood and held my credentials in my right hand as I took the five steps to the corner booth.

Rhea looked up at me and said without emotion, "Lucy took my order already."

"Ms. Wellmy-Steinberg, I'm not a waiter."

"Then I'll ask you to step away from me. I don't talk to reporters."

This was the second time someone had mistaken me for a reporter. I wondered if I needed to upgrade my wardrobe. I said, "I'm not a reporter. I'm a New York homicide detective looking into the murder of Emily Parker."

She didn't flinch or give anything away. She was confused but not skittish.

Rhea surprised me by saying, "What have you found out? I've been sick thinking about what happened to her."

I took the opportunity to sit across from her in the booth. I might have been in a little shock. This was too easy. I was already in an interview and almost at a loss for words. Almost.

I looked at her with my best sincere face and said, "I wish I had information to give you. I'm still gathering facts. When was the last time you saw Emily?"

She paused and looked at me. I noticed for the first time that her eyes were a little bloodshot. Finally, Rhea said, "You think I don't realize who you are. I do talk to my husband once in a while. I even talk with my sister-in-law, Beth. You've met Beth. You're lucky she thought you were a joke. Otherwise you might not be sitting upright."

I tried to push forward with the interview. "So when was the last time you saw Emily?"

Rhea just stared at me. Then she said, "Am I a suspect, Detective?"

"Not at the moment."

"Is my husband?"

"I don't think either of us has the time to sit here all day while I exclude suspects one at a time. If you're telling the truth and you really want to know who killed Emily, I don't see why you won't speak with me." Sometimes logic wins out in a situation like this.

Rhea said, "Because I already spoke to the FBI and the DC homicide detectives."

"And what did you tell them?"

She smiled. She had the kind of perfect, straight white teeth that a combination of nature and good orthodontia can produce. "You're a funny guy, Detective. You see, I'm not only married to a Supreme Court justice. I also graduated from Columbia Law."

"Impressive."

"And I don't waste time on people like you."

"Like me? What am I?"

"An irritant. Not much more. Now you can go about your business and tell whoever sent you here to back off."

"I hope—"

"I said, move on, Detective."

Her tone and inflection were as good as any beat cop's in the Bronx. I still had no idea who had killed Emily, and I was definitely not impressed with her friends.

CHAPTER 46

ABOUT FORTY MINUTES later, I found myself on a park bench, looking at my friend Roberta Herring. I liked the sun on my face.

We both ate gyros bought from a street vendor. Roberta said, "This guy has the best gyro I've eaten in DC. Still not as good as the guy near Claremont Park in the Bronx."

I agreed the food was good, though it had taken a stack of napkins to stem the flow of tzatziki sauce.

Roberta looked at me and said, "So your whole interview with the justice's wife was a bust?"

"Not a complete bust. I didn't have to eat that shitty food. But she shut me down pretty quick."

Somehow Roberta had kept her blue business suit spot-free while munching on her gyro. All I could do was look at her and think how far she'd come from working a foot patrol in the Bronx.

Our bench was next to a running trail. I felt a pang of guilt every time a runner darted past us. Each giant bite of the gyro seemed to calm me down.

I said, "Harry Grissom told me to come home."

"Will you listen?"

I cocked my head at her and said, "What do you think?"

Roberta started to speak in a stream of consciousness. She said, "I wonder if there are politics involved. Are agencies guarding their turf? Even though the kid from the FBI is working with you, is he telling the truth? Is that why the DC cops talked to you? I wonder if you're close to something."

I said, "I don't feel like I've gotten far."

"Compared to what? You're used to working mostly drive-by shootings. You can solve those with a few interviews. This one might take some time. There're just too many factors. Hell, for all we know, Emily Parker's murder could be random."

I liked this sort of spitballing. It helped me form my own ideas. But when Roberta suggested Emily's murder might be random, I said, "What about Michelle Luna's death? They were in the same social circles. They died by similar methods."

Roberta said, "What angle are you looking at? You think it could be a lover? If you think someone's going to let you talk directly to the justice, you're crazy."

"I don't know why this investigation feels so different to me."

Roberta said, "I know why. I can't believe you don't see it. You're used to working cases in New York. No matter how bad a serial case can be or how bloody a domestic murder is, you still go home to the kids and Mary Catherine every night. I think you're overwhelmed. You don't get to take a break. All you hear is information about Emily's murder all day and all night."

I just stared at my friend. "Oh, my God, I think you're right."

"You, of all people, need your family. You're a classic 'family man.' Don't try to run from it. Embrace it."

I swallowed the last of my gyro. "Thanks," I said. "You always seem to know what's bothering me."

CHAPTER 47

I DIDN'T DRIVE to my hotel. My recent experiences told me nothing good happened at that place. I'd had to talk to people I didn't want to. I'd even had a scuffle with someone. And everyone seemed to know the address.

Instead, just a few minutes after I left Roberta, I found myself headed north. North on I-95. The only slowdown I hit on my four-hour trip to New York City was in Philadelphia. And it wasn't too bad.

It didn't matter how rough the trip was. It would be worth it when I saw the faces of my wife and kids as I stepped through the door. It was a risk. I might catch them on a night when everyone was out. Or I might catch everyone in a bad mood. It didn't matter to me. I just needed my family. Even if it was for only a single night.

The first face I saw as I stepped through the door was

Juliana's. She was working on the dining room table, frantically writing on a legal pad as she paged through books spilling all across the width of the table. I stood in the doorway and stared at my beautiful oldest daughter.

She had the tip of her tongue stuck out the left side of her mouth. A sure sign of concentration since she was a little kid. She turned her head to see who'd opened the front door but not come through the dining room yet. That's when I saw the grin spread across her face. I didn't know what was more stunning: the dimples from her smile or the white, perfect teeth giving me faith she'd make it as an actress one day.

She was on her feet and running to me as she squealed, "Dad."

That brought a chain of responses throughout the house. I could hear Mary Catherine asking what the commotion was about as she marched toward the front door.

Juliana literally leapt into my arms. She hadn't done that since she was a little girl. Instantly, I realized I'd made the right decision to come home.

Then I was hit by guided missile after guided missile. Chrissy, Shawna, and Fiona would've made good linebackers the way they hit me and held on.

My world seemed to freeze as I saw Mary Catherine. She was wearing jeans and a T-shirt and looked like she'd been helping Fiona craft. Sparkles and some glue globs clung to her fingers. A blue ribbon was stuck to her leg, but I wasn't going to mention it. I just stared at her beautiful face. Her blond hair was tied back in a loose ponytail. Her blue eyes opened wide as she saw me.

The kids made way, and she came right at me. She wrapped her arms around my neck and planted a big kiss on my lips. Big enough for a couple of the younger kids to turn away in disgust. To me, the kiss was just right.

When Mary Catherine stepped back, she said, "Where's your bag?"

That's when I had to level with her. "I'm only home for a visit." It hurt to see the kids' smiles drop almost immediately. I thought Chrissy was going to cry.

I looked to soften the blow. "I just missed you guys so much that, after lunch, I couldn't go back to my hotel. Once I got on I-95, I didn't even think about turning back."

Brian and Ricky wandered in from the living room. Their greeting was much more restrained. "Hey, Dad." They both gave me a quick hug. But the others were still staring at me like they deserved an explanation.

I said, "I have to go back to DC tomorrow. I hope I won't have to stay long. What I'm doing in DC is really important to me."

Mary Catherine still had her arm around my waist as she said, "If it's important to you, it's important to us." When she didn't get the rousing response she'd expected, Mary Catherine looked at the kids and said more forcefully, "It's important to us, right, guys?"

Now I saw where the term *commandant* came in. Every kid immediately chimed in. It was very impressive to influence so many people with just one command. She could work for the NYPD. Maybe even the marines. Either way, I was glad she'd taken on this job instead.

I owed Roberta Herring a lunch. Hers was the best advice anyone had ever given me. I'd been home only a couple of minutes and I already felt like a new man.

CHAPTER 48

I TOOK MY time making the rounds. I was careful to spend alone time with each of the kids.

Most everything was the same. Shawna was working on some secret project with my grandfather. She only hinted that it had something to do with artwork.

Jane was a little tougher to corral. I sat next to her at the dining room table, where most homework was completed. I said, "How's school? Anything giving you a problem?"

The teenager let out a laugh. "I'm a little stuck in Calculus II. Think you can explain it?" Her look effectively communicated what she thought of my math skills.

"What about creative writing? I'm good at that."

"If you mean supportive, you're right. All you ever say about any of our essays is 'Good job.'"

"Can I help it if you are all so talented?"

Jane scowled as she looked at the empty page in front of her.

I gave her a few seconds and said, "Talk to me. What's wrong?" I knew each of the kids' moods. Jane got frustrated but not openly angry.

She looked at me, and I saw a tear in her left eye. "I'll admit I'm annoyed. I've been journaling since I was eight and always get an A on any English or writing assignment. Trent, who spends more time thinking about sports, gets recognized for the first thing he's ever written."

"But his subject matter might have helped. He has a unique view of adoption and culture."

"And I don't? I've written essays on being one of ten adopted kids. On what it's like to be obviously Asian in a multicultural family. I never even had a teacher bring it up. Trent writes the same sort of essay and he's going to meet the mayor."

"I've met the mayor. It's not much of a thrill. In fact"—I lowered my voice to sound conspiratorial—"he's a bit of a dick."

That made her laugh. She gave me a spontaneous hug. If I'd made her feel a little better, she had put me in a great mood.

Then I found Brian, who wasn't in school anymore. He was also the source of most of my concerns. Since coming home from prison, he'd given us a few scares. At first, he had been sullen and he disappeared all day long. Later, I learned he was going through air-conditioning repair school. He had wanted to surprise me. And he had.

We sat together on the couch. He was still wearing his gray uniform shirt that said BILL in lovely embroidery across his right chest.

When I asked him about the name, Brian said, "At first it was just because they didn't have a uniform for me. Then everyone thought it was funny. Now I just sort of answer to the name Bill."

I laughed. "That's exactly how things happen at the police department. Usually it's with a nickname. You do one thing you regret and the next day you're stuck with some nickname you don't like. I almost got hung with the label Kickback."

"What'd you do? It doesn't sound like that bad of a nickname."

"Unless you're on your third week in uniform and you step behind a mounted unit, then slip in the horse's poop." I paused as Brian laughed. "What made it worse was, the cop on the horse looked behind me and shouted, 'Get out of there, you idiot. Do you want to get kicked back into the Stone Age?'"

Now a couple of the other kids had wandered in to hear the story.

"A few of the other rookies heard it, and I had the nickname before I went home for the night. Thank God it was the end of my week and I had a two-day break. The nickname was forgotten by the time I went back to work. I think I would've been named Kickback to this day if I would've had to go right back and face those guys."

We were holding dinner until my grandfather arrived. He was polite enough to call and say he was being held up at Holy Name, but then Bridget let it slip that I was home. I had kinda wanted to see how surprised he would be to see me.

When Mary Catherine cautiously approached the couch, I knew there was a problem. She gave a quick look to Brian, who took the hint and found somewhere else to go. Most of the other kids were busy again with their own projects.

I hate waiting to hear bad news. All I could say was "What's up?"

She brought a piece of paper clipped to an envelope from behind her back. "I was going to break the news to you this evening."

"No one is getting suspended from Holy Name, are they?"

"I wish it was that simple."

I knew it was important, then. Mary Catherine took church and school at Holy Name very seriously. Some of it had to be her love for Seamus. I gave her my full attention.

She said, "It's a certified letter from the IRS."

I had an idea where this was going.

"We're being audited going back five years."

For some reason Senator Lom Wellmy's face popped into my head. I glanced at the paper Mary Catherine handed me and said, "I think six years is the legal limit for review. I'm not sure I make enough money to worry about it."

"You think they'll ask questions about the apartment? Or the trust set up to pay the taxes?"

"I don't know. I wonder if we need a lawyer. An accountant at the very least." Years ago, my first wife, Maeve, had cared for an elderly man who lived in this apartment. She had completely changed the man's perspective and life. He had gone from being a sour old curmudgeon to wanting to come to the kids' birthday parties. When he died, with no heirs and few friends, we had been shocked to learn he had transferred the title of this beautiful apartment to Maeve and me. He had even set up a trust fund to pay the taxes. I thought I'd been straight with the IRS concerning the apartment. I guess that was about to be tested.

CHAPTER 49

AS USUAL, MARY Catherine made dinner an event. And clearly she'd had the meal planned long before she knew I was coming. A pork roast with sauerkraut and mashed potatoes, with a healthy assortment of vegetables on the side.

The food was heaven, as was the chance to listen to the kids chat about every possible subject, from the NBA to a Wolverine comic book.

Jane asked Fiona about joining the basketball team. Fiona's smile confirmed I'd made the right decision. She said, "I'm going to play, and Dad is going to coach me. Coach the whole team."

My policy of treating each of the kids equally could come back to haunt me. Though I could already picture myself having to coach a half dozen other teams, I shrugged and said, "Sounds like fun."

After dinner, while all the kids pitched in on cleanup, my grandfather and I had a talk on the couch.

Seamus said, "Where is Mary Catherine?"

"Taking a well-earned hot bath."

"Good plan. The girl deserves it. You should see the way she holds down the fort while you're gone. And those kids love her. They may give her some grief, but they've got her back."

"And she has mine. I would've gone crazy if she hadn't surprised me in DC this week."

"That why you had to come home now?"

I nodded. I was tired physically, psychically, and spiritually. That's one of the reasons I was talking to my grandfather. I joke about him being ill-tempered and giving me a hard time, but it's pretty much an act. He has more insight into the human condition than anyone I've ever known. And he knows me better than anyone else.

I said, "It's getting a little late. Are you going to stay the night?"

He shook his head. "Not tonight. I'm hosting a community outreach meeting tomorrow morning. I've been pushing to open our playground to at-risk youth. The YMCA said they'd provide at least two coaches to help us keep an eye on everyone. The Y is a great outfit. I hope we can team up with them." He paused and I knew he was framing a delicate question. Finally, he said, "When do you plan to go back?"

I sighed. I couldn't hide my exhaustion. I said, "I guess tomorrow."

"You don't sound so enthusiastic about it."

I shrugged. "I'm here with my family. That's what I want. It's all I ever want."

"It may be what you want, but it's not *everything* you want."

I thought about it and said, "You're right. I can't stand the idea of Emily's killer going unpunished. I'll admit I didn't think through all the problems my going to DC would cause. No one's making it easy."

"You've been in tough situations before. Even when Maeve was dying, you stayed on the scene of a hostage situation. And you did it because you have a sense of duty. A strong sense of duty. This is no different. You can't stand the thought of any killer going unpunished."

"Emily was my friend. I can't even tell you how much it means to me."

Seamus nodded. "I understand. I liked Emily too. She was a lovely woman."

"What I'm saying is, I'm torn. I miss my family when I'm not here. But I know it will haunt me the rest of my life if I don't find Emily's killer."

"You have to follow your heart."

I smiled and looked at my grandfather. "You used to say, 'Trust in faith.'"

"It's essentially the same thing."

"Sometimes I worry that wanting punishment for the killer is too close to vengeance. I'm not sure how Jesus would feel about that."

"God threw down some punishments over the years. Everything from a flood to turning a woman into a pillar of salt. He did what he needed to do. Just like you need to do this for your friend. I truly feel we both found the right careers. You just did it at a much younger age."

I turned on the couch and embraced my grandfather. When I felt his thin body in my arms, it made me worry about life without him. But at least I had him for now. And once again he was making sense.

CHAPTER 50

I WAS UP early. I knew I would be. It wasn't even light outside when Mary Catherine murmured, "Are you awake?"

Staring at the ceiling, I mumbled, "Yes."

"What time do you have to leave?"

It hurt to say it out loud. "Harry wanted me to meet him for coffee around eight. That way I can be back in DC by early afternoon."

"I'll miss you." That was all it took for me to spin in the bed and face my beautiful wife. We wrapped each other in a tight hug. As soon as she kissed me, my resolve to go back to Washington started to fade.

We made love in the early morning darkness, before any of the kids were stirring. It was the kind of intimate encounter that made me feel like everything was fine. I could lose all my worries anywhere I was with Mary Catherine.

It was only after, as we lay in bed with our arms around each other, that I heard some of the kids start to move around. Jane was our early bird who liked to shower before anyone woke up. I could also hear Brian as he got his gear together for another day at work.

Mary Catherine said, "You need to get up and get ready as well. As much fun as this was, you need to finish your business in DC. Then come back here and take up the easy job of raising ten kids." We both started to giggle.

As we all sat together around the breakfast table, the kids were much more subdued. Sort of like they were every morning. It was tough saying good-bye to them as I headed out the door.

Thirty minutes later, I found myself at a coffee shop on West 42nd named Romeo & Juliet Colombian Coffee. I liked it because I could take the Lincoln Tunnel under the Hudson River and be on I-95 headed south in just a few minutes. The small place was busy, and we grabbed a tiny table in the corner where we could talk.

I couldn't help but look at Harry and once again think how much he reminded me of an Old West gunfighter. The crags on his face had been earned over a career as a cop. His nose had been broken on the job four different times. His mustache dipped a little below both sides of his mouth. He was definitely pushing the NYPD grooming policy. But given that he was a twenty-seven-year veteran of the force with more decorations and commendations than any one person could count, people tended to give Harry some leeway.

Harry said, "I'm glad you're back in New York."

"I'm not. In fact, from here I'm heading back to DC. It's not something I want to do, but I'm going to do it." I hadn't wanted to be so blunt, but I didn't want to ruin our reunion either. Harry was my friend and needed to hear the truth.

Harry kept his gray eyes staring straight ahead. It was a habit he had whenever he was about to deliver some bad news. I'd seen it a dozen times. If he wasn't looking at you, you didn't want to hear what he had to say. This time Harry said clearly but not directly at me, "They want to transfer you."

"You're kidding me. Where?"

"Staten Island. They're talking about starting some kind of opioid task force for all the kids of city workers who use that poison."

"Sometimes I forget Staten Island is still part of New York." I thought about it and couldn't wrap my head around that kind of punishment. "Aren't all of our bosses cops? You'd think they'd understand what I'm trying to do and how cases can unfold at different speeds."

Harry let out a heavy sigh. He turned to face me, which made me relax a little. For the first time I could see his age more clearly. To me he was almost like my grandfather: ageless. Even though he was older than me, I always thought of Harry as part of my age-group. But now I saw the deeper creases and the gray advancing in his eyebrows and hair.

Harry thought about my question and said, "They may be cops, but they work for politicians. In fact, a lot of them have become politicians to get to where they are. If they feel the heat, their answer is to turn off the oven and run out of the kitchen. Speaking of bosses, how's Roberta Herring?"

I liked the way his face lit up when he said her name. I said, "She's doing great. I've had a couple of meals with her in DC."

Harry said, "I miss her. She's old-school." After a moment, he said, "I guess I'll have to cover for you a while longer. Do you at least have some decent leads?"

"There was another woman from DC who was strangled in Baltimore. She and Emily traveled in the same circles. Something tells me my suspect lives in the DC area."

"I trust you to do what's right. Keep working on it and I'll figure out a way for you to stay employed. If I can."

I smiled. In his way, Harry was telling me to follow my heart. It was one of the many ways he reminded me of my grandfather. And I rarely regretted it when I listened to either of them.

CHAPTER 51

LUCKILY, I WAS on the road and out of the city early enough to reach DC by lunchtime. It wasn't that I was hungry or planned my meals that carefully. I knew exactly where I was going and what I wanted to accomplish.

I was running out of time in DC. Something had to crack and had to crack fast.

In a way, surveillance was my only available tool. Cops have a love-hate relationship with surveillance. You can accomplish a lot by seeing someone do something illegal. You can make a case, you can make an arrest, or you can follow that person back to the boss. That's all theoretical. In most cases, surveillance is messy, long, and not as productive as cops would like.

I drove right into the Capitol Hill area of DC and parked across the street from Gold's Gym. The security guard at the Supreme Court had let it slip that Beth Banks worked out there every day around lunchtime. I had already deduced that Beth Banks looked at things differently than most people. But I sensed she was nothing if not consistent. She had the kind of orderly life that many of us aspire to but none of us really want. Same schedule every day. Same problems to deal with. Same time to work out. I knew to be here by 1:30 or else I'd miss her.

Now, from my vantage point across the street, I could see through the only unobstructed window of the gym. I didn't have any surveillance equipment with me. No binoculars, nothing like that. But I had learned a few tricks over the years. I zoomed my iPhone all the way and looked through the camera. It gave me a good view of some of the people inside the gym. And after only a couple of minutes I saw Beth Banks.

She was in a black unitard. Now that I could see her arms, I wouldn't describe her as a swimmer. She had better biceps than most men I know. She wasn't fooling around either.

I now understood why the security guard at the Supreme Court Building had said a government gym wasn't good enough for Beth Banks. She needed a challenge. It looked like she was getting it. I first spotted her on a treadmill, running at a frightening pace. My lungs hurt just watching her. Then she moved to a set of dumbbells beside the treadmill and did ten reps of shoulder presses. After that, she balanced as she lifted a knee and the opposite arm while still holding the dumbbells. Then she jumped back on the treadmill. I didn't ever want to have to tangle with her.

I made a few notes, then wondered if I would see her meet with anyone from the case. That really had to be my goal. She was hardly going to buy cocaine from a known dealer on the street. I had to see something that would let me draw some conclusions or at least create a theory about how she could be involved in Emily's death.

I really was reaching for straws at this point. All I could tell from this quick surveillance was that Beth Banks was capable of overpowering Emily Parker. Even with Emily's FBI defensive tactics training, I'd have to give the edge to Beth Banks.

As I watched her, I started to realize why she could be a good suspect. If she had felt Emily might jeopardize her brother's reputation, maybe she would have done something drastic.

The only way to figure out if she had committed a homicide was more investigation. More questions. And more time spent in DC. The math didn't seem to be working out in my favor.

CHAPTER 52

IF BETH TURNED out not to be a suspect, I wanted her on my side. That's why I continued the investigation in half measures. I left my rental car parked on the street. Then I strolled across to the gym, walking casually in front of the big bay window to get a better look inside.

I could remember a surveillance I was on in Brooklyn about fifteen years ago. I was helping a narcotics borough unit. We'd set up on a coffee shop where an informant was supposed to meet one of the bigger heroin dealers in Brooklyn.

While I sat alone in my car, looking at the coffee shop, I noticed two men rush into a liquor store next door. It was a robbery, and people could get hurt. I knew what I had to do. I popped out of my car, and two of the local detectives followed me. The robbers were so shocked when they burst out the front door and saw us standing there that they surrendered instantly.

The funniest part to me was the fury of the narcotics detective that I would blow a drug deal for a good armed robbery arrest. Sometimes you had to question people's priorities. Like someone who'd do anything to protect the reputation of their brother.

I walked past on the sidewalk as casually as possible to see if Beth Banks was still working out. I didn't see any sign of her. The treadmill she'd been using was now occupied by a large hairy man in a fluorescent-orange shirt.

When I turned from the window, I felt the world tumble in front of me. Or maybe I was the one tumbling. I was on the sidewalk in an awkward sprawl. My vision went dim, my stomach heaved, and I felt like I might be having a stroke.

When my senses started to return, someone was standing directly in front of me. I looked up from my humiliating position like a dog on all fours. To make matters worse, I looked up into the stern face of Beth Banks.

As I slowly rose to my feet, I realized Beth had just kicked me in the head with her long, limber legs. Hard. It didn't matter that I stood a head taller than her and probably weighed seventy pounds more. I was impressed.

I rubbed my temple where her foot had caught me so squarely, knowing that she had a clear shot to prolong the attack.

Beth Banks put her hands on her hips and cocked her head a little to the side. All she said was "Don't be creepy. It's bad enough you barged into my office. Are you going to follow me around the rest of the day? If I catch you stalking me again, I'll break something. And it will be something you use a lot."

The vagueness of what she was going to hurt made her threat that much scarier. She turned and walked away confidently. Even in the business suit, she was clearly fit.

I kind of liked her.

CHAPTER 53

I SAT IN a nearly empty sub shop a few blocks from Gold's Gym. The half eaten turkey sub on my plate was evidence that my head hurt too much for me to eat. My remedy, for the moment, was to sit quietly with a bottle of cold water pressed against my temple. Almost the exact spot Beth Banks had kicked me. I thought I could reasonably say I was the only person ever kicked in the head by a Supreme Court justice's chief of staff. I figured she'd kicked someone in the head before this. I just assumed it was before her tenure with the Supreme Court.

I recognized I was feeling a little sorry for myself. I'd just had my ass kicked by a woman 70 percent of my size. I wasn't on the trail of a killer, nor did I have any decent leads. Most of all, as I sat there wallowing in self-pity, I missed my family.

My quick trip home had only made me realize how desperately I needed my family. And that was a joyous realization. Most people would be thrilled if they could actually say they enjoyed spending time with their family. But I really *did* love spending time with them. Yet I couldn't do it. At least not now.

The three other people in the sub shop all had their own problems. The kid behind the counter clearly didn't want to work here. A woman sitting near the front looked clinically depressed as she picked at a salad with brown lettuce and two whole tomatoes thrown on top. A guy in a delivery uniform didn't have time to enjoy lunch, downing his six-inch sub in four bites. My problems seemed more manageable when I looked at the big picture.

I took a pen and my little notepad from my sport coat and started to make a few notes. I wrote down the names of my three best suspects.

Beth Banks, who was certainly physically capable, had a motive to protect her brother and was just plain mean.

The next name was Robert Steinberg. I knew it was far-fetched to think a Supreme Court justice might commit murder. But in the real world, almost 80 percent of women who disappear or are murdered are attacked by their husbands or boyfriends. Domestic violence is real. It doesn't care what aggressors do for a living.

The last name I wrote down was Jeremy Pugh. He was strong, crazy, and apparently pretty smart. That's a dangerous combination. If it weren't for the fact that Emily had an open case on his group, The Burning Land, he wouldn't even make the list. His aggressive behavior since I'd first met him kept him as a potential suspect.

I'd spoken to both Beth Banks and Jeremy Pugh. That left Justice Steinberg as the only one of my potential suspects I hadn't spoken to face-to-face. If I wanted to do it, I had to plan. Clearly I wouldn't get into his office again. Even if I did somehow manage to make it there, I doubted I would survive my next encounter with Beth Banks.

I couldn't conduct an interview at Steinberg's home. He'd call the cops so fast I wouldn't even get out a greeting. And all the locals would need is some kind of criminal charge like trespassing or a beefed-up burglary charge to send me home. Permanently.

I took another bite of tasteless turkey, then drank my cold water. As I sat there, thinking about buying another bottle of water just to keep on my head, my phone rang.

I looked down and saw it was Bobby Patel. I wondered if Beth Banks had even bothered to report my lurking around her gym. There was no sense in putting off bad news. That seemed to be the only thing Bobby called me with.

I put on the most cheerful voice I could, answered the phone, and said, "Hey, Bobby, how's it going?"

"Metropolitan Police Department just called me. They have someone in custody for Emily's murder."

CHAPTER 54

IT DIDN'T TAKE me long to meet Bobby in front of an off-site building used by the Metropolitan Police of DC. The square, two-story building with a cheap decorative brick facade was a street crimes/narcotics unit in an industrial area just outside the city proper.

Most larger city police departments have something like it, a nondescript office where plainclothes officers can meet without the risk of inmates or prisoners seeing them. That way they can continue making undercover drug buys or connect with informants in public. Besides, all the narcotics guys think it's cool.

I saw a few younger officers near the front door. They looked pissed off, and I knew exactly what had happened. Some homicide detectives had commandeered their building. No one appreciates shit like that. Every unit thinks it is the most vital police unit in the city.

The other thing I noticed was the number of new Ford Crown Victorias and Chevy Tahoes in the parking lot. That told me there was command staff on-site. Bosses tend to grab the nicer vehicles. Maybe there was something to this arrest story after all.

Bobby trotted up to my car. He slid to a stop and did a double take when I crawled out of the Prius.

I asked, "What's wrong?"

"I was going to present you as an FBI agent without going into much detail. But I don't know any self-respecting FBI agent who would wear that jacket."

I looked at him in a gray business suit with a nice dark tie. He did look sharp. I held up my arm and looked at my jacket. "It's a dark green plaid sport coat. It goes with my khakis. It also hides my pistol and keeps me warm in the shitty weather down here in DC. I'm pretty sure clothing is all the cops in there are going to care about. Is it functional, does it have holes? Welcome to the real world, Bobby."

As I suspected, Bobby ignored my prediction about DC cops' take on fashion. Instead, he scowled and said, "Just follow me and keep your mouth shut. And definitely don't say out loud that you're an FBI agent. We need to have plausible deniability if anyone complains later that you were here."

"Bobby, the cops inside this building don't give a damn about any of that shit right now. They want to make a case. If they have a suspect they like, they'll barely notice we're here."

"But their bosses will notice and ask questions."

I just nodded and followed him into the two-story building, which had a sign for JOHNSON'S WEB DESIGN AND VIDEO EDITING. It was just modern and flashy enough to seem real. Just vague enough to never have anyone stop and ask what they do.

Each office had one or two people in it. Most were in some sort of serious discussion. I figured there were already some district commanders and certainly a public information officer or two formulating some kind of press release. After all, the story of Emily's murder had been on the news.

A tubby man wearing a tan, short-sleeved shirt with a brown, checked tie greeted Bobby. Bobby didn't bother to introduce us. All I caught was his first name, Perry. He had the burned-out look of a longtime homicide detective. A quick haircut without care for the lines of his head. A gut that hung over his belt from too many fast-food meals thrown down while reading reports. And a slight limp from a torn MCL that he was too busy to have anyone look at. I guess homicide detectives in every city are about the same.

I listened as he and Bobby started talking about the case.

The detective, Perry, said, "This guy lives in some bushes exactly on the route your agent used to run from the Whole Foods. We were canvassing the area for about the tenth time. We started from the Whole Foods where she left her car and worked toward the river. Then we noticed a brand-new Fitbit on this guy's wrist. That's what started it. It didn't take long to confirm that it was Emily Parker's Fitbit. I'd say we're looking at a pretty solid case."

I couldn't contain it anymore. I blurted out, "Are you kidding me?"

191

CHAPTER 55

BOBBY TRIED TO brush by my comment. An old-school homicide detective like Perry wasn't going to let it go.

Perry used his bulk to shove past Bobby. "What d'you mean, am I kidding you? Hell no, I'm not kidding anyone."

Bobby tried to redirect the detective's attention. "He didn't mean anything by it."

The detective ignored him. He broke into my personal space and raised his voice. "What do you mean? How many goddamn homicides have you worked?" It was just under a shout, and his face was turning red. A scary shade of red.

I knew not to say *Calm down.* That never helps when someone is upset. I think whoever started saying it, maybe back in the Middle Ages, meant it ironically.

Instead, I said, "I've worked a few homicides."

The burly detective lowered his voice and said, "You don't think he's a good suspect?"

"I'd like to talk to him. Having someone's Fitbit doesn't mean you killed them. What else have you got? There's gotta be something."

The detective just stared at me.

I asked the next logical question: "Did he confess?"

That froze the detective in place. He looked at me and said, "He's answered in the affirmative to questions about grabbing the FBI agent."

I wanted to call bullshit. But I kept my mouth shut. No matter how hard it was.

The detective said, "The suspect has three arrests for violent crime. That counts for something."

"Unless he didn't do it. Then it doesn't count for shit."

The detective's face flushed again, but he didn't say anything.

Bobby chatted in a low voice with the detective, then said, "Can we talk to him for a minute?"

The detective hesitated. "I might need to clear this with one of the bosses."

Bobby kept an even tone. "We're not trying to steal your case. But I have to be able to brief *my* bosses. We just want to get in and ask him a couple of questions. Obviously, you can stay with us the whole time."

It was too reasonable of an argument to ignore.

The detective led us through a narrow hallway to an interview room. The room was small. Maybe ten feet by ten feet. The ceiling tiles were almost low enough to touch. I wondered if that was intentional. To give people a claustrophobic feeling. There was a camera in each corner. Perry gave us a briefing sheet with the man's name, age, and criminal record. As soon as we stepped in, a young female detective stood up. She was in the corner, and the suspect was cuffed in the middle.

The tall, skinny man of about fifty-five looked to be six three and probably didn't break a buck forty. He was mostly bald, but the rim of gray, messy hair still on his head was long and uncombed. He had a ruddy face made tough by years of living in the sun.

We slid into the seats across from him. Bobby had already warned me that he was going to ask the questions.

Bobby said, "Are you Jason Hagensick?"

The man had a wide grin. Several of the teeth in his lower jaw popped past his lips, giving him the look of a bulldog. All he said was "Yep." His eyes were focused on something on the far wall. When he turned and looked at me, I noted that his eyes looked clear. I didn't detect any drug use.

"You know why you're here, right?"

"Yep."

I started to have an uneasy feeling. I looked down at the briefing sheet and saw that he had been arrested twice in the early nineties for some kind of fighting. He'd had another arrest a couple of years later for stalking. I couldn't contain myself and said, "Did you see a woman running near where you live in the bushes?"

"Yep."

Bobby cut in. "Did you hurt her?"

"Yep."

Now I raised my hand to stop everyone. The young female detective was still standing in the corner. The lead detective, who had tried to sell us on this guy's guilt, stood by the door.

I said, "Are you the president of the United States?"

"Yep."

I shot a nasty look to the detective. I even mumbled, "He answered in the affirmative."

CHAPTER 56

IT'S RARE THAT I lose my temper. Perhaps it's a side effect of having ten children. But in reality, before we adopted our first child, I was pretty good at keeping a level head. I attribute most of that to being raised by Seamus Bennett.

But looking at that homeless man's face and knowing what the homicide detective was considering, I lost it. I stomped out of the interview room. And kept stomping all the way down the hallway. I saw half a dozen sets of eyes fall on me. I couldn't have cared less. I hit the exit door like a fullback.

I didn't realize I'd been holding my breath until I got outside. I gulped in the fresh air and appreciated the afternoon sun on my face.

Bobby eased out of the door a minute later. He took a moment to straighten his tie and pulled the cuffs of his shirt. Then I heard him take a deep breath as he turned to face me.

Bobby said, "What was that hissy fit about?"

"Are you kidding me? If you're making a joke, that's fine. If you think that poor guy in handcuffs actually killed anyone, you need to find a different line of work."

"I don't need a detective from a local agency telling me what I should do with my career. I don't care if you're with the NYPD, the LAPD, or the Hattiesburg, Mississippi, PD, you're still not the FBI."

"For all the faults the FBI has, I haven't known any agents who would railroad someone into a charge just to clear a case."

"You're right. It's a local cop who's more likely to do something like that."

In that moment, I wanted to smack the arrogant prick. For all the goodwill we had built up, he was wasting it awfully fast.

Bobby said, "I'm not saying I would've gone along with it. I just wanted to hear what the detective had to say and what the suspect looked like."

"I'm beginning to think the suspect might be better-looking than that guy. Maybe wear a suit. Maybe even wear a dress. I have a few suspects in mind, but that guy ain't one of them."

The door to the building burst open, and the chubby homicide detective stuck his head out. He glared at me and said, "You blew any chance we had of making a case on that guy." He pointed a crooked finger at me.

I just stared at him. I didn't say a word. I didn't trust myself.

The detective came out to us. I couldn't wait to hear more excuses. He leaned against a blue Ford Taurus and crossed his arms in front of him. "I wasn't going to charge him unless we had enough. But after your little outburst and the way the command staff reacted, I won't even get a chance to question him."

"You talked to him for a while. Did he say anything you could use?" I waited through a couple of moments of silence, then added, "Besides 'Yep.'"

"You got no idea the kind of pressure I'm under. The stories on the news. The FBI calls every day. My bosses want this cleared up. I'm just making sure we don't miss anything. But pulling stunts like that makes us miss stuff."

I took a few steps closer until I was only a foot away from the detective's face. "Tell me what you're missing by not talking to the poor guy you have in there. You think any prosecutor would have accepted a case like that? Or would you have made a probable cause arrest and hoped that it got through first appearance? I didn't become a cop to ruin people's lives. I became a cop to help people." I glared at him without having to say *What about you?*

The detective let out an exasperated sigh. Without a word, he turned and stormed back into the building.

Before I could say anything to Bobby, an unmarked Chevy Tahoe pulled into the lot. It had the look of a command staff car. When the door opened, I was even less happy.

CHAPTER 57

THERE WERE LITTLE things about the Tahoe I should've detected before the door even opened. It had just a little too much wear and tear and mud splattered across the door. Very few command staff people would allow a vehicle to get that sloppy. That's why they have assistants. That's why there are rookies: to clean cars occasionally.

Instead, when the door opened, and the tall black man emerged, I recognized him. It was Paul Daggett, from the Special Investigations unit. I remembered him from when he and a couple of his friends had visited me at my hotel.

The first thing out of the DC detective's mouth was "You don't listen so well."

I said, "It's Daggett, right?"

"Good memory. Too bad you don't have any common sense to go with it."

"Last time we met, you had a couple of minions with you."

Just then the doors to the Tahoe opened. I heard a woman's voice say, "You mean us?" The physically fit woman, about thirty with long dark hair, stepped out onto the asphalt. She was dressed in a Nationals T-shirt and had a Glock model 19 in a holster on her hip.

The driver was the heavyset white man who'd been quick with the comebacks. He casually leaned on the hood and let the others do the talking. He didn't look any better dressed today than he had a few days ago. Over stretch jeans, he wore an old light-blue sport coat that looked like it came from a leisure suit.

I looked at the three of them and said, "Now you're complete. You look like a middle-aged Mod Squad."

Only the chubby guy laughed.

I said, "What's the matter with you two? You never watch any reruns?"

Daggett had a deep, resonant voice. He used it to good effect. "Fun and games are over, *Detective* Bennett." The way he'd emphasized *Detective* told me he wasn't trying to be respectful. "You just ruined a potential lead."

"I just kept your detective from looking like an ass."

"Why? Because you're NYPD and so much smarter than the rest of us?"

"That's part of it. Yeah. But your man in there is under too much pressure. He was considering charging the wrong person. A poor homeless dude who doesn't sound like he's all there. It would've looked bad for everyone."

Daggett took a minute to consider that. Of the three partners, he was the only one wearing both a tie and a coat. He could've been a lawyer, with his neatly trimmed goatee and just a few specks of gray in his close-cropped hair.

I said, "I'll make you an offer you can't refuse."

"I'm listening."

"You go in and talk to the so-called suspect. Just for a minute or two. Then, if you think that I'm wrong and he's good for Emily Parker's murder, you come out here and tell me that with a straight face. If you honestly think he's a good suspect, I'll go home."

I paused and appreciated the anticipation on the faces of the three DC cops. Daggett was smart enough not to say anything.

So I dropped in the second part of my proposal. "On the other hand, if you agree with me, if you talk to him and realize the only thing he might have to answer for is why he has Emily's Fitbit, then you come out here and wish me a good day. I'll go about my business and you go about yours. But maybe you could appreciate someone trying to look out for one of your detectives. And the reputation of your department."

Daggett would've been a good poker player. His face gave nothing away. It felt like the city had gone silent. Bobby was off mingling with some new arrivals. They were all wearing suits, so I assumed they were Feds.

Finally, Daggett said, "You have yourself a deal, Detective Bennett."

CHAPTER 58

I DIDN'T MIND waiting outside while Daggett took me up on my offer. I kept an eye on Bobby and wondered what he was telling the two men and two women he was talking to so earnestly at the corner of the building.

I hoped I'd read Daggett right. He seemed like a decent guy. One who would stick to a deal. He also didn't impress me as someone who would meet this potential suspect and then lie to me. It didn't matter now. I'd made my deal and I would stand by it.

The female detective—who had never given me her name, and I didn't ask—looked over at me. I always liked to see sharp younger people on police forces. The way the police are treated in the media has made it harder and harder to recruit good cops. I couldn't blame anyone who didn't want to give their heart and soul to a job that didn't really offer much.

She said, "Seriously, why are you in DC?"

I kept a very even tone. "Emily Parker was a friend of mine. I owed her a lot. Finding her killer doesn't seem like that much to ask."

The female detective looked off into space. After a few moments, she nodded. "I've gotta say, that's a pretty good reason."

The fat guy moved from the front of the Tahoe and now leaned on the SUV next to his partner. He said, "I still think it's sort of arrogant to believe you're the only one who can find the killer."

I shook my head. "That's not how I feel at all. I'm just another set of eyes and ears. Look at what happened here. I didn't see the same thing your detective did. If your man, Daggett, disagrees, then I misjudged him. But I always keep my promises. If he honestly thinks this is the killer, I'll leave."

The fat detective said, "Tell you what, if Daggett walks out here, looks at you, and says, 'Have a good day,' lunch is on me any day you want."

We shook on it. He said, "My name is Swinson. My friends call me Dave."

The female detective said, "I'm Nancy Gorant. Nice to meet you. Maybe you're not the asshole I pegged you for."

I wagged a finger. "It's awfully early to say I'm not. Trust me, I know we're all in this together." It was a feeling many cops shared. These two were no exception. I felt like I'd made a couple of friends. But I still didn't have an answer from Daggett.

Bobby broke off from his meeting. When he came over to us, I explained exactly the deal I'd made with Daggett.

Bobby said, "I almost wish he'd come out here and say the guy's a good suspect, if only to get you out of my hair. I just had a long talk with supervisors from my office. One of them noticed you. I hinted indirectly that you were here with the DC police and not me. Please don't rat me out."

Nancy Gorant said to Bobby, "We were just getting used to Detective Bennett being here. Are you as interested as him in finding the FBI agent's killer?"

"I'm all in on finding Emily's killer. That's all I work on. I thought that Bennett would be a help, but so far I'm wasting too much time trying to explain him to other people."

Before the debate could progress into whether I was worth saving in any way, the door to the office burst open and Detective Daggett stepped out. He'd been inside a little longer than I thought necessary.

He walked right up to me, cleared his throat, and said, "Have a nice day."

I had a free lunch coming from Detective Swinson.

CHAPTER 59

IT DIDN'T TAKE long for Bobby to get nervous hanging around the DC police's off-site building. There were just too many FBI supervisors and people who would ask questions about me. I'd noticed that Bobby was helpful and supportive, unless it interfered with his ambition. Finding a fellow FBI agent's killer would go a long way toward propelling him to the top. And I was sure he didn't care if I figured it out or he did, as long as he got the credit.

I was good with that. But I wasn't about to send some mentally incapacitated homeless man to jail just to make it look like we'd solved the crime. That's not how cops make their reputation.

Bobby broke off his conversation with a group of DC police supervisors and returned to me. He tugged at his collar and tie. Not a sign of inner peace.

I said, "Is that your Rodney Dangerfield impersonation?"

"Who?"

"Great stand-up comedian. Been in some classic movies."

Bobby gave me a blank stare.

"Easy Money. Caddyshack." After still no response, I said, "Are you more of a superhero-movie kinda guy?"

Bobby leveled a look at me. "I am a raised-by-Indian-parents kinda guy. The only movies I've seen are historical or documentary. The only TV shows I was allowed to watch played on PBS. Now, if you're asking me about a writer, I've read them all. My parents would make me read a book before I could even go out and play soccer."

I said, "Truthfully, I don't know whether to feel sorry for you or give your parents a prize."

Bobby glanced around the parking lot and said, "Let's go somewhere we can talk in private."

"Follow me," I said. About five blocks away I had noticed two picnic tables in a shaded spot beside a convenience store/gas station.

I hustled inside while Bobby stayed in his car on his cell phone. The place was only two rows of junk food and a couple of big freezers. Merchandise was stacked from the floor to the low ceiling. Everything from cases of beer to portable Bluetooth speakers. The young woman behind the counter never looked up from her phone. I grabbed my traditional grape Gatorade and a big bottle of water for Bobby. I motioned to him that I was headed to the picnic tables.

Someone had put a flat-screen TV in the window facing the picnic tables. With the closed-captioning on, I didn't mind having a few minutes to watch the prelude to the local news. It was just tilting into late afternoon, and the traffic was picking up.

I found a clean corner of one of the picnic benches. A lot of people clearly ate their lunch here every day. Only about half of them cleaned up after themselves.

Bobby finished his call and sat down across from me with his hands folded on the table. I handed him the water bottle, and he stared at me like he was about to give a confession.

Finally, Bobby said, "What you did wasn't cool."

"You mean keep someone from being wrongfully charged with murder?"

"You know exactly what I mean. You're supposed to be an observer. You were present as my guest. Anything you say or do in a situation like that reflects on me. When this is over, you can just go back to New York and the life you have there. Some of us have to stay in DC and work with these cops on a daily basis."

I understood what he was saying. Most cops would. They have their way of doing things and I have mine. I refused to apologize for doing the right thing. But I understood why Bobby was angry. And he had expressed it pretty clearly.

I looked at the younger FBI man and said, "So what does this mean going forward?"

"There is no 'going forward' as far as you and I are concerned. We can talk on the phone. Maybe even chat in person. But I'm not going to take you to any crime scenes or interviews. And—I can't stress how important this is—I don't want to know about it if you talk to Justice Steinberg. Or his wife. Or his sister. That can be your part of the investigation. The FBI has already spoken to them. I doubt our agents pushed any of them particularly hard. I can see the value in you talking to them. But I can't see losing my job over it. So not only will this give me *plausible* deniability. I also can outright deny any knowledge of your dealings with the Steinbergs."

I made the calculated move to keep quiet. People hate awkward silences, and they fill in the gaps by putting forward how they really feel. I didn't have to wait too long.

Bobby blurted out, "This doesn't affect how I feel about you. You're a sharp detective. Clearly you're a loyal friend. But I can't risk it anymore."

I slowly nodded my head and said, "I understand."

Bobby took a swig of the water I'd bought him. Then he looked down at his phone. The guy got more texts than a teenager on a Saturday night. I took the opportunity to look up at the TV.

It was midway through the local afternoon newsbreak. I saw protesters in front of the Supreme Court Building. I looked more closely and realized from The Burning Land T-shirts that the group was stirring up shit. The closed-captioning confirmed it.

I watched carefully for a few seconds, hoping to catch a glimpse of Jeremy Pugh or one of the others I might recognize. The closed-captioning mentioned that the anarchist group was protesting a Supreme Court ruling about schools requiring vaccinations for students.

As they were interviewing one of The Burning Land protesters—a woman, about twenty-five, with a spear tattooed on the side of her face—I looked past her to the people swarming the front of the Supreme Court Building. That left those who worked inside only one exit route.

This would be my best chance of finding Justice Robert Steinberg.

CHAPTER 60

EVEN IN MY sluggish Prius, I made it to the Supreme Court Building in less than half an hour. The protest seemed to have gone downhill from the time when I'd seen it reported on the TV. Bottles smashed in the street right in front of the Prius. A rock sailed past the windshield. I knew I couldn't assist the DC and Supreme Court Police in their containment efforts.

A young woman wearing a sundress held a flower up to a police officer. She smiled as she stepped forward. I wanted to yell through the car window to the cop, *Move back! Keep space between you!* But I couldn't.

The cop stared at the young woman with the flower just as she raised a plastic cup. She splashed something into his face. He dropped his nightstick and reached up to grab his eyes as two other cops moved him off the front line. I hoped it wasn't pool acid or something as dangerous. I'd seen the chemical used in other protests. The media rarely picked up on it.

I knew the justice typically drove a black Mercedes sedan. I'd barely pulled my Prius to the curb when I saw the gate to the underground parking garage open.

I held my breath as a blue Cadillac SUV emerged from the exit. Before I could react, I saw a black hood ease out behind it. A moment later, Justice Steinberg's Mercedes pulled into the street and headed north. There was no way he would notice something like this Prius following him.

Not long after leaving the Supreme Court Building, he pulled into the one place most Americans looking to complete a home project eventually go: The Home Depot. This one was on Rhode Island Avenue in the Brentwood section of DC. And I had an opportunity to intercept him.

I hung back in the parking lot and let him walk inside. He'd gone for the casual disguise of removing his suit coat and loosening his tie. As I sat in my rented car, I realized this was the first live view I'd gotten of the justice. I'd never heard Justice Steinberg speak other than answering some not-so-difficult questions during his televised confirmation hearing.

Maybe my thinking had been off. Since when had I looked at a murder and not bothered to see each suspect in person?

Justice Robert Steinberg was a moderate with good bipartisan support. He had a trim figure and a steady stride that radiated athletic vitality. He looked younger than his forty-one years. He shied away from all the talk in the media about being the youngest justice ever appointed to the Supreme Court.

It didn't take me long to catch up to the justice. As I edged closer, I could see the resemblance to his sister. The justice was fit, but few people outside the US Navy SEALs could rival Beth's level of fitness.

He picked up a couple of things in the paint department and was heading toward the rear of the cavernous store. And no one recognized him. Not one person. If Steinberg had been an actor or singer, he would've been mobbed. But no one recognized one of the most influential people in the US.

I tried to anticipate where he'd go. I got ahead of him and waited.

CHAPTER 61

I DECIDED TO make my move in plumbing. The justice was meticulously inspecting three or four brands of toilet parts. I suppose close study is how one becomes a successful lawyer, college professor, and Supreme Court justice.

Interviewing well-known people can breed false familiarity, the feeling of knowing them from TV or movies or speeches. In fact, all you're seeing is the character they play. I don't care who you are or what you investigate, having a preconceived notion about a suspect influences the interview.

I once interviewed a well-known music producer who was accused of running down a rival with his SUV. I'd seen the music producer on TV and concluded he might've been talented making albums, but he wasn't particularly smart. At least in the way we normally define smart people.

It wasn't till we got into the interview, with his attorney

present, that I learned he was a graduate of the University of Michigan and had earned a master's degree in accounting before his music career had taken off.

I didn't need that surprise right at the beginning of our interview. It turned out, even with a master's from a good school like the University of Michigan, the music producer had poor judgment. And a temper. That combination rarely works out well. In fact, he had threatened his rival the night before, and the rival's girlfriend had the voicemail recording.

Eventually he pled guilty to manslaughter, and he was still at a prison in upstate New York. Common sense is always more important than money or even a decent education. The problem is that you can't teach common sense.

I stood, looking up at a wall full of replacement parts for sinks. Like a fisherman, I remained patient. I was letting my fish swim toward me. The justice moved on from toilet parts until he was about five feet away from me.

That's when he surprised me. Maybe *shocked* is a better word.

Justice Steinberg turned to me just as I was glancing in his direction. His brown eyes showed no concern or apprehension. He just looked at me and said, "I wondered how close you'd try to come to me in here."

My throat went dry. I could think of nothing to say. Then I blurted out, "So you know who I am?"

He chuckled. "Detective Bennett, at this point everyone in Washington, DC, knows who you are. It's just that most people don't realize *what* you are."

"A homicide detective."

The justice smiled and said, "I was thinking more along the lines of a giant pain in the ass."

CHAPTER 62

JUSTICE STEINBERG AND I squared off in the aisle. Faucet displays and toilet parts were our audience. When I say *squared off,* I mean it figuratively. We faced each other. Each assessing the other.

The justice was a hair under six feet tall. He had sort of that rugged outdoorsman look. It always went well with an Ivy League education. Not to mention the money his family had or the money he had married into. It looked like he was working just a little too hard at being a "regular guy."

Steinberg smiled. "You may want to make this quick. My sister is meeting me here to look at kitchen appliances." He made a show of looking up and down the empty aisle. Then he stared straight at me, a grin still on his face. "You're familiar with my sister, Beth, aren't you?"

His smile told me there were few secrets between the two of

them. It also told me he didn't care how physical she got with me. He impressed me as one of those jerks who thinks they're better than everyone else and above the rules.

I tried to keep cool. "Yes, I've met your sister." I rubbed my temple where she'd kicked me. "She makes quite the impression."

He snorted and said, "You have no idea. She's been like that since she was a kid. You know how embarrassing it is when your sister is suspended from high school for breaking the nose of the captain of the football team? Then there was the incident at Stanford. A swimmer got a little frisky with her at a party." He paused and looked around for Beth again.

When he didn't finish the story, I said, "I kinda want to know what happened to the swimmer."

"Let's put it this way: it was tough for him to compete for a few months while his dislocated shoulder and broken ribs healed." The justice shook his head. "Stanford has a dedicated room in their business school with thirty state-of-the-art computers for students to use. That was my father's gift. Basically, a thank-you for not kicking my sister out of school."

"Did the swimmer bring any charges?" I followed the cop's line of questioning.

Steinberg shook his head. "He knew he was in the wrong. If he had kept going and my sister had filed a complaint, he would've only gotten a slap on the wrist. I think this worked out better for everyone."

We stood there for a moment in silence. I tried to break the ice by saying, "I'm impressed you recognized me."

"The NYPD isn't the only agency with briefings. You know the Supreme Court has its own police force. And they are definitely aware of you. Even though they say you're no threat.

At least physically. My sister confirms that." He gave me another smile. This guy was not easily rattled.

"So what's next for us?"

Steinberg kept his eyes on me. "You tell me. You're the one stirring the shit."

"And you're the one living in it."

"I don't follow you, Detective."

"You were having an affair with Emily Parker. It is not the first one you've had. Everyone in town knows about your antics. One person even called you a 'wild child.' That puts you at the center of a homicide investigation."

"No, it puts me at the center of *your* homicide investigation. I've already told everything I know to the DC police and the FBI. I'm not a suspect for either of those agencies."

"Did they know about your wild personal life? Or is that a fact you decided was not important enough to mention?"

"I didn't tell them I dated two women at the same time in law school. Who are you? The morality police?"

Holy cow, he had a point. It made me pause for a moment. Then I regained my senses. "I couldn't give a shit about your personal life. But it does give you a motive to kill Emily."

Now his smile turned into a smirk. "How the hell do you figure that?"

"There are a thousand different ways I can see why you'd have a motive. Domestic violence has no single catalyst. Or, if I want to use a really simple theory, maybe you were afraid she could ruin your reputation."

That brought a genuine guffaw. When he was done with this laugh, he wiped his eyes with the back of his hand, looked at me, and said, "I'm married to the daughter of the most investigated active senator in Congress. He was once photographed on a date with a model half his age while his wife was undergoing chemotherapy. That didn't even ruin his reputation. The people of New York have elected him three times since his indiscretion. That's not even considering the public Justice Department investigation on his scheme to get campaign money from every corporation in New York. The fact that the Department of Justice didn't file charges rarely makes a difference in public opinion. But the people in New York like what he does, so they reelected him. I doubt my relationship with Emily would do anything to my reputation."

I could see why this guy was a great trial lawyer. At least at the moment he seemed to have an answer for everything. Without really having to think about it.

After a few more seconds of silence, the exasperated Supreme Court justice sighed. "Detective Bennett, what would it take to make you go away?"

"I'd go back home if I could find Emily's killer."

"I'd like that as well."

Then I heard a woman's voice behind me say, "What the shit?"

It was Beth Banks. She was eyeing a two-foot-long pipe sitting on the shelf. I could already see how she could use it as a weapon.

CHAPTER 63

BETH BANKS PACED back and forth across the width of the aisle. Her measured and determined movements reminded me of a boxer too hyped-up to sit down before a big match. Or maybe she was more like a tiger in a zoo, pacing back and forth, eyes always on the people watching her.

I would say she was sizing me up, but she'd already done that. Quite effectively. That's when I realized she was waiting for word from her brother to let loose on me. It was really a no-win situation. Even if I defended myself, all witnesses would see was a tall man fighting a much smaller woman. It didn't matter that she'd already knocked me off my feet and proven to be twice as athletic as me.

Now she stopped and looked at me as she opened and closed her fists. Maybe it was just a warm-up. She didn't want to risk pulling a muscle while she beat me senseless.

She looked at me and said, "How's the head feel?"

"I'm Irish. I'm more worried about your foot." I figured it was better to engage her verbally.

Beth let a smile slip out. She had a lovely smile. Just a flash of warmth. I wondered what she was like when she wasn't trying to punch someone. Too bad that smile didn't go with her personality.

Beth said, "Good one. I didn't know if a New York cop would have any kind of a sense of humor."

"I didn't realize you had a sense of humor until just this moment."

"I'm sorry I gave you that impression. I like finding humor in things that scare most people. Take clowns. Normally, they make me laugh. What about you, Detective? Do you like to find the bright side to scary situations?"

I cocked my head to the side. "I swear to God, I can't tell if you're trying to intimidate me or flirt with me."

"Trust me, Detective, you wouldn't have any doubt if I was trying to intimidate you."

I couldn't resist. "Why is that?"

"Because you'd be looking up at me from the ground. Similar to our last encounter." She turned to her brother like *Do you need me?* He gave her a subtle shake of his head. To me, Beth said, "I'm off to refrigerators. Don't worry, Detective, I'm not looking for something big enough to store your body. From what I hear, no one in DC would care much if someone killed you. I doubt I'd even have to hide the body."

I took the little comment, then said, "You know, in some places that could be considered a threat of violence."

"More of a hypothetical threat. Just something to make me smile tonight over dinner."

Beth stuck out her hand for me to shake. When I did, she showed me what a powerful grip she had. I didn't wince or make any noise. I didn't try to squeeze back. I let her have her fun. There was no doubt she was mostly muscle. She was also her brother's muscle. She was forcing me to notice it and acknowledge it.

That's why I had her as my number one suspect in Emily Parker's death.

CHAPTER 64

AS SOON AS Beth Banks had turned the corner of the aisle, her brother looked at me. He lowered his voice and had a conciliatory tone. "I appreciate your loyalty to Emily. I knew her since she graduated from Quantico. She meant a lot to me."

"Thank you, Justice Steinberg. But it still makes me wonder about a lot of things."

"Like what?"

"Like what would a guy like you do to keep Emily from talking to your wife?"

He just stared at me. Then his mouth dropped open a little. Finally, I had struck a nerve with someone in this damn case.

It was almost a full ten seconds before he regained his senses. "Is that it? You think I'm worried Rhea would find out about me and Emily? Have you been operating on that assumption from the beginning?"

I said, "In your long legal career, you never saw a man take drastic steps to keep his wife from finding out about a girlfriend?"

"I know the theory. I agree that it happens. Much more frequently than is reported. But I think you should've spent a little more time digging into my relationship with Emily. Or maybe, more accurately, Emily's relationship with my wife and me."

Now it was my turn to stare silently. Eventually I said, "I'm not sure I'm following you. Your wife knew all about Emily?"

He gave me a little laugh. "Knew about her! They spent a lot of time together. I'm not sure I even saw Emily alone. My wife and Emily were close. They'd share a cigar once in a while. More important, we always considered our relationships private. As in it's no one's business but ours. I wish you would consider it the same way."

I couldn't hold it in any longer. I unleashed a verbal haymaker. "What about the relationship you had with Michelle Luna? Should that be considered private too? Or the fact that two different women who were friendly with a powerful man are now dead? What are the chances that both women who were close to you end up dead by strangulation?"

I had to wait. The mention of Michelle Luna had affected the justice. He was visibly emotional for a moment. Then he focused back on me. "As far as I know, Michelle and Emily never met each other. They were actually quite opposite. Michelle was on the wild side and also reckless. She had her own demons."

"Is that what choked her to death in Baltimore? A demon? Or did Emily smoke one too many cigars?"

"Now you're just trying to be cruel. Saying something like

that doesn't further your investigation. All that does is play on my emotions."

I didn't care if I hurt his feelings. When this was over and I had found Emily's killer, if it wasn't him, I'd apologize. Until then he could kiss my ass.

Justice Steinberg held up his hand and said, "We're not getting anywhere. I hope someone finds Emily's killer. I really do. I also hope you go back to New York City soon."

Then I found myself alone and surrounded by toilet parts.

CHAPTER 65

I IMMEDIATELY DROVE back to my hotel. I'd gotten in the habit of driving through the parking lot once to see if there was anyone suspicious hanging around. Although I was pretty sure I'd already run through the entire list of people who planned to threaten me.

I got to my room, pulled out my notepad and everything I'd collected on the case. I spread a few sheets of paper on the small desk, some on the bed, and a few more on the cheap sofa. I didn't realize how much information I'd gathered until I stepped back. My room looked like a disaster scene at a recycling plant.

I also considered my conversation with Justice Steinberg. People think that a cop needs to hear a confession during an interview for it to be worthwhile. That is absolutely not true. Every interview teaches you something. It may teach you that the person you're interviewing has nothing to do with the crime. But there are dozens of levels between that and a confession. For one thing, Justice Steinberg had been much less interested in talking about Michelle Luna's death than in talking about Emily Parker.

The mention of Michelle Luna's name had seemed to throw the justice off a little bit. But my perception didn't confirm a theory or motive. There were plenty available. Protecting the justice's reputation was the most likely possibility.

As far as suspects go, the justice was believable. I'm not saying I'm a human lie detector, but after a hundred classes on interviewing and twenty years of asking the tough questions, I have a pretty good sense of when people are lying. Justice Steinberg was a smooth operator who was smart and well educated. But if he had committed a homicide, he didn't have the street sense to hide it. I was leaving open the question of whether he'd ordered someone else to do it.

Then I looked at the details of both murders. They were similar but not identical. Michelle Luna had been choked from behind. That's how the Baltimore forensic people were able to lift DNA from the back of her earring. The medical examiner in DC had said Emily was strangled with two hands by someone facing her. Then she was dumped in the water. They were unable to recover any usable DNA from the body.

The DNA from Michelle Luna's murder was the only physical evidence that meant anything right now. The biggest problem with a DNA sample is that you need a sample from a suspect to compare it to. The earring sample had been run through the DNA databases and had received no hits. That meant it was up to someone to supply a sample from a suspect not in the database. That gave me a whole host of new problems to think about.

Maybe I'd been too focused on this investigation. I'd really been looking only at Emily Parker's murder. I should've been looking at it like two murders. And if there was evidence connected to only one victim, I could run with that.

Then I thought about my suspects. Jeremy Pugh was still in the mix. Leaving out the idea that it was two random murders, I kept coming back to Beth Banks. A good upbringing and education could disguise a lot of traits. Maybe she was smart enough to hide the fact that she was a killer.

I wasn't sure if Roberta Herring could do anything more for me. I also had no more support from Bobby Patel. But by stepping away from Bobby, I was stepping away from some of the arbitrary rules he had laid down.

It looked like I had a lot of work still to do.

CHAPTER 66

MY PHONE RANG and knocked me out of my deep thoughts on this case. I almost couldn't take my eyes off the bed where the papers were still spread out. I figured the call was probably Bobby. He'd realized he'd been a dick and wanted to apologize. Maybe I did like working with that guy more than I thought.

I glanced at the phone and saw it was Mary Catherine. I snatched the phone up without thinking. I realized I was grinning like a bookie before the Super Bowl when I said, "Hey, beautiful, how are you today?"

"Better now that I hear your voice."

She would never lose her light Irish accent. And I was glad of it.

Mary Catherine said, "I was just calling to see how you're doing. I was wondering if there's anything I can do to help."

"I hope that means there haven't been any more bomb-shells at home. The city building inspector isn't condemning the apartment or anything like that, right?"

"No, nothing new. In fact, it's been quite the exciting day."

"Everything all right?"

"Your grandfather burned his hand while working with Shawna on their secret art project. It is nothing serious. I had some ointment and put a bandage over it just so he'd know not to knock it around. But the devilish look in your grandfather's eyes when he's trying to keep a secret is the best thing ever. He loves doing projects with the kids and is really good about working with one of them at a time."

"Did he tell you anything about the art project?"

"That's the best part. Both he and Shawna are keeping their mouths shut like spies in custody. I'm really impressed."

I chuckled, thinking about Mary Catherine's superhero-level abilities. She kept the house running and my pack of feral kids in line. At least some of them could pass for feral. In New York City.

Mary Catherine said, "And Fiona is over the moon about basketball now that she knows you're going to coach. Sister Lora is quite happy too. I wonder if her plan all along was to get you to coach."

I said, "I wouldn't put anything past Lora. She's sneaky like that. I heard she wanted to live in the dorm at Holy Name so much that she gave up her entire life to serve Christ. I'm sure she has diabolical plans to manipulate a lot of people."

"Oh, you're terrible. You don't think she used Fiona to trick you into being a basketball coach?"

"I'm sure she did. But she'll brag about it to me when I get back. You can't really be sneaky when you're proud every time your trick works. Besides, I saw the smile on Fiona's face when I said I would coach. That's all that really matters."

Mary Catherine enthralled me by describing her day of volunteering at the school. She took my mind off my problems. I could listen to her all night long.

Unfortunately, a kid problem popped up and ended our long chat. And I was left alone in my hotel room to think about how nice it would be to see my family again.

CHAPTER 67

WITH ONE ANNOYING phone call, Bobby Patel prolonged a day that already felt like it had gone on forever. He was in the lobby waiting for me. I was surprised to see a trickle of sunlight leaking through the giant windows.

Bobby sat on one of the large sofas, looking out on the busy entrance to the hotel. He was still dressed in a dark suit like a junior banker.

Bobby stood as soon as he saw me and extended his hand. The first words out of his mouth were "Sorry. I didn't like how we left things."

"You mean you severing all contact with me?"

"That's a brutal assessment. But I have to keep you at arm's length. I can't risk my career. It's too hard for someone like me to move up in the FBI. I can't give them any easy excuses."

I nodded, noncommittal. I understood his reasoning, even if

I didn't agree with it. I asked about my main concern. "What did they do with our homeless suspect, Mr. Hagensick?"

"No charges. But he couldn't respond to any questions, so they placed him in a psychiatric ward for a seventy-two-hour observation. He seemed quite happy to have a bed and food. Last I heard he hadn't said anything but 'Yep' since they'd found him."

I chuckled. "I respect commitment in almost any form." I motioned for Bobby to sit on the couch with me. I turned to him and said, "What really brought you over here to see me? I know you weren't worried about my feelings."

He paused and then sputtered. Finally, he let out a sigh and said, "The FBI has several theories and even a suspect."

I interrupted him. "Whoa, a good suspect?"

Bobby shrugged. "I'm not part of that team. I don't know the specifics."

"Tell me what you do know."

"They've got surveillance on a house painter. He worked in the Steinberg house for almost six days."

"So someone's admitting that Emily visited the Steinberg house? It was beginning to feel like the FBI didn't realize the Steinbergs existed."

Bobby frowned. "Do you want to listen to why I'm here or bitch about the FBI?"

I nodded and mumbled, "Sorry."

Bobby waited a moment to ensure I was properly contrite. Then he said, "This house painter is a convicted sex offender and may have been in the area where Emily disappeared. They haven't arrested him. They're just trying to figure out if he has any hidden apartments or anything like that."

"Why tell me?"

"Because my supervisor already gave me something else to look at in addition to Emily's murder. That means the bosses are either losing faith that we'll be able to solve the case or they're losing faith in me. I want to make sure there's someone out there looking out for Emily. Sometimes I wonder if the Bureau is afraid of what it might find out if it looks too deep."

I thought about all of this. Finally, I looked at Bobby and said, "The surveillance of the painter feels more like a desperation move."

"I agree, but what else do we have? Do you have some secret insight you haven't shared with any of us?"

I said, "Just this afternoon I thought about looking at the case a different way. What if we considered Michelle Luna tied to the case after all? Maybe there's something from her investigation we could use on this one."

Bobby shrugged. "At this point I'm not sure what to do. But I don't want to be the guy who ruins *your* career. I'm also here to warn you."

"About what?"

"A couple of the supervisors at the off-site office were asking questions and figured out who you are. I heard the special agent in charge was going to make a call to your police commissioner. You might want to keep that in the back of your mind."

I let out a laugh. "After the threats I've already gotten, I'm not terribly afraid of the FBI boss calling someone at the NYPD."

Bobby stuck out his hand. "Still proud to be working with you."

CHAPTER 68

BOBBY WASN'T OUT of the lobby before my phone rang. It took me a moment to recognize the Maryland number. It was Emily Parker's sister Laura.

After I answered, she said, "My mom and I remembered a few things we thought we'd pass on. We also have a favor to ask."

"I'll do anything I can to help you guys."

"My mom is really shaken by Emily's death. She thought Emily would show up like she had in the past. Anyway, we're supposed to pick up Emily's personal effects at the FBI office. Would you consider coming with us?"

"Of course. When do you need me?"

"The FBI was open about timing the appointment. My mom thinks she'll be up to it later in the week."

"Happy to do it."

"I also found a business card at Emily's apartment. It made

me remember her telling me about someone she was close to. A lawyer named Reggie Balfour. I think he's a high-end attorney who works by referral only."

I wrote down the contact information Laura gave me. I looked at my watch and realized it might be a good time to intercept the hardworking attorney leaving his office not far from the swanky Capitol Hill area. Better to catch this guy late, as he was leaving, than try to wrangle an appointment.

The lawyer's elegant three-story office building resembled an art gallery, with wide, tall windows and paintings and sculptures in the lobby under spotlights. When I arrived, I was surprised to see at the very reasonable hour of seven only four cars left in the covered parking lot. Two were small, practical vehicles, like the Prius I was driving. One was a nice SUV that had two car seats in the back seat. That left a black Lexus LS. A nice car even for an attorney. Even an attorney who worked at a firm so exclusive it had no need for a sign.

I parked a few spots down from the Lexus, then called NYPD dispatch. I gave them my ID and the license plate. They had no way of knowing I was off duty and not even in New York. A moment later my theory was confirmed. The black Lexus came back to an R. Balfour. The address on the registration matched the office. I didn't want to push my situation and ask for any other information.

I decided to avoid startling anyone. I waited in plain sight, right next to the car. I was dressed in a sport coat and hoped that I didn't look too menacing. At least not to an attorney who drove a black Lexus LS.

Two young women, each carrying a box of files, walked out of the door with barely a glance in my direction. I caught snippets of their conversation. "Meet you at seven tomorrow morning." All I could think was these poor women had only twelve hours off before they had to return to work. My police job didn't look so bad in comparison. The women separated and each got into one of the practical cars I'd noticed when I first arrived.

I tried not to check my watch constantly. I had to tell myself I wasn't hungry, I wasn't in a hurry, and I had no plans. Sometimes you can talk yourself into patience. I surfed the internet on my phone, checking Facebook to see if my kids had posted anything interesting. I also scanned Instagram for the same reasons. I heard the door. My head snapped up. But it didn't look like Reggie Balfour. It was an attractive African American woman about thirty-five. She wore a pretty designer skirt and blouse and carried a briefcase that looked like it was designed by Vera Bradley—a symmetrical pattern with a lot of color on the sides of the case. Her professional hairstyle was fashionably short. The diamond earrings looked like they cost more than I made in a year.

She looked up from her phone and saw me standing at the rear of the Lexus. She stopped about halfway between the door and the car. I smiled to put her at ease.

The woman said, "Can I help you?"

"I'm sorry, I didn't mean to startle you. I was just waiting to talk to someone from the building."

"I'm the last one in the building. Who were you hoping to talk to?" She was careful to keep her distance, and I noticed her take a couple of small steps backward toward the door.

I showed her my badge and said, "I was hoping to talk to Reggie Balfour for a moment. He's not in any trouble or anything."

She smiled and said, "I should hope not."

"So you know Mr. Balfour?"

She had a wide, lovely smile. Like the girl next door. "I'm Regina Balfour. My friends call me Reggie."

Now, this was a surprise.

CHAPTER 69

CAUGHT COMPLETELY OFF guard, I stared at the attractive woman, searching for the appropriate response.

Even in the low light of the parking lot her smile was remarkable. She let out a quick laugh. She said, "My real name is Regina Balfour, but my dad was a huge Reggie Miller fan. He started calling me Reggie when I was little, and it stuck."

"It's a good way to throw people off."

"I noticed your badge is from the NYPD. What brings a detective from New York all the way down to Washington, DC? I hope it's not just to ask me some questions. The high-tech contracts I work on really have nothing that could be criminal."

"I actually wanted to ask you a few questions about Emily Parker." Now it was my turn to spring a surprise. And it clearly wasn't the surprise she had been expecting.

I thought I might have to catch her at the edge of the Lexus.

Instead, she turned, set down her briefcase, and leaned on one of the car's driver's side doors.

Reggie Balfour said, "I'm sorry, still mourning. I've been so upset since I read about Emily. How did you know we were friends?"

"Her sister gave me your name. They were close, and Emily apparently spoke fondly of you."

"We had fun hanging out. Good dinners, the occasional cigar—Emily was great. Sometimes it's tough to find another professional woman who shares my mindset. She made me laugh. She got me."

"When was the last time you saw her?"

Reggie Balfour looked off into space, concentrating. Then she shrugged her shoulders and said, "I'm not really certain. Maybe three months. I might've talked to her on the phone, but I didn't see her." She looked at me and asked, "Why is an NYPD detective working on a homicide in Washington, DC?"

I explained that I was a personal friend of Emily's, then fudged a little bit, saying that I was helping the FBI with the investigation. "I'm also closer with her family, so I've gotten more personal leads. That leaves the FBI open to investigate other angles." That seemed to satisfy her.

Reggie explained that she and Emily had met at a professional women's group about two years ago. "There was a rumor that Emily and I were lovers. Emily thought it was funny and told me not to stop it. She got a kick out of people talking about her. She said it was like performance art. That was one of the reasons Emily was linked to so many people. She was an interesting and entertaining friend. But she didn't care about labels. She didn't care what people thought of her."

"Were you aware of any threats against her or any concerns she had?"

"No, none at all. In fact, she seemed to be pretty stable in her relationships."

We chatted for a few minutes more. I picked up a little bit here and there I might find useful later.

I asked, "Was there a reason you hadn't hung out with Emily in the last three months?"

She hesitated, and the pause filled me with anticipation. Anytime someone hangs back during a casual interview, pay attention for a spill of something interesting.

Finally, Reggie said, "She was spending a lot of time with other people."

I said, "One of the advantages of me doing part of the investigation is that it is completely confidential. I won't even make notes of our conversation. I've spoken to her family, and I know about some of her relationships. I don't want you to worry about repercussions."

Reggie visibly relaxed. "You probably heard she was close with Robert and Rhea Steinberg."

I nodded.

"Emily was really committed to them. To their relationship."

"Both of them?" I tried to keep my surprise hidden. I don't think I did a very good job.

Reggie smiled. "Yes, Detective, both of them. Might sound shocking to you. I assume you're married with children. And that kind of multiple-partner relationship can be hard to get your head around. I know that Emily loved the Steinbergs. Maybe Rhea more than her husband. And to tell you the truth, I have no idea what she saw in that entitled little brat."

"You know the Steinbergs personally?"

"I would say I know them personally but not socially. The justice is a little bit of a loner, and his wife believes most people are beneath her. I guess that's the best way to describe it. I never saw Emily around them. I don't know how they interacted. But I've talked with Rhea plenty of times. I've had to put up with her long soliloquies about her 'art.'" The air quotes around *art* told me what she thought of Rhea Wellmy-Steinberg's talent.

Reggie's confirmation of what Justice Steinberg had tipped to, that Emily and both the Steinbergs were in a relationship, changed my thinking a little bit.

"It doesn't sound like you're a fan of Rhea."

"She's not an enemy. She just never impressed me. I know she's got a law degree from Columbia. Not something an idiot can achieve. But her interpersonal interactions are usually all about her. I never understood what a smart woman like Emily saw in an empty bottle like Rhea." Reggie shrugged. "I guess the heart wants what the heart wants."

That's when I started thinking about the possibility of Justice Steinberg's sister, Beth Banks, being jealous of their relationship with Emily.

CHAPTER 70

I DID HAVE some access to databases. Bobby had given me a password to get into a state police site that showed tolls someone might pick up driving on several of the paid highways. There was a chance I could get lucky and run one of my suspects' license plates and find a hit. But it would have to be a hit on the day Michelle Luna was murdered in Baltimore.

There were also my regular NYPD access databases, generally public records aggregators. Nothing too fancy. Who pays the light bill at a certain address? Does someone have a specific professional license? That kind of thing. Information that comes in handy when trying to piece together an investigation.

Bobby also had given me access to an aggregate of security cameras, including the Whole Foods where Emily had parked, located within the city limits of Washington. The missing footage from the Whole Foods still hadn't turned up. There were hundreds of other feeds I could tap into if I needed to. Useful if I had a team to help me. A little overwhelming by myself.

I searched for the license plates I had collected both during surveillance and after digging through public records for vehicle registrations in the last two years. The first plate I plugged in was Beth Banks's. There was nothing.

Just for fun, I ran both Justice Steinberg's and Rhea Wellmy-Steinberg's. They had lots of tolls but nothing to or from Baltimore other than one trip about a month ago.

I was about to move on to another website when I decided to look up Jeremy Pugh's vehicles. At the time of Michelle Luna's murder, Pugh was driving a three-year-old Ford F-150 pickup truck. I knew he'd lived in the Northern Virginia area.

I was surprised to see Pugh had been close to Baltimore the day before and two days after Michelle Luna's murder. If he lived in the area, that wouldn't be unusual. Still, it made me think. I hadn't heard much from the boisterous Burning Land extremist lately.

I went back to the security surveillance website and checked the Whole Foods on the day Emily Parker made her last run. After more than an hour of poring over different video feeds, the best I could find was a Ford F-150 parked in the lot of the Whole Foods. It was in a cluster with several other vehicles. I would bet it was one of the managers who had arrived early to get some work done.

Thinking about Pugh, and the fact that The Burning Land claimed to not know the FBI was looking at them, made me wonder. Had Pugh known Emily in some other way? Could he have been a source of information for her? He could have been an informant for his own group. As with any case, there were more questions than answers.

At least I managed to suppress my urge to call Detective Holly from the Baltimore homicide squad this late in the evening. If she was working, it was because they had an active homicide. If she wasn't, I didn't want to bother her at home. I managed to force myself to lie on top of the sheets and doze off.

First thing in the morning, still wearing my clothes from the night before, I decided to call Detective Holly. Her cheerful voice and positive attitude this early annoyed the shit out of me. But I kept my comments to myself.

After we got the small talk out of the way, Detective Holly said, "I know you didn't call to see how I'm doing on the job. For the record, I'm crushing it. What can I do for you this morning?"

"I was curious about the DNA you collected at the scene of the Michelle Luna homicide. I know you ran it through the CODIS. Did you ever have any suspects good enough to collect samples from?"

"Never developed anyone enough to worry about DNA. I was still hoping we might get a random hit at some point in the future. They're always adding samples to the CODIS database."

"What if I had some suspects in the Emily Parker homicide I've been looking at? Could we compare them to the Michelle Luna DNA?"

"That's fine with me. In fact, it sounds like a good idea. The FBI has the profile, and their evidence unit is holding our DNA sample." She paused, then added, "Will your suspects give you consent, or will you have to get the samples surreptitiously?"

"I know for sure that no one is giving me consent to take a sample. Some think they're above the law, and one suspect probably thinks it would be a conspiracy to charge him. It's going to take some work to get samples. At least that gives me something concrete to do."

"Call me if I can be of service."

I wasn't sure if she was being sarcastic. "I'm sure you're a credit to the Baltimore Police Department."

I heard a cheerful "Bite me" just as the line went dead.

CHAPTER 71

I SAT AT the small desk in my hotel room, staring at a blank legal pad. Somehow I had a feeling things were starting to move. Maybe it was just me thinking about a different aspect of the case. Maybe it was Detective Holly's good-natured personality. Somehow, still wearing yesterday's clothes, I had a faint feeling of hope. But it's hard to exploit hope without some hard work.

Trying to get a DNA sample surreptitiously is one of the trickier investigative jobs. DNA can be derived from a number of sources, like someone's sweat, saliva, hair, mucus, or, of course, blood. Think about the challenge of taking any of those things without a person knowing about it. A stealthy investigator might be able to pull out a strand of a suspect's hair without her knowing it. But probably not. You could follow her around for a month until she got a haircut. Then you'd have to prove there was a 100 percent chance you had picked up the right hair. After that, the sample would have to match. It was an endless maze that ended in a puzzle.

The three suspects I was focusing on were Beth Banks, Justice Steinberg, and Jeremy Pugh. I didn't even want to think how I'd manage to get a DNA sample from someone who worked at the Supreme Court. Jeremy Pugh might be a much easier case. Especially if he accosted me again. A decent punch and I might end up with plenty of DNA sample on my knuckles.

The other more direct, and efficient, way was to see how the NYPD was doing on the investigation into Jeremy Pugh's altercation with the *New York Times* reporter. That reporter had been hospitalized for three days. I had left the details with a friend of mine at the Special Investigations Division.

Detective Sergeant Lisa Mulé had worked with me in a couple of squads over the years. Her nickname was Lisa "Chaos." That's because chaos seemed to follow her. Or, more often, she seemed to cause it. More than that, Lisa seemed to thrive in it.

At home, she had four kids, each smarter than the last. That made for a wild mix. Our theory on the squad was that she was so used to chaos at home, she needed it at work to feel normal. She was definitely a punch-first-ask-questions-later kind of cop. To make all that even more interesting, she stood a statuesque five foot ten, with a smile that could stop traffic.

The flip side to the idea she caused chaos was that she got results. That accounted for her meteoric rise to Special Investigations. To me, she was a really good cop, but more important, she was a good friend.

She picked up her desk phone on the second ring. She had a very professional greeting. "Sergeant Mulé, Special Investigations."

"Chaos, what's going on?"

"Hey, Mike. It's the usual bullshit around here. Some dick at One Police Plaza thinks that we can tie more than half of our homicides to serial killers. Somehow he thinks that'll show how good the PD has been in reducing overall violence. I swear to God, Mike, I have no idea where some people get their ideas."

"You're preaching to the choir, sister."

"This jackass just pulled it out of his butt. Now I have to do a two-year survey. I looked over the initial data, and it feels like you were the lead on about half the homicides. What a waste of time."

"Everyone gets interfered with. Teachers hate all the dictates that come down from school boards. Nurses hate some of the rules that come down from hospital directors. Cops just hate rules."

Lisa said, "Are you still in Washington, DC?"

"I am."

"If I was your wife, I'd go down there, grab you by the hair, and drag your ass back to New York."

"If you were my wife, I'd be smart enough not to let you know where I was staying."

We both laughed, and she brought me up to speed on her family. She ended by saying, "I'm guessing you called me about this shithead Jeremy Pugh."

"You guys done with the case? Anything we can do?"

"You mean you didn't hear already? This is just a coincidental call?"

"What are you talking about?"

"I've got the warrant right in front of me. We can't identify who was with Pugh the night they beat the poor *New York Times* reporter. We figure Pugh might talk after we arrest him."

"Do you know what precipitated the fight?"

Lisa let out a laugh. "It was no fight. The reporter was trying to get reactions on the president's latest poll numbers. That's it. He spoke to these two and somehow his question didn't sit well. They put him in the hospital. Three broken ribs, broken left wrist, ruptured eardrum, and a collapsed lung. Nice people you hang out with, Mike."

"This makes it much easier for me, Chaos. I needed to get a DNA sample, and now we can get it when he's booked."

"I'll email you the affidavit and warrant."

"What was the exact day of the attack?"

There was a pause in the conversation, and I could hear Lisa searching through some paperwork. She came back on the line and said, "The assault occurred on the second. The victim picked out Pugh from a photo lineup. Plus, we have two different security video sources on the attack. It's a good case."

I was silent as I processed what she just told me.

Lisa said, "Mike, you still on the line?"

"If it happened late on the night of the second, it puts one of my suspects in New York just before Emily Parker was murdered. Unless he went through some extraordinary transportation, Jeremy Pugh isn't a good suspect."

Lisa said, "We verified that Pugh was still in town two days later."

I muttered, "Shit."

"Since I worked this case because of information you gave me, can you do me a solid and make sure the DC police arrest this mope?"

"I know the perfect unit to handle it."

Just before I hung up, Lisa said, "Mike, you're being careful down in DC, right?"

"I'm trying to."

"They're nothing but a bunch of sharks."

"It's nice to know someone cares." I wasn't being a smart-ass. Sometimes when you're working on a case you forget about real life. It was nice to be reminded I still had friends.

CHAPTER 72

I HATE TO admit it, but I always feel a twinge of excitement before an arrest. For veteran cops, I'm an outlier. All rookies feel this way. After all, an arrest is the ultimate validation of your work. It means you conducted a thorough enough investigation and you have probable cause to believe you solved the crime. It's a great feeling, and even after all these years, it's good to have some excitement.

Detectives Swinson and Gorant were going to meet me at the National Mall. Their partner, Detective Daggett, was stuck in a briefing at the DC police headquarters. I couldn't believe that I was looking forward to seeing Swinson and Gorant after everything that had happened. It proved to me that first impressions aren't all that important. It takes time for people to show their true colors. Even if we had started our relationship with them threatening me to leave the city, I now believed they had been acting in the best interests of their department as they saw it at the time.

We'd made a simple plan to meet at the mall, then find where The Burning Land was protesting. It was a good bet that Jeremy Pugh would be with them. If not, we'd fall back on good old-fashioned police work. We'd go to that warehouse they hung out in, or Barbucks, find out where he was living, and check there. Generally ask a few questions until one of his friends got so annoyed they gave him up.

Before I started to walk over toward the mall, my phone rang. I immediately noticed it was my grandfather. My first thought was that it could be bad news. I took the call.

"Hey, Seamus. Everything okay?"

"Of course it is, my boy. I wouldn't burden you with my problems when you have the weight of the world on your shoulders."

"It sounds like you're buttering me up for something."

"It was more of a sarcastic impression of you. But I really am calling to see how *you* are holding up."

I smiled. This elderly man, who never shrank from a challenge and did the best he could raising me, was still worried about me. Some people might say he was treating me like a child. I preferred to think of it as true parental concern. It was just one more reason to admire him.

Forget the fact that he ran a successful bar for decades and decided to join the priesthood in what many would say was the twilight of his life. He fooled them all. He had been a priest for many years now. He made a serious impact, not only at Holy Name but also around the entire Upper West Side. I felt honored that he would be so concerned about me.

I decided to change it up on him. I said, "Mary Catherine tells me you burned your hand."

"It doesn't look too bad. It's about the width of a pencil and runs maybe two and a half inches along the back of my hand. It hurt like a son of a bitch."

"Should a Catholic priest use that kind of phrase?" I knew I was setting him up for a great retort.

After the slightest hesitation, Seamus said, "I don't know. Should a New York City detective be working a homicide in Washington, DC?"

"Touché. Seriously, how did you burn it?"

"For the sake of art and my beautiful great-granddaughter. Shawna is very excited about this. No injury or other catastrophe will delay its unveiling. Besides, the burn isn't bad and it makes me look tough. At least tough for an old priest."

We chatted for longer than I expected. It was just nice to hear the old man's voice. To hear little details about each kid and Mary Catherine from a different perspective.

Seamus said, "I swear you must've been a saint in a previous life to find a woman as perfect as Mary Catherine." He paused, and I knew that impish grin was spreading across his face. "Or maybe Mary Catherine was a sinner in a past life. Yeah, that makes more sense."

I glanced at my watch and realized I had to pick up my pace to the National Mall. But I wasn't done with my grandfather yet. "Can I ask you a philosophical question?"

"That's my specialty. You may have the degree in philosophy, but I have the experience."

"That's why I'm asking. I'm headed to the arrest of a man who assaulted me a couple of times. You're one of two people I told what he did to me the first time. His name is Jeremy Pugh. He beat a *New York Times* reporter half to death."

"So what's your philosophical question?"

"Not only am I excited about the arrest. I'm also in a good mood. It almost feels like vengeance."

"Would you describe your job as getting revenge on people?"

"Absolutely not."

"And are you doing your job?"

"Yes, I am."

"Then vengeance is just a perk. There's no reason you can't enjoy your work. Every once in a while God gives you a little blessing you can smile about."

"While I was thinking about it alone, I went back to what you used to say: 'What would Jesus do?'"

Seamus laughed. "First of all, even Jesus would not let someone pee on his back."

That made me laugh the rest of the way to the mall.

CHAPTER 73

I WALKED TO the edge of the National Mall, where two of my three new friends with the Metropolitan Police Department's Special Investigations unit had told me to meet them.

David Swinson and Nancy Gorant were standing with two big, uniformed officers. One of them, a muscular black man about thirty, looked bored. The other uniformed cop, a white guy a few years younger but just as big and muscular, looked excited. If I'd had to choose, I would've chosen the bored one. Bored veterans cause fewer problems than enthusiastic rookies. But to be honest, the idea of seeing Jeremy Pugh in handcuffs made me kind of excited as well.

Nancy Gorant said, "I'm going to go with them. Maybe he'll be less likely to cause problems if there's a woman talking to him."

Dave Swinson let out a good laugh. "That's bullshit. You

just want to be there to get a good lick in if this mope tries anything. You're hoping you can get in your workout during company time."

Nancy just smiled and shrugged.

I knew I'd do nothing but upset the big asswipe. I stayed put. I was content to stand thirty feet away with Detective Swinson and watch.

There was a fair amount of activity on the mall today. Competing groups protested various issues. Others were on the mall as well: tourists, two groups of schoolchildren, and what looked like residents of a retirement home on a field trip. Even with all the people, I figured we were close enough to see and hear what would happen during the arrest.

Swinson said to Detective Gorant and the two uniformed cops, "You guys don't want to call in any more help? He's a pretty big dude."

The big black cop said, "Shit no. He might not resist if there's too many of us. We've got to give him a chance."

I liked the cop's sly smile as he said it. I also liked his confidence.

I watched as the detective, now wearing her badge on the outside of her shirt and showing her pistol on her hip, approached Jeremy Pugh. The two big uniformed cops flanked her.

The first thing she did was pull an old police trick. She said his name in a sweet, sexy voice to confirm it was him. As soon as she said, "Jeremy Pugh," like Jessica Rabbit in *Who Framed Roger Rabbit*, Pugh turned to look at her. That was his mistake.

I could see the smile spread across Nancy Gorant's face. Immediately, both the uniformed cops stepped up to either side of Pugh.

The tall black cop said in a professional tone, "Please turn around and place your hands behind your back."

Pugh didn't move.

In a slightly louder voice, the cop repeated his command. But he added the dreaded "Do it now."

Jeremy Pugh looked outraged more than anything else. He stared at the cop, then said in a loud voice, "No, you don't understand. I'm here for America." He still didn't move his arms, and he had to look up slightly at the big cop. "What are you doing? I'm out here helping your people."

Now it was the cop's turn to look astonished. "My people?"

"Yeah, black people. Black lives matter, man."

"You also protest when a black cop is murdered?"

That earned the cop a blank stare from Jeremy Pugh. The other cop forced Pugh's arms behind his back.

The black cop said, "Time to go to jail, Gandhi. Maybe you'll be able to help us from inside."

Pugh yanked his arms away from the cop trying to cuff him. He jumped back a few feet from the cops. He shouted, "This is bullshit! They're trying to silence me! We live in a Nazi state!" He looked around, trying to gain some support from the crowd. He found little. Even the other Burning Land people looked away or wandered off. Everyone's a tough guy until the cops show up.

The black cop kept his voice calm. "I'll give you another chance to comply."

I'll admit, there was some part of me that wanted to see this cop punch Jeremy Pugh in the face. The memories of him peeing on my back and confronting me at my hotel kept flashing in my mind.

Instead of seeing a big muscle-bound cop pound Jeremy Pugh, I got a more enjoyable show.

While Pugh focused on the cop talking to him and tried to make his case to the crowd, Detective Gorant quietly slipped around to the rear of Pugh. She gave some kind of signal to the two uniformed cops. They both took a couple of steps back. That made Pugh think he had scared them away. He never even looked behind him.

The attractive detective calmly placed her foot between his legs and then jerked his right arm so that he tripped and fell facedown on the ground quickly. She had his hand cranked behind his back before he could even let out a yelp.

Pugh squirmed in the armlock. The detective leaned in close and said, "Put your other arm behind your back."

When Pugh didn't act immediately, she twisted his right arm a little more. That got the reaction she wanted. In a matter of seconds, he was handcuffed and yanked to his feet.

And I was down one suspect in a homicide.

CHAPTER 74

AFTER I WATCHED the DC cops cart away Jeremy Pugh, I walked from the National Mall back to my hotel. I'd just orchestrated the arrest of a dangerous criminal. I had acted as liaison between the NYPD and the DC police. And yet I was not in the mood I had expected.

Instead of feeling upbeat and positive, all I could think was how few suspects I had in Emily Parker's murder. And that's why I was in DC. Not to clear an NYPD assault case. I hadn't realized when I first considered Jeremy Pugh as a suspect that he would end up wasting so much of my time and energy. But that's the way things generally happen in major investigations.

Now I was determined to look at both Michelle Luna's and Emily Parker's murders as somehow connected. That meant I was going to focus a little more on Michelle Luna's murder. And I had an idea what I was going to do.

As soon as I got back to my room, I called the tech investigative division of the NYPD. I tried not to be like some of the dinosaur cops, or, as the young guys called us, Detectivesaurus Rex. I was prepared to move with the times. And that meant embracing new technologies.

I knew cops who bragged about shunning technology and doing things "old school." That's fine to say, but it never helps an investigation. As the world speeds up and adopts the latest technology for even simple things, cops have to do the same thing. Luckily, I don't have to be an expert in emerging technologies. All I have to do is be aware of these new trends. There are always experts I can turn to.

This time I was going to focus on cell phone technology. It's amazing what a cell phone can do. It's also amazing how a cell phone can be tracked. Real criminals, professionals—well, at least *smart* professionals—will take the battery out of their phone before they go somewhere they don't want to be tracked.

Regular people who commit crimes don't think that way. Usually, a crime like murder is spur-of-the-moment for a nonprofessional, a so-called crime of passion. This was my opinion, of course. And I wanted to see how accurate it was.

I didn't recognize the voice that answered the phone by saying, "Tech Unit, William speaking."

"Hello, William, this is Mike Bennett at Manhattan North Homicide."

There was silence for so long I thought we had lost our connection. Then I heard William sputter, "Detective Michael Bennett? Really? I've never gotten to handle any of your stuff before. I read about it in the newspapers and hear people talking about your cases. This is a real honor, sir."

I like compliments as much as the next guy, but I really didn't have any time to waste hearing flattery like this. I had to get this done before someone shipped me back to New York, whether I wanted to go or not.

I said, "I appreciate all that, William. But I need to talk to one of your best techs about a Google warrant to figure out if someone was in a certain area during a homicide." A Google warrant was a general term for a glorified subpoena to the tech giant. Once a judge signed a Google warrant, the company could provide information on the subscriber. It had to do with how often their phones, even iPhones, interacted with Google programs, such as Google Maps. It was a new process that cops and Google were still trying to navigate.

William said, "As luck would have it, I'm your guy. I'm the official liaison with Google and Microsoft. I know all the Google reps in their law-enforcement liaison office." His voice kicked up a notch with every sentence.

I had to smile at his enthusiasm. "Good deal. The only thing is, I'm looking in the Baltimore area. Is that a problem?"

"Not at all. I know your cases take you all over the place. I heard about you going to Estonia. Baltimore is like a suburb of New York compared to that."

I started to scribble a few notes. I said, "William, what's your last name?"

"Patel. P-a-t—"

I interrupted him. "I know how to spell Patel. Are you any relation to Bobby Patel?"

"Sure, he's my cousin."

CHAPTER 75

I FELT MY world start to spin a little bit. What are the chances I would call the NYPD and reach Bobby Patel's cousin?

Then William Patel said, "In fact, I have six cousins named Bobby Patel. You do realize Patel is the most common Indian name in the US, right? We're like the Smiths in India."

"What about Bobby Patel the FBI agent in Washington, DC?"

"Oh, *that* Bobby."

I suddenly felt like I couldn't catch a break. Was this some kind of conspiracy? All I could say was "He's your cousin?"

William chuckled on the other end of the line. "No, I was just testing your gullibility. You failed. Now, let's see if we can help you solve a homicide in Baltimore."

I liked this guy's attitude. I briefly explained the circumstances of the homicide. I left out why I was involved. I let him assume that it was somehow connected to a homicide in New York.

William said, "It helps if you can narrow down the parameters of your search as much as possible. The fewest possible phone numbers. The smallest spread of dates. And a relatively small geographic area."

I gave him the date of Michelle Luna's homicide. I even gave him the exact location within Baltimore.

William said, "Fairfield doesn't sound like such a bad neighborhood. It's not like Compton."

"Bad things can happen anywhere, William."

Then I gave him the phone numbers to Robert Steinberg's, Rhea Wellmy-Steinberg's, and Beth Banks's cell phones. I didn't want to risk using the names. Although William might keep things quiet, there was no telling what people at Google might leak. I decided to keep the suspects' names to myself.

William asked, "Do you have enough probable cause for the Google warrant?"

"I'm trying to see if any of those three were in Baltimore. They knew the victim. I'm just trying to build a case. I'm not trying to charge anyone based on the information from the warrant."

William's enthusiasm didn't fade. "Got it. I have a lot of friends over at Google. I might be able to do a quick check just to see if there's anything worth sending them a warrant for. They're good about little things like that. Know what I mean?"

I knew exactly what he meant. The world of investigations depends on people helping one another. I was a little worried about this being a major case. Then I remembered I wouldn't be the one bringing charges. The FBI or the DC police would. I just had to hand over information to them.

It was an odd conundrum. If I waited on a warrant, the

information wouldn't come back until after I was sent home. Possibly by force. I made an executive decision. I said, "Go ahead and check first. All I need is a yes or no. I don't need any details yet."

William said, "I'll call Google right now."

CHAPTER 76

I HAD TO do something to keep occupied. I sat at the little writing desk in my hotel room. I gazed down at the eight file folders I'd created. Each held a different screwed-up pile of information. I shuffled them around for a moment and then felt a wave of relief when my phone rang. Not that I expected any answers from my friend William in the Tech Unit, it's just that it gave me something to do.

When I looked at the phone, I was surprised to see it was Mary Catherine. A smile spread across my face as I answered, "Hello, beautiful."

Mary Catherine said, "How are you doing today?"

"Trying to get things done. How about you?" I waited during a long pause on the other end of the line. Every second made me more apprehensive about what was coming.

Finally, Mary Catherine said, "I don't know. I guess I'm lonely. I'm a lonely newlywed. Aren't you lonely too?"

"When I stop for a moment, yes, I get down and lonely. But in the spirit of always speaking honestly with each other, most of the time things happen so fast here I can't think of much. I'm on the move and concentrating."

"I'm sorry. I didn't mean to remind you."

"Don't be ridiculous. Just hearing your voice cheers me up. Even if your voice sounds a little sleepy and scratchy this morning. Are you okay?"

"Just tired. Glad the kids are all at school. I will say I was a little queasy earlier. Now I'm fine."

"Are you sure?" My mind started to race with all the possibilities.

Mary Catherine said, "I ate some kind of breakfast sandwich Seamus brought over. It didn't agree with me."

"What did that old codger want?"

Mary Catherine giggled on the other end of the line. I could picture her beautiful smile. Dimples in both cheeks. Blue eyes flashing. God, did I miss her.

Mary Catherine said, "All Seamus needed was some sandpaper and a pair of your locking pliers for his project with Shawna."

"Any idea what this super-secret project is?"

"None at all. And I don't ask questions. It's nice that your grandfather can get so committed to a kid's project. We are really blessed to have him in our lives." Mary Catherine sighed, and I could hear the exhaustion in the exhale.

I said, "Are you sure you're okay? Say the word and I'll be home in a few hours. I'll come back home for good."

"Really? You'd do that for me?"

"Of course I would." I waited in silence to give Mary Catherine plenty of time to think about my offer.

Eventually, Mary Catherine said, "I know you'd come home. I know the kind of man I married. I also know you'd never hold it against me. But it's important to do the right thing. Finding Emily's killer is the right thing to do." She paused for a moment and added, "As long as you don't forget Trent's ceremony with the mayor."

"There is no way I'll miss it."

Mary Catherine said, "You stay in DC. I've got it nailed down up here."

I had to smile. I knew she had it nailed down. I doubted if there was anything that could defeat Mary Catherine. And through it all, she was still supporting me. Supporting a job I didn't have to be doing.

What a woman.

CHAPTER 77

I LAY ON my hotel bed, thinking of Mary Catherine. Wearing all my clothes, including my shoes, with my feet dangling. It was a loser's pose, taken when everything had gone to shit. And it felt like one, accomplishing nothing except making me realize I could barely move.

I felt like a lovesick teenager. I missed her so much. But I couldn't see her. All the threats and commands to return home had made little impact on me. But hearing the loneliness in my wife's voice almost broke me. I considered giving up. Going home. Living my life.

My stomach roiled in acid, in part due to stress. I had to consciously unclench my jaw. This was not my usual state of existence. I forced myself off the bed. I plodded to the tiny writing desk under the wall-mounted TV. I plopped down in the chair and grabbed a random file folder.

Was it fate that a four-by-six print of Emily's FBI identification photo fell onto the desk? It forced me to stare down at her pretty and solemn face. The FBI didn't care much for agents smiling for their ID photos. That's when I realized I was going to keep trying to find her killer. Until I had no other options. As far as I knew that could be in a day or two. Fate or not, Emily's photo stiffened my resolve.

Then my phone rang. It was a blocked number, but I was confident it was William Patel from the NYPD tech division.

William jumped right into it without even a greeting. "I just talked to a buddy at Google. You had narrowed down things so much that he could check it quickly and easily. There was one hit."

William gave me the number and I immediately recognized it as Beth Banks's phone.

"Could he go into any details about the hit?"

William said, "He explained to me that Maps and some of the other Google programs randomly interface with satellites. It's a way to keep the GPS as accurate as possible. He couldn't narrow down the exact location of the phone on that date but knew that it had been in Baltimore. He said that it accessed several programs in the evening of the date you gave me. He couldn't go into much else."

I made some notes in my main notebook. Maybe I'd stumbled on a good suspect. Frankly, Beth Banks was about my only suspect now. This was a case we had to get exactly right. A jury would be sympathetic to a Stanford-educated woman who was the chief of staff for a Supreme Court justice. There could be no doubt. That's why I needed a DNA sample. And she wasn't going to give it to me. Not voluntarily, anyway.

William said, "My buddy says that if you're going to use any of that information in a report, we have to send him a signed court order."

"That sounds more than fair. I should know shortly."

William said, "May I ask why we're worried about a homicide in Baltimore?"

"You may ask, but I won't answer. Trust me, William, it's better that way."

"Then can I make a request?"

"Of course. But once again, I can't guarantee I can grant it."

"If I give you my personal cell, will you deal with me directly? Now you've got me hooked."

"You got yourself a deal, William. And when I get back to New York, I'll explain it all to you in person."

As soon as he hung up, I wondered if I'd still be employed when I got back to New York. I also wondered if that would influence whether I gave William the briefing he wanted. I figured if I really was unemployed, I would have plenty of time to meet William at a coffeehouse.

I stood up with new energy. I had a lead, a suspect, and a job to do. I had to follow Beth Banks until I could figure out a way to get a DNA sample.

CHAPTER 78

I HAD SOME time before I thought I could find Beth Banks easily. I knew her schedule by now. There were a few little things I wanted to settle first. I view every potential piece of evidence in a homicide as vital.

The gap in the security footage from the Whole Foods bothered me. Bobby had mentioned something about their DVR not working and the backup system missing one DVD. It would've shown exactly what time Emily Parker had pulled into the lot. If the killer was someone she knew, maybe the killer knew her schedule. It's possible the killer had arrived in the parking lot before her.

The timeline could be important.

The FBI had talked to the manager at the Whole Foods, and no one knew what had happened to the DVD. In my opinion, no one was particularly upset about it either.

It was an odd feeling to be working on my own in a city not New York. There, I would've had a team helping me, and all of us would have been raising holy hell to find the DVD. Doing a surveillance solo required cutting corners.

I pulled into the surprisingly crowded lot. I had seen some of the prices at this place and wondered who the hell shopped here. But once inside, it was quiet and calm, and the produce was well stocked. I had to acknowledge that it was an extraordinarily pleasant experience.

A clerk turned to me and said, "May I help you, sir?"

I looked at the young African American man and said, "Is there a manager around?"

The young man stood up taller. He was damn near as tall as me. And probably weighed as much as Mary Catherine. He closely embodied the term *beanpole*.

He said, "I'm Archie Hart, manager on duty. What can I help you with?"

I liked his attitude and his infectious smile. He was tall and gangly but had a handsome face and perfect teeth. I went through a quick introduction and flashed my badge. It was as if Archie had been expecting a visit from law enforcement. I explained to him about my interest in the security footage and that I knew about the missing DVD.

The young manager led me through the store and past a set of double doors in the back. We worked our way through a maze of shelves and stacked crates of snack foods and health drinks. I didn't even recognize most of the brands.

We ended at a door that was slightly ajar. It looked like a closet with Christmas tree lights inside. It was their security office. At least that's what they called it. We peeked inside, and

I could see four TV monitors, two on the outdoor cameras and two on cameras inside the store.

He said, "You said you knew about our system and how one of the DVDs of the day in question is missing."

"That's really what I wanted to talk to you about. Is it common to misplace DVDs with security footage?"

"It's not really a fair question. Ninety-five percent of the time the DVR records and backs up everything automatically. We don't even check the feed unless there's a problem. A few days before this terrible incident, one of our cashiers decided to take a break, choosing this room as quiet and relaxing. Anyway, she tipped over a Coke she tried to set down on the DVR. That's why we had to use the other DVR with a lot less data storage."

"How long had you been using the other system before the FBI came in to ask to see the footage?"

"I don't know. Maybe five or six days. Generally, on that system, backing up all the camera feeds uses two DVDs a day. We have no idea what happened to the missing DVD. I wasn't the manager on duty when the FBI came to take a look. That manager told me she thought everything was in order the night before. She had no idea what happened to the DVD."

I looked at the neatly arranged DVDs. Each had the date and time written in red Sharpie. The same person appeared to have marked each DVD. The number one was written with a small base and a flair at the top, like a professionally printed sign.

I gave the helpful young manager my card. He didn't even look at it, so there were no questions about why a detective from the NYPD was in Washington, DC. We shook hands, and I had one more puzzle to solve.

CHAPTER 79

IT WAS TIME to get serious. At least that's what I was calling my surveillance of Beth Banks. I was seriously looking at her as a legitimate suspect. And I timed my surveillance perfectly.

I slowly drove past Gold's Gym. Beth's BMW was in the front. My secret weapon in this surveillance was my nondescript purple Prius. No one would notice it. No one would ever think it was a police car. And I was starting to dig the way it made me feel like a giant every time I tried to cram myself into it. It made me smile when I thought about how my family of twelve would deal with having a Prius as the only family vehicle. My guess was it would not work out well.

My plan was simple. Watch Beth Banks until she did something that left a DNA sample. It could be sweat on a door handle if I got there fast enough. It could be a strand of hair, blood, a fingernail. It didn't matter. And I didn't care. I was determined to stay with Ms. Banks until I accomplished my goal.

I pulled into a parking space one building away and across the street. I had a perfect view of the Gold's Gym's entrance. Generally, a surveillance is conducted with a number of unmarked police vehicles. Follow a suspect in the same car all the time and they will probably notice. Depending on which direction your suspect turns, you have to have a car ready to make that turn.

Beth Banks zipped out of the gym to her BMW. Soon she pulled out onto the street and drove past me. I fell in behind her, leaving a vehicle between us.

She headed back toward the Supreme Court Building. Her route was uneventful until a block before she might normally veer left toward the office, where Ms. Banks turned right instead—abruptly. She surprised me, making me worry she was doing countersurveillance. I thought she'd noticed my car and was trying a technique common among drug dealers looking to shake surveillance, making a quick turn to see if I followed.

I had no choice. I took the turn. Maybe not as dramatically as Ms. Banks in the BMW had, but I could feel a hint of centrifugal force as I kept my foot on the gas and turned hard to the right.

My concerns about countersurveillance were for nothing. In another half a mile the BMW zipped into a spot in front of a Dunkin' Donuts about ten blocks from the Supreme Court Building. I was able to park on an adjoining street that gave me a full view of the inside of the small, drab donut shop. Only two of the six tables were occupied.

I turned my attention back to the BMW. As soon as she was out of the car, Beth Banks gave someone inside the shop a halfhearted wave. I looked back into the shop and saw her recipient. A smile spread over my face. Sometimes luck favors the simple.

Beth Banks slipped through the Dunkin' Donuts doors and met her sister-in-law, Rhea Wellmy-Steinberg, sitting at a table next to the window. These relatives by marriage were both about the same age and well educated. They probably had a lot in common.

Personality-wise, they didn't seem to be particularly similar. From everything I'd heard and my limited personal experience, Rhea Wellmy-Steinberg was a little self-absorbed and entitled. Whereas Beth Banks was just a badass. I knew her family had money, but I didn't get the idea that it mattered much to Beth.

I noticed Rhea already had a coffee for Beth sitting on the table. This might be a rare opportunity to get samples from two of my suspects at the same time.

CHAPTER 80

I COULDN'T BELIEVE how clearly I could see both women through the main window of the Dunkin' Donuts. I couldn't hear what they were saying, but I could see the animated expression of Rhea Wellmy-Steinberg. If they weren't arguing, it was a deep, earnest discussion.

All I needed was for them to talk long enough to finish their coffees and leave the cups on the table. I still hadn't worked out exactly how I'd recover the right cups if they threw them in the trash. Sometimes you have to improvise.

Surveillance is a tough gig. It tends to be more of a narcotics activity. Following people around. Trying to catch them in the tiny window when they actually commit a crime.

There's not too much surveillance when you work homicide. Narcotics cops at the NYPD call it "the unparallel universe," because they are always amazed at how no one ever notices surveillance teams. While half a dozen cops might be focusing on one criminal as he sits at a café, everyone around that criminal has no idea about the surveillance. I used to think it was because people are not particularly observant. Now I prefer to think of it as the cops doing surveillance are particularly effective.

By most standards, this was not much of a surveillance. Clearly, seeing two women talking in a nearly empty Dunkin' Donuts is not that big of a challenge. I leaned back in the front seat of the Prius and made a few notes about the time and place. If I did recover DNA and it proved useful, I'd have to be able to explain exactly when and where I had retrieved the sample.

I watched the subtle signs of their discussion. It seemed that Rhea was doing most of the talking. She was also more upset than Ms. Banks. Rhea scooted her chair a little closer during the discussion.

I took a quick look around the rest of the Dunkin' Donuts. There were two bored baristas, absently wiping down the counter to fill time. Another couple who had been sitting a table away were just throwing their trash in the garbage can on their way out the front door.

That left two other people in the Dunkin' Donuts. I wouldn't be going inside until after my two suspects left, but I still wanted to know who or what might be waiting for me. It never paid to be surprised while working on an investigation.

It looked like the conversation was wrapping up. I pulled my seat back to a completely upright position. Both the women were standing now, and Ms. Banks kept shaking her head.

I watched with interest as Ms. Banks took a sip of her coffee, then turned on her heel and marched out of the Dunkin' Donuts. Unfortunately, she took her coffee with her.

I sat in my little car and watched in complete disappointment as Beth Banks raced away in her BMW.

I looked back toward the Dunkin' Donuts just as Rhea Wellmy-Steinberg was opening the front door. Dammit, I could be distracted too easily. My eyes darted back to the table that she had been sitting at with her sister-in-law. Her cup was still sitting on the table in front of the chair she'd used.

I started to grin. Completing part of the task was better than not completing any of it. I'd have to resume my surveillance of Beth Banks later.

CHAPTER 81

NO MATTER HOW Bobby Patel was feeling about me, he agreed to meet me quickly. I told him I had a break in the case. I'd wait until I saw him face-to-face before I told him it was a DNA sample for the Michelle Luna homicide. From there the only question was whether he'd submit the sample to the FBI lab. He could claim that it wasn't his case and, technically, not mine either. Then I'd have to go through Detective Holly in Baltimore.

I'd thought about using the detective earlier. If she submitted the sample, there wouldn't be any questions. If there was a hit, then we could move. We would try to tie the two murders together with Rhea Wellmy-Steinberg as the connection.

If there was no hit, life went on. In all likelihood, I'd go back to New York with my tail between my legs.

In the end, I decided it was more efficient and more honest

to approach Bobby directly. I knew he'd get a little pissy about it. At this point in my career I expected most FBI agents to get pissy about something.

We met at a Chinese restaurant not far from the FBI field office on Fourth Street, about a block from I-395. Bobby was waiting for me as I walked in. He sat in the very back of the restaurant, dressed in his typical business suit with a bold tie. This one had a purple hue.

Before I sat down, he said, "Whatcha got in the bag?"

"Possibly the break in our case."

"What kind of break would physically occupy a Dunkin' Donuts paper bag? That sounds like a DNA sample. We don't have any DNA markers in this case. So I'm curious what this meeting is about."

I handed the bag across the small table to Bobby. "This meeting is about a legitimate DNA sample from a legitimate homicide. We may disagree on Michelle Luna being tied to Emily Parker. I recognize that both cases could be random killers. I recognize that the victims never met. I'm still asking if you could expedite comparing the sample to the Michelle Luna homicide."

Bobby was silent. I don't think I ever realized how intense his brown eyes were until they fell on me. He just stared at me. It was unnerving. If you had told me when I first met Bobby that he could make me nervous, I would've laughed out loud.

Finally, I said, "C'mon, Bobby, we got nothing going on in the case. I visited Whole Foods earlier and was reminded that we don't even have a full set of security videos. Nothing is going right in this case. We need to shake things up."

Bobby said, "Obviously I know about the missing DVD. I talked to the manager and corporate security manager for hours trying to figure out what happened. We just have to chalk it up to a bad break. They don't care about security footage as much as cops do. They don't have to make cases based on what's on their videos. They just want to make sure they're covered if someone slips and falls and tries to sue them."

Bobby looked away for a moment. Then he focused back on me again with those intense, brown eyes. "Who's the sample from? I thought you ruled out Jeremy Pugh as a suspect because he was in New York. Who else do you have that you could get a sample from?"

I hesitated. "I don't think I should tell you who the sample is from just yet. It's for your protection more than mine. I'll take full responsibility if anything breaks bad from it."

I almost chuckled at the expression on Bobby's face. He looked like one of my kids when they got left out of something. Then he said, "It sounds like you don't trust me."

"On the contrary, I doubt you could lie. That's why I don't want to tell you. There might be some blowback later. You need to be able to say you didn't know who the sample was from. That might be a problem."

Bobby said, "Okay, I'll submit it as a John Doe sample. Shouldn't be a problem. If I do it under Emily's case number, the sample will get processed immediately. Or maybe sooner."

"I'll believe that when I see it."

For the first time today, Bobby smiled. "Hey, that sounds like a knock on the FBI."

"Yes, of course it is. What did you expect?"

CHAPTER 82

I STAYED AT the Chinese restaurant after Bobby left. The area DC calls Chinatown is a small historic district just northwest of Capitol Hill. I don't mean to be a snob, but the only real Chinatown on the East Coast is in New York. I don't care what Boston or Philadelphia or any other big city has to say about it. But for the record, the chicken chow mein at the restaurant was outstanding.

The five customers in the quiet venue were spread out. That's why I was hesitant to answer my phone when it rang. I looked down and saw the main number to One Police Plaza. I wondered if it was William Patel with more information from the Tech Unit.

I answered it like I always do. "Michael Bennett."

A man's voice said, "*Detective* Michael Bennett?"

"That's right. Who's this?"

"This is Alfred Brocious."

That one caught me by surprise. I knew the dead silence on the phone line didn't help my position. And the commissioner of the NYPD didn't help me out by saying anything else. He just let the silence hang there.

Finally, I managed, "What can I do for you, Commissioner?" I tried to picture our new commissioner's face. I'd met him only once in passing while I was at One Police Plaza. It was right after the city had hired him away from Philadelphia, where he had been a respected deputy chief. His deep voice made everything sound like a grave matter.

"Your lieutenant, Harry Grissom, says he can't reach you. Is he lying or are you not taking his calls?"

The wording of the question made it sound like something a politician would say. "I was about to call him back, Commissioner."

"No matter what else happens during this conversation, please don't lie to me again. Is that clear, Detective?"

"Yes, sir."

"I was a detective once. Back in Philly. I thought I was slick too. You know what got my head out of my ass?"

"No, sir."

"I realized we all have jobs to do. We're all in this together. No matter how the media might twist stories. No matter what a segment of the public may think about cops. We're lost if we don't try to help each other any way we can. You're not helping in DC. In fact, it sounds like you're a hindrance."

I said, "None of that is Harry Grissom's fault, sir. Please don't take anything out on him. This was my choice and my decision. I've been on leave for a while. I had a lot of days in the vacation bank."

"I don't want to crush a respected lieutenant like Grissom. I wasn't trying to get you to rat him out. I don't even want to punish *you*. In fact, I don't really have time to talk to you. So I want to keep this quick and to the point. Where are you?"

"As I said, I'm on leave, sir."

"I didn't ask your status. I asked you where you are. As in a place. A tangible, real-life location."

"Washington, DC."

"You see, I knew that. Would you like to know how I knew that?"

"No, sir, not particularly."

The commissioner just rolled along with that sonorous voice. "I knew you were in DC because it feels like every swinging dick with a law-enforcement title of some kind has called me this week to bitch about you." His voice increased in intensity at a steady pace.

I didn't answer. Mainly because there was no answer to it.

After a moment, the commissioner said, "Well?"

"I-I-I'm not sure what you want, sir."

"Now, that's a good comment, Detective. No one ever seems to care about what I want. It shows me you're a considerate and intelligent detective. What I want, Detective Bennett"—his voice continued to build—"is for people to stop annoying me. In this case, the solution to my problem is quite simple. You are to come home. Come back to New York. Right now."

"But, sir—"

The commissioner cut me off. "It sounds like you may have misinterpreted this call. Maybe it's my friendly demeanor." Now he was almost shouting. "This is not a negotiation. I'm giving you an order. Come back to New York."

The line went dead. I pictured the commissioner slamming the phone down in the cradle. Of all the requests for me to go back to New York, I think his was the most eloquent and compelling.

I didn't know what to do. So I did what I always do when things seem overwhelming. I called my wife, Mary Catherine.

CHAPTER 83

THE CALL WITH Commissioner Brocious had unnerved me. Usually I'm not too susceptible to threats. The commissioner knew how to deliver the best kind of threat. He didn't make one. He simply told me to come home. He was smart enough to know my imagination would come up with worse punishments than he ever would. And my imagination was working overtime. I pictured myself directing traffic in Flushing Meadows when the US Open was on. Or maybe I'd be working in some sort of sex crimes unit attached to a precinct. I shuddered, thinking what my future held.

That's why I needed a change of pace. I wanted to hear a friendly voice. I didn't hesitate to dial Mary Catherine's phone. Just talking to her always made me feel better. Her voice was like a soothing balm on my nerves.

I also had a second agenda. I wanted to hear how she

sounded. During the last few calls, Mary Catherine had sounded exhausted. She also had mentioned that she hadn't been feeling well. That concerned me.

I could hear a certain level of scratchiness in her voice when she answered. I always thought her sleepy voice had a sexy edge to it, but I was preoccupied.

I asked if she was feeling okay.

Mary Catherine said, "It's weird around here during the day. It's so quiet. With you gone and all the kids at school for the majority of the day, I get a little lonely. I'll admit it. I even went down to Holy Name this morning to say hello to Seamus. To be honest, I was also trying to get a look at the art project he and Shawna have been working on."

"Did you get to see what it is?"

"Nope. And Seamus is so tight-lipped it makes me think he would've been a good spymaster during World War II."

I laughed and said, "He might've been. He rarely talks about his life before coming to the US. No one is able to figure out how old he is. Carbon dating failed. Chemical tests are inconclusive. Our next step is to cut him in half and count the rings." I loved her laugh.

We chatted about nothing for a few minutes. Then Mary Catherine ran through the kids and what they were doing. Most of the issues were school projects or interest in joining outside sports leagues. The usual. When you have ten kids, you tend to take most issues in stride. If you don't, you'll go crazy quite quickly.

A couple of things caught my attention as Mary Catherine was talking. Especially when she got to my oldest daughter, Juliana.

Mary Catherine said, "Juliana went on a date last night."

"What did you think of her date?"

"Seems like a nice young man. He's a sophomore at Manhattan College."

I said, "Of course my next two questions are: How old is he? And what is he studying?"

"Don't worry. He's not an old man. He's probably a year or two older than Juliana. And he's studying creative writing."

"Ugh."

Mary Catherine said, "What's wrong with studying creative writing?"

"Nothing if you want to live with your parents the rest your life. I'm more interested in her meeting engineers, medical personnel, or at the very least a law student."

"*You* studied philosophy at Manhattan College."

"And look where it got me."

"In a beautiful apartment on the Upper West Side, with ten wonderful children and a wife who misses you."

"When you put it that way, I think I might be crazy to stay in DC any longer."

Mary Catherine laughed, then said, "What's new on your case?"

I told her about the DNA and how I was able to get a sample without riling up a Supreme Court justice's wife. I made it sound like I'd risked my life at a cave in Tora Bora. But that's the nature of most police stories: they need to be exciting and interesting.

Mary Catherine said, "I don't understand why a homicide in Baltimore is related to Emily's murder."

"I'm not sure it's related. Maybe I'm getting a little desperate.

But if the Baltimore homicide and Emily's homicide are related, we might get lucky with this DNA angle." After I thought about it for a moment I had to add, "Or they could be unrelated. If that's the way it turns out, but we do get a DNA hit, at least I helped solve the Baltimore homicide. Even though I didn't know the victim, I know there have to be family members and friends mourning her and hoping for justice."

Silence lingered between us. Finally, Mary Catherine said, "What prompted you to call? Really?"

I told her about my conversation with the NYPD commissioner less than half an hour ago. This time I left it up to Mary Catherine to draw her own conclusions.

Mary Catherine said, "I think you should stay in DC. It doesn't matter what the NYPD wants. You've given them plenty of your life. If you get fired, it won't make one bit of difference to me. We'll be destitute anyway once the IRS's through with us. And with you out of a job, maybe I'll finally see more of you."

I chuckled and said, "I do love how you're a glass-half-full kinda girl."

CHAPTER 84

THE NEXT DAY I got a call from Bobby Patel. He wanted to talk in person. Right away. He swung by the hotel and met me in the lobby.

He had lost a lot of his nervousness at us meeting in public. He scanned the room only twice instead of once every thirty seconds. Though he was dressed in his usual suit, he resembled a kid bursting to tell someone big news. I guessed, in this circumstance, that was exactly what he was.

In jeans and a pullover, I felt underdressed sitting next to him at the small, round table. Our two cups of hotel coffee sat steaming in front of us.

I said, "What was so urgent? Do you have results from the DNA sample I submitted?"

"Why else would I insist we meet in person?"

"That was a really fast turnaround. I'm impressed."

"The FBI has access to cutting-edge technology. I stressed to the forensic scientists the importance of this test, and they used a speedy new technique for 'preliminary' analysis. They're working on a full profile now. But they're confident that the DNA you submitted matches the DNA that came from the Baltimore homicide scene."

"Good work." Frankly, I was shocked that this long shot had actually resulted in a match.

I thought of ways to stall for time, but I didn't have to. Bobby went on about the FBI lab. He bragged about their capability and training. I would too if I had FBI-level resources. I liked it when any cop was proud of their agency. No matter how I felt about the FBI, I had to admit they had moved things along quickly.

Bobby focused his intense eyes on me. "Okay, I came through for you. Now you've got to tell me who the sample came from. We can't close out the case until we have all the information."

Now I really had to stall. This was a tough one. I trusted Bobby. I didn't necessarily trust the FBI. The Bureau had rarely done me any favors in the past. But I had a responsibility to the investigating detectives. I needed to tell them about the hit and let them decide how to handle it before I told Bobby.

I decided to take the quickest route. Sort of like ripping a Band-Aid off quickly instead of a little at a time. I looked at Bobby and said, "I can't tell you who it's from right now. I'm sure you'll understand I have to talk to the Baltimore homicide detective first."

Bobby simmered. This was not the answer he'd expected.

"You haven't talked to me about that many suspects. It's gotta be one of a handful of people. I don't understand why you won't confirm it."

"I just explained it to you. I have a duty to talk to the investigating detective first. There are no hidden agendas here, Bobby. I want to wrap this up as quickly as you do."

"What's your plan? Just because we got a hit on a Baltimore homicide doesn't mean the same killer attacked Emily. I don't know of any evidence that links the two homicides."

"That's true. My plan is pretty simple. As soon as we make an arrest, start with a good interview. See if we can convince the killer to confess to Emily's murder as well. Anything the killer says might point us in a new direction."

Bobby grumbled. Then he looked at me and said, "You better stop treating me like a servant who doesn't need to know why he has to clean the toilet."

"C'mon, Bobby. Everyone knows why it's important to clean the toilet."

CHAPTER 85

I FELT THE pressure escalating. I needed to move quickly on the DNA information Bobby had given me so that I could solve the case and get back to New York in time to keep my job. And with a Supreme Court justice's connections, the Steinbergs might be tipped off about the DNA hit before we could even do a proper interview.

That's why I wasted no time in calling Detective Holly at the Baltimore homicide unit. After a quick hello, I told her about the matching DNA.

Detective Holly said, "Are you trying to keep me in suspense? I know you had several suspects. Which one provided the DNA sample?"

Normally, I'd milk a big moment like this. You know, pause for dramatic effect. Instead, I jumped right in. "The sample belonged to Rhea Wellmy-Steinberg."

There was dead silence on the line. It went on so long I had to say, "Hello? Stephanie?"

"Sorry. That one took me by surprise. You told me the Steinbergs were possibly involved in the case, but I never thought one of them would be a suspect. A *legitimate* suspect."

"Can I ask a couple of favors?"

Detective Holly said, "Are you kidding? You just provided me with a good lead on an ice-cold case. Granted, a suspect like Rhea Wellmy-Steinberg complicates things, but it's still a cleared case. This one will get me noticed. Ask any favors you want."

"Can you move quickly on a warrant? I think my time here in DC is almost up."

"Again, are you kidding me? My bosses will want me to arrest her in the next hour. I have parts of a warrant already written up. All I have to do is fill in some names and the DNA information. It's certainly enough probable cause to move forward. So, yes, we'll be making an arrest today."

I hesitated, then made my second request. "The initial interview when you serve her with the warrant will be vital. I need to be there. I need to tie her to the murder of Emily Parker. Right now, the only way to do that is through an interview. We have no other information linking her to the homicide."

"So your working theory is that if she committed one homicide of a woman she knew, she might do it twice?"

"Something like that."

Detective Holly put me on hold to work out a few details. About three minutes later she came back on the line. "My lieutenant wants us to move quickly as well. He's not as sold on you being part of the interview. He says it may look bad later on. He's not sure why an NYPD detective is in Washington anyway."

"I haven't heard that question before." I appreciated her courtesy laugh on the other end of the line. Then I thought of a way to force my way into the interview. I said, "You guys are going to need me to testify about how I obtained the DNA sample later. Would you prefer to have a friendly witness on the stand instead of a pissed-off cop from New York?"

All Detective Holly would commit to was calling me when they were coming into Washington to make the arrest.

CHAPTER 86

I DIDN'T KNOW what to do with myself after I called Detective Holly. I was nervous. This was the break in the case I'd been waiting for, but the Baltimore cops weren't going to care as much about Emily Parker's homicide as I did. What if they didn't let me into the initial interview? They might just ask a few preliminary questions and book Rhea Wellmy-Steinberg on the Michelle Luna homicide. Then Rhea would never talk about Emily.

I had bet the entire Emily Parker case on this roll of the dice. I knew the Baltimore homicide detectives were already pushing it to get a warrant based solely on DNA evidence. It would pass initial appearance and maybe a few evidentiary hearings, but I doubted it was enough to get a conviction. There were too many ways to explain the DNA on the earring. The explanations wouldn't necessarily be believable, but they only had to convince one person on a jury.

I ran down my task list. It was pretty short. I called Emily's mother to arrange collecting Emily's personal effects the next day. Her desk was not at headquarters on Pennsylvania Avenue but in the DC field office where Bobby worked. We would meet there.

Then I called Dave Swinson over at the Metropolitan Police's Special Investigations unit just to give him a heads-up.

Swinson chuckled and said, "That's one hell of a job. But I already knew the Baltimore cops—or as we call them, *the minor league*—were coming to make the arrest. They called our homicide team to make sure someone was available to help them. Special Investigations hears about all of that."

"I may have to call you if I get frozen out of the interview."

"You think there's a chance in hell a suspect like Rhea Wellmy-Steinberg is going to say anything? Doesn't she have a law degree from NYU or someplace like that?"

"Yeah, Columbia. She hasn't practiced in a few years and isn't a current member of the bar."

Detective Swinson said, "I'm saying, despite the hippie artist demeanor, she's probably pretty sharp."

"Lawyers are generally good when they're dealing with clients. You can never tell how someone under stress will react. That's why I want to be in that first interview. I need to ask her about Emily Parker while she's still in shock."

Detective Swinson hadn't calmed me down. All I could do was wait.

It was late morning when Detective Holly called me to say they were in DC and intended to make the arrest. I managed to convince them to talk to me first. I raced over to a city office where the Baltimore cops and the DC homicide unit were meeting. From the front of the conference room, Detective Holly gave me a quick wave as I slipped in behind assembled law enforcement.

Of course a lot of detectives were involved in a case that would be a national news event. Though there was agreement that the arrest needed to happen right away, the location was up for debate. Someone suggested going to her house. Someone else argued for alerting Justice Steinberg.

I was happy to see Detective Holly speak up. "We've got to conduct an interview as soon as we confront her. We have to rely on the element of surprise. We can't let her surrender and have time to get her story straight with a lawyer."

As the group discussed potential ideas, I slipped over to Detective Holly.

I said, "I have a pretty good idea where Rhea is right now."

"Great. Where is she?"

I gave her my best evil smile. "All it will cost you is a seat at the interview table."

I could tell Detective Holly was impressed with my negotiating skills.

CHAPTER 87

I LET DETECTIVE Holly make the pitch for me to be in the interview. When a DC detective asked why, Detective Holly said, "I think he can help us find her quickly."

Detectives generally aren't stupid. They knew some kind of secret deal had passed between Stephanie Holly and me. None of them looked happy about the high price of the trade-off.

We sat in silence. This wasn't a gangster movie. I didn't know how far I should push this.

I risked it and told the entire room how Rhea tended to visit Rose's Down-Home Diner after her morning work at her art studio. The DC cops knew the place immediately. A tall female detective said, "The food there sucks."

We made a plan. That's what cops should do every time they make an arrest. At least a *planned* arrest. After some haggling, the group agreed that Detective Holly would be the lead. A DC detective and I would go in with her.

I looked over at the DC detective. He hadn't said a word during the entire meeting. He was in his late forties and dressed in a rumpled suit. This was not a cop looking to make a reputation. He was a token. He'd have no real role in the interview. By the looks of him, he had no real interest in it either.

It was clear someone in the DC police was getting nervous. They wanted to limit their exposure. After all, it sounded crazy on the face of it. The spouse of a sitting Supreme Court justice arrested on a homicide charge. Who'd believe it? But the DC police command staff couldn't let the media think that cops from another agency had walked into DC and made an arrest by themselves. Politics—it follows us everywhere.

Stepping through the front door of Rose's Down-Home Diner, I felt a strong sense of déjà vu. It was as if the tiny restaurant had been frozen in time since my last visit. One person sat at the counter. The tattooed, unfriendly waitress just stared at us as we walked casually toward Rhea Wellmy-Steinberg, sitting by herself in a corner booth.

I noticed she was eating the super kale soup as she read the *Washington Post*.

No one in the diner paid much attention to us. We walked casually, trying to avoid any commotion. Detective Holly slid into the booth right next to Rhea so calmly that it seemed natural. I'm sure the waitress thought we were meeting Rhea.

Rhea's mild reaction didn't raise any alarms either.

The DC detective and I slid into the booth directly across from Rhea.

Detective Holly and the DC cop had their badges and IDs

out almost before Rhea's eyes came off her *Washington Post*. No one wanted Rhea to think she was being kidnapped.

The other detectives may have identified themselves, but it was me Rhea looked up at. She said, "Now you have to bring friends when you annoy me?"

"I'm glad you remember me."

"Barely." She looked around the table, then focused on me again. "I thought I made it clear the last time you approached me that I didn't want to talk to you." She looked directly at the DC cop. "This man is stalking me. I'll file a report with you. I don't want him near me anymore." When the DC cop didn't move, Rhea added, "Do I need to make a phone call? You won't have a very good day if that's what I have to do."

Rhea was definitely not making any friends at this table. I was impressed that the other two cops kept quiet. I always liked to let a suspect's imagination run wild. Thoughts of what might happen were almost always worse than the reality.

Rhea looked at me again and said, "If no one is going to tell me why you're bothering me, I have work to do back in my studio." She looked at me with the intense disdain Brahms might've leveled at Kid Rock if the two of them had had the chance to talk.

Rhea pointed at me and said, "I already told him I have nothing else to say about Emily Parker. I miss her enough without you reminding me every day."

I didn't say anything. This was Stephanie Holly's show. She didn't disappoint me. She took control of the interview immediately.

Detective Holly pulled out a sheet of paper from the inside of the windbreaker she was wearing. She said in a very calm and reasonable voice, "Rhea Wellmy-Steinberg, we have a warrant for your arrest on the charge of first-degree murder."

"What! That's crazy. I would never hurt Emily."

Detective Holly calmly explained, "The warrant is for the murder of Michelle Luna in Baltimore."

That had a decidedly different effect on Rhea Wellmy-Steinberg.

CHAPTER 88

I CAREFULLY WATCHED Rhea Wellmy-Steinberg's face as Stephanie Holly read her constitutional rights from a card. The emotionless mannequin I'd spoken to days earlier displayed a gamut of feelings, from annoyance that we were bothering her to anger that we weren't leaving her alone. That switched to shock as she understood why we were there.

Rhea sat quietly for a moment. We gave her the time to process her shock, which then seemed to slip toward inattentive exhaustion. Like all the years of living in the fast lane had finally caught up with her.

Detective Holly said, "Ms. Wellmy-Steinberg, do you understand the rights that I just read to you?"

Finally, Rhea collected herself. She looked at Detective Holly and said, "Yes, yes, of course I do."

Carefully, Detective Holly continued to talk and engage with Rhea. Then she said, "Will you speak with us?"

"Why?" There was no arrogance in the question.

Detective Holly said, "We'll listen to explanations. Perhaps it was self-defense. Maybe we can work something out. Things might go easier for you."

"Nothing is ever easy. Nothing." There was a disturbing finality in her voice. Rhea didn't fidget or show any nervousness. If anything, she was withdrawn. I had the distinct feeling she had been expecting this to happen at some point.

Detective Holly gently prodded her. "I have a few questions. Will you talk with us?"

She didn't ask for an attorney and kept talking. That's all an investigator could hope for.

I was on edge, anticipating Rhea's refusal to talk. I expected Detective Holly felt the frustration every detective experiences at a slow-to-start interview.

Rhea's usual arrogance could work in our favor. She viewed us as uninteresting drones who couldn't trick her into revealing information. That was fine with me.

The waitress walked over toward us, but Rhea waved her off.

I've often found that the most powerful people have the fewest friends. She looked lost, lonely. My guess was she didn't have anyone to confide in. Rhea Wellmy-Steinberg looked like someone without a friend in the world.

Then she started to cry. It sounds horrible, but I had been waiting for this moment of vulnerability, when her guard fell. She used a napkin to blow her nose. Her eyes were watery and red.

I leaned on the table a little and said, "Are you okay?"

After another mild honk into the napkin, Rhea nodded.

I had to keep going. If Rhea didn't talk, I had nowhere else to look. At least not before I got sent home to New York. I felt my stomach tighten with anxiety as I looked into Rhea's face. I honestly couldn't tell if she was going to break or not.

I said, "I know you were close with Emily Parker. You and your husband both. Was it the same way with Michelle?"

I didn't know exactly what cord that hit, but it hit hard. Rhea sucked in some air and stared at me like I had slapped her across the face.

Then she started to sob.

CHAPTER 89

RHEA WELLMY-STEINBERG recovered faster than I thought she would. In less than thirty seconds, she was wiping her nose with the same soggy napkin and looking up like she was waiting for more questions.

It was Detective Holly who was able to strike a hammer blow to Rhea's confidence by playing up the evidence. "We have a DNA match. Your DNA was found on Michelle Luna's body. It could only have come from you during the struggle with Michelle."

Rhea didn't deny any of it.

Detective Holly said, "Were you reacting to a threat from Michelle?"

Solving a homicide in Baltimore was important. But now that the conversation was focusing almost exclusively on Michelle Luna, I worried I might not get a chance to ask anything more about Emily Parker.

Rhea chose that moment to look at me and say, "I love my husband. I love him more than anything."

All the detectives stared at one another in acknowledgment that Rhea's nonsensical statement had come out of left field.

Rhea turned to Detective Holly and said, "Men can be fickle. They certainly don't like to share the same way women do." Then she was silent.

What the hell was she talking about? I caught a look from Detective Holly. She was as confused as I was.

I said, "Did Michelle Luna threaten your husband?"

This time there was a long hesitation. "It wasn't a physical threat. And it wasn't to my husband. It was a threat to my *marriage*. She got her hooks into Rob and wasn't going to let go. He became obsessed with her. The more power she had over my husband, the more she enjoyed it. And she liked to rub it in my face."

This wasn't quite a confession, but it was close. I could feel the excitement build in my stomach. Like I was on a roller coaster about to drop from the top of the lift hill.

She wore a blank look on her face as she took a clean napkin to wipe her eyes and blow her nose again. Rhea said, "I just wanted to talk to Michelle. We were at her apartment building in Laurel, in the parking lot next to her car. It was evening, the first time in a week she'd left our house. The first time I could get her away from Rob to talk to her alone. She said she was part of his life now." Rhea trailed off to nearly a whisper. "It was nothing planned. It just sort of happened." Then she sat there without saying a word.

Twenty seconds passed in what felt like an hour.

Detective Holly prompted her. "What happened? I mean exactly what happened?"

Rhea was still operating in that weird time warp. She waited ten seconds more, then said, "Michelle turned away from me. Looking at her back and neck reminded me of all the self-defense training I'd taken with Beth." She looked around the table, then said, "Beth Banks is my husband's sister. She's really quite good at Brazilian jujitsu."

Then she returned to her original story. "Anyway, when Michelle turned her back, I wrapped my arm around her throat. Just like Beth had taught me. I locked my arm in place with my left hand. By that time, I was furious. I don't even know how long I held her throat. But when I released my grip, she dropped to the ground. I panicked. We were right next to her car, so I shoved her into it. Then I drove out of the parking lot. Before I knew it, I was headed north toward Baltimore. I parked the car in a desolate-looking section of the city."

Detective Holly said, "Did you do anything to the interior of the car?"

This was important. If Rhea knew the details, she couldn't claim later she invented the story.

Rhea said, "Yes. I found a small can of WD-40 in the glove compartment. I'd seen a brief my husband had read where the defendant sprayed WD-40 to remove oils that leave fingerprints on surfaces. I gave it a try before I placed Michelle behind the wheel of her car. Then I just walked away. I took three different cabs to get back to my car at her apartment complex."

Now it was our turn to be speechless. We all stared at Rhea Wellmy-Steinberg.

CHAPTER 90

I SAT QUIETLY and listened as Detective Holly carefully walked Rhea through the rest of the interview. She asked all the usual questions. Rhea seemed more in control now, but she hadn't stopped talking. Amazing. It was as if she didn't think she had done anything wrong.

Maybe I was giving her too much credit for her law degree, but I almost thought she was setting up a defense of mental incompetence. She legitimately thought she was justified in her actions. After about twenty minutes, my opinion evolved from Rhea setting up the parameters of a mental incompetence defense to realizing she was batshit crazy.

I felt a wave of nerves. Detective Holly caught my eye to let me know she was winding up the interview. She set me up perfectly with a line of questioning. Detective Holly said to Rhea, "Was Michelle Luna the only woman involved in a romantic relationship with you and your husband?"

"Why would that matter?"

Detective Holly looked at me and I fired my first and most important question. This was going to be my only chance before someone ripped me off this case. Whether it was the NYPD terminating my employment or the FBI kicking me out of DC.

I looked directly at Rhea and waited until she focused on me alone. Then I said, "It matters because we are still investigating the murder of Emily Parker. Remember, I asked you questions about Emily just a few days ago right in this spot."

Rhea Wellmy-Steinberg stared at me, with a look of surprise that quickly changed to anger and then to outrage. Rhea said, "How could you think I would ever hurt Emily? She was everything to me."

I had to keep up the pressure. "Did Emily get her 'hooks' into your husband like Michelle did?" I lifted my hands to use air quotes for possibly the first time in my life.

Now Rhea looked positively pissed off. "How dare you. You claim to be Emily's friend. How could you ever think she'd try to manipulate my husband? We were all soul mates together. If anything, Emily and I were closer than she and Rob."

"So you're saying you had nothing to do with her abduction and murder? I just want to be absolutely clear."

"If you think that little of Emily and can't read when someone is telling the truth, I don't think you're a particularly good detective."

I believed her. I could read people well. I also had years of experience. Someone didn't admit to one homicide then deny another one so vehemently.

After a couple of standard questions, I hit Rhea with "Was she concerned about anyone? Did she feel like she was in danger?"

"From whom? She was a physically fit FBI agent. She never mentioned any concerns."

I asked, "Had anything changed in her life that you're aware of?"

Rhea looked off into space as she considered the question. She took her time. Then she said, "Emily wasn't specific, but she might have gone on a date or started seeing someone before she disappeared."

"Would she usually talk about her romantic life with you?"

"We had no secrets. Apparently, the person gave her some sort of expensive gift. She wasn't sure what would happen or how to handle it."

"Can you tell me anything about this new person? Male, female? Did she mention a name?"

Rhea shook her head. "No. We only talked about it on the phone for a few minutes."

The interview had run its course. Rhea mentioned something about calling her husband. Then she added, "Or perhaps I need an attorney." At that point, the interview was effectively over. We weren't going to ask her any other questions.

Detective Holly handled it perfectly. She said, "Let's get back to Baltimore so you can make some phone calls and we can straighten this all out." It was a classic police line to keep a suspect calm until they were booked. It worked more than 80 percent of the time.

By the way Rhea stood up and laid a twenty-dollar bill on the table, I would say she was no exception.

CHAPTER 91

I WAS SURPRISED Bobby wanted to meet me at an Irish pub called Sullivan's to celebrate the arrest. I'd thought he'd be upset when he found out I'd facilitated the arrest of a Supreme Court justice's spouse. Apparently, I was wrong. He seemed to be in good spirits.

As soon as I sat down at his table in Sullivan's—a name seemingly shared by one in six Irish pubs—Bobby said, "You guys are all over the news."

I was surprised to find Bobby drinking a beer. Most shocking of all, he had removed his tie. It was the first time I'd seen him look like he was off duty since I had arrived in DC.

"I wasn't mentioned, was I?" I felt a little panic rise in my throat.

"No. The Baltimore police were credited with the arrest. I have to confess, you were right. Too bad you couldn't get Rhea to confess to Emily Parker's murder. But I guess there's no doubt she did it. Not now, anyway."

"I don't think she killed Emily."

Now Bobby looked shocked. "How can you say that? She admitted to strangling Michelle Luna. Emily Parker's murder was also a strangulation. That was your whole damn theory."

"Trust me. I was at the interview. We got into details about the Michelle Luna homicide. Rhea never flinched. She even admitted using WD-40 to screw up the forensic scientists. She had nothing left to hide. She denied any involvement in Emily's murder. Frankly, I buy it."

Bobby was shaking his head. "Maybe you're too close to this thing. Something will turn up that shows Rhea was involved. We've got to give it more time."

I respected Bobby's determination. I wanted to find Emily's killer just as badly.

I tried to change the subject. "This is the most casual I've ever seen you."

"I'm calling it a night. I'm wiped out from the last few weeks. I'm going to head to my apartment in Alexandria and crash until my alarm goes off at seven tomorrow morning.

"You're not going to give up on Emily's investigation, are you?"

"No. Never. But it sounds like you're getting ready to go back to New York."

"My son is involved in a ceremony tomorrow afternoon. I can't miss it." I explained about the essay and a little about the family dynamics. Bobby seemed fascinated.

Bobby said, "It was just me and my sister at home. It allowed my parents to focus on us completely. Now my sister is a neurotic orthodontist in Dover, Delaware. I escaped some of the neurosis, but I know my parents' constant attention warped me somehow." He chuckled.

We chatted a while longer. I didn't bother to tell Bobby I might be at his office in the morning with Mrs. Parker and Emily's sister. Those were the tentative plans. I wanted to pick up Emily's personal effects, then head to New York. I could already picture the look on Trent's face when I showed up at the apartment.

I had a big family meal planned at Trent's favorite restaurant. It was an interactive sports bar. Luckily, the boy was more interested in games than expensive food. Although with ten kids and your grandfather tagging along, no meal in New York is ever cheap.

I was surprised when Bobby gave me a little hug good-bye. He even threw in a "I still might make it to New York. We'll have to work together."

"I'd like that." I meant it too.

CHAPTER 92

I WOKE EARLY the next morning as the sun was creeping up in the east. I lay in bed, grappling with a feeling of finality that was veering toward guilt and depression. It was certain I had let Emily, a woman who had never failed me, down.

I ran the interview of Rhea Wellmy-Steinberg through my head over and over. At no point did I *not* believe her denial of killing Emily. The breaking news had been unrelenting. Virtually every channel ran specials about the arrest of the spouse of a sitting Supreme Court justice.

Even if it had been almost two years since Michelle Luna's murder, the reporter interviewing her father took a far too aggressive tack toward a man who had lost his daughter. It brightened my mood to hear him say that he had found a sense of closure, and he and his family could move forward now. He placed a hand over his heart as he thanked the Baltimore police for never giving up. Though he may never know how lucky he was that Detective Stephanie Holly had been assigned to the case, I did.

I grabbed a quick hotel breakfast of stale English muffins and cereal. Mrs. Parker had said she and Laura would meet me at the FBI field office at eight o'clock. The thought of heading home after that lifted my spirits. All I could think was *Home to my family. Home to Mary Catherine.*

I'd been worrying about her even more than usual over the last few days. She sounded tired. Somewhere deep in my heart, I thought she might be pregnant. The thought was not upsetting at all. I know, I know, I already have enough kids. The other way to look at it is that one more kid can't be much more effort. Either way, my first concern was Mary Catherine's health and comfort.

At exactly eight in the morning, I rolled into the visitors' area of the lot across from the FBI DC field office. My nondescript little Prius held a single suitcase and a big case folder. I was in the middle of deciding whether to give it to Bobby Patel or the DC homicide unit. If I saw Bobby this morning, I might try to feel him out on the subject.

I got a surprise hug from Mrs. Parker and Emily's sister Laura. I understood Laura's hug, but Mrs. Parker did not impress me as a fan of personal, physical contact. You live and you learn.

I'll admit I was a little disappointed in our reception. I had assumed the special agent in charge or another high-ranking Bureau official would meet us. Instead, it was the personnel director. And I guessed she had never even met Emily.

The personnel director was about forty with neat blond hair and reflective glasses that looked like they could incinerate ants if she held them up to the sun. She was professional if somewhat curt as she ushered us into a conference room four doors down from the lobby. In the hallway, agents and analysts hustled back and forth.

Sitting on the table in the conference room was a box with all of Emily's personal belongings from her desk. At least it was an official FBI evidence box and not a paper towel box from Costco.

I didn't say a word. I was just there for support. As the FBI personnel director left us, she said, "Take all the time you need. When you're done, just come out the door, turn left, and the lobby is straight ahead."

I had to admit she had a very nice voice.

I watched as Mrs. Parker grimly poked around in the box. She pulled out a framed photo of her, Emily, and Emily's two sisters. Another photo showed Emily on a treacherous mountain-bike trail.

Emily's sister Laura saw me looking at the photo and said, "She picked up mountain biking in LA. Just loved it."

The rest was the usual stuff crammed into a cop's desk. Notebooks, a Rubik's Cube, and a few mementos from different cases. There was also an unmarked metal cigar tube.

Mrs. Parker set the cigar holder down on the table. "I'm glad I never saw her smoke."

Laura said, "It was like five cigars a year. But they were expensive ones. She loved to smoke Cuban cigars despite the ban."

When I picked up the cigar holder, it rattled with a weight that didn't feel like a cigar. I quickly unscrewed the brown base and tipped the holder. A blue pen slipped out and clattered onto the table, breaking the silence in the room.

I picked it up. It was a really nice pen. Expensive. A blue Montblanc.

Laura looked at it in my hands.

I said, "Recognize it?"

Laura shook her head.

I held it close to my face to read the tiny inscription on the pen's silver clip. It said *From BP with love.* I read it aloud. Then I looked at both women and said, "Any ideas?"

Mrs. Parker and Laura looked uncertain, then began to chat about who it could be. They mentioned a couple of names. Mrs. Parker said, "Oh, what about Bill Parker?"

Laura looked at me and said, "He's our cousin." Then she looked at her mother and added, "He's too cheap to buy extravagant presents. This seems more like a boyfriend gift."

Something about the words *boyfriend gift* made me pause. Then it hit me. BP was Bobby Patel. The pen was a gift from Bobby. I recalled Rhea Wellmy-Steinberg saying Emily had received an unwanted, expensive gift. Despite Bobby claiming that he and Emily were work friends, he had wanted more.

Thinking back to Bobby's commentary on Rhea Wellmy-Steinberg, I realized he had been leading me toward Rhea. Had he really been trying to cover his own involvement in Emily's death?

I felt a little shaky as I considered all the possibilities.

CHAPTER 93

I FOUND MYSELF still holding the cigar tube in my hand. My mind worked overtime. I desperately wanted to find some reason that discounted Bobby as a suspect in Emily's death.

Mrs. Parker dug around in the box a little more. Then she said, "I thought maybe her ring was in here. It wasn't found by the police when they recovered her body." She choked on the word *body*.

My brain was working on a different frequency. I barely heard her.

Laura said, "Her emerald ring?"

Now I looked up, and Mrs. Parker explained it to me. "When the girls were little, I took them to Tennessee. When we were in Pigeon Forge, Emily wanted to go to the campy little place where you buy sacks of sand and strain it through an old-time waterwheel. Like panning for gold. She found an emerald, and we had it made into a ring. We had to resize that ring six times as she grew older and refused to take it off."

I noticed Mrs. Parker look off wistfully. I knew she at least had good memories of her daughter. To confirm it was the same ring I recalled, I said, "Can you describe the ring?"

"It had a thin gold band that twisted into a heart at the top. The little square-cut emerald sat right in the middle of the heart. It was sweet. She held it very dear."

Yes, that matched my memories as well.

I lifted the cigar tube with the pen inside. "Can I hang on to this for a little while?"

"You may have it. In fact, I'd like that."

I appreciated the sentiment, but I promised I'd give it back.

We packed everything back into the box. Just as I opened the door, I heard a familiar voice. It made me freeze in place. Then I peeked out the crack in the door and saw Bobby Patel chatting up a secretary. He was a different guy in this setting. Cheerful, charming. He even looked well rested.

I had to get Mrs. Parker out of here. We were already committed to going down the hallway. I didn't want her to have to face Bobby Patel. Even if she didn't have any idea why she shouldn't be seeing him.

I quickly ushered the women out of the room. I didn't take the route the personnel director had mentioned. We turned at the first corner. It made for a much longer trek to the lobby, but I felt like we were moving away from Bobby.

My heart pounded. I couldn't even think what I'd say if we ran into him. And I certainly didn't want Bobby to know I was here.

We burst through the door and found ourselves in the

opposite corner of the lobby again. I tried not to be obvious as I rushed Mrs. Parker and Laura across the lobby and through the front door. Then I walked them directly to Laura's Chevy Suburban.

Mrs. Parker gave me a long good-bye hug. This time I was a little better prepared. I was also touched. Then, just as she was about to get into the SUV, she leaned up on her tiptoes and kissed me on the cheek.

She said softly, "We'll get through this, Michael."

I couldn't tell her that now I thought maybe we would.

I watched them drive away, feeling exposed as I stood in the FBI field office parking lot. I didn't even turn to look back at the building. In my imagination, Bobby Patel was watching me from a window.

I shook my head to clear my thoughts. I was getting paranoid.

I forced myself to turn and peek. I wanted to relieve my anxiety. Instead, I swear I saw someone standing by a window, staring out at me.

CHAPTER 94

I DISMISSED MY paranoia that I was being watched as I left the FBI field office. I needed to focus. I looked down at the cigar tube in my hand. The pen was a really big deal. It would have cost a couple hundred dollars minimum. Maybe double that amount. That was a special present. Especially for a young FBI agent. That was not a gift between casual friends.

I couldn't waste time if I wanted to make any kind of credible accusation against Bobby Patel. I needed to find his car. It had to be close by, and maybe there was more evidence in it.

I quick-stepped out of the parking lot. The number of Ford Crown Victorias, Chevy Impalas, and Ford Tauruses on the street told me a lot of the agents parked there for quick access. My guess was that Bobby wanted to be out front and able to get to his car quickly. As much time as he spent out in the field, he struck me as the kind of guy who wouldn't waste time parking in the lot.

Trees along the sidewalk around the building blocked some of the view from the windows. I stopped beneath one and took a quick look up and down the street. There was no one around. And no traffic. I spotted Bobby's five-year-old brown Taurus at the end of the block.

I walked quickly, pausing in front of the Taurus. I took another moment to glance around. The coast was clear. I took a deep breath, then searched the ground for a rock or some object to break the driver's side window. I'd never learned to pick car locks like most cops on TV.

I found a chunk of broken concrete loose in the sidewalk around the base of one of the trees. I calculated how quickly I would have to act once the window shattered. I'd have only a minute to search the car. Then I had another idea. It was simple and not necessarily a long shot.

I got down on all fours and felt under the bumper at the rear of the car. I felt along the metal frame, then I found what I was looking for: a hide-a-key. Any cop who has ever worked a crime scene and locked his keys in the car knows to hide a key somewhere convenient. As a cop, you never live something like that down.

I pulled the key case off the frame. The key was old. It had rusting crud on it. Probably whoever had had the car assigned to them before Bobby had put it there.

The interior of the car was clean. No surprise. Bobby was a little bit of a neat freak. There was nothing in the console or the glove compartment. Then I noticed something catch the light. It was under the passenger seat. I reached down and was able to just touch the silvery sliver.

When I pulled it up to look at it more closely, it took me a moment to realize it was a fragment of a broken DVD. Just a tiny chunk of it. And there was a little writing on the chunk. The upper part of the number one written with a flair at the top in red Sharpie. Just like the other DVDs for the security system at the Whole Foods where Emily had started her run. Bobby was the one who had taken the DVD. He had broken it up into little pieces right here in his car. Maybe he did get flustered and make stupid mistakes.

I was careful to only touch it on the edges. I used my phone to photograph it in place and leave it there. Just in case things didn't work out the way I planned. Now I had no doubt that Bobby had killed Emily Parker.

Just as I was about to scoot out of the car, I noticed a set of keys at the bottom of a cup holder. They were clearly Bobby's apartment keys along with a small mailbox key attached to the key ring. I kept the keys because I knew I could find out where he lived.

I was on my way to Alexandria, Virginia.

CHAPTER 95

PUSHING MY RENTED Prius to its limits, I had a few minutes to think about what I was doing. I couldn't believe I was contemplating one of the most bush-league, unethical moves of my career. Basically, I was going to commit burglary.

I had already called my new best friend William, the tech wizard, on his cell phone, because I needed an exact location, and the public records aggregators I'd been accessing over the past two weeks don't cut it when it comes to federal law-enforcement personnel. No questions asked, the young man was thrilled to tiptoe into some less-than-public data on the fly as I headed across the Potomac. It took him about thirty seconds. Five minutes later I was pulling up in front of a big, modern apartment building on Patrick Street, not far from Alexandria's historic district.

The city itself was basically a nice suburb for federal workers to live. It was trying to hang on to the old Southern town feel with trees lining many of the streets and older homes preserved. Its fake veneer felt to me like a Disney-run community.

I wasted no time once I parked outside Bobby's building. It was a nice place, if not particularly secure. I didn't run across any security cameras or personnel as I hustled through the lobby and up the stairs. Thank God I had his keys.

It was a typical single guy's apartment. A few groceries and three six-packs of beer in the refrigerator. I don't even know why I checked. Just curious, I guess.

The place was clean, and I noticed three photos on a shelf near the bedroom. All three were Bobby, his sister, and his parents. The Patels were a good-looking family. Each photo had been taken in a different vacation spot. One looked like Disney World when Bobby was about twenty.

There were a few photos on the wall of Bobby in his judo gi. One looked like a big-time tournament. Bobby must be pretty good at it.

I was prepared for a thorough tossing of the entire apartment. I also knew I had limited time so I might have to compromise. I had started right at the front door with a quick sweep of the area. Nothing unusual. Circuit box hidden by a Georgetown banner. Nothing behind any of the hanging photos.

Bobby was bright. He might have a wall safe. Although I doubted apartment management would allow that kind of re-inforced wall for a really secure home safe.

I looked at the giant fish tank that sat in a nook next to the kitchen. There were a couple of clown fish and a weird-looking sea anemone floating around. There was also a model of a pirate ship with a treasure chest. A mermaid sat on a rock with a tail that waved in the water.

As much as I didn't want to, I slipped off my jacket and rolled up my shirtsleeve. That's right, even with a college degree and years of homicide experience, I still have to do shit like this. I reached down and opened the treasure chest. Nothing. Just a tiny, fake, plastic pile of gold.

I'd seen things hidden in fish tanks on TV and thought I had a chance. As I pulled my hand out of the tank, I made a quick decision to check the mermaid. Her tail continued to flutter in the water. I pulled her off her rock. Then I froze. Stuck to her bottom was a key held in place by a piece of gum. *No way.*

I pulled the mermaid out of the water and inspected it. The key came off easily. It wasn't a safe deposit key. My guess was the small, plain key belonged to some kind of safe. But I had been unable to find one in the apartment. Where would an FBI agent hide a safe? I wandered through the apartment, checking behind furniture. Nothing.

I sat on the bed, thinking. When I looked up, I noticed Bobby's closet. One of the bifold doors was open. The closet was filled with suits. Four of them looked the same color to me. Bobby loved suits. The view drew me toward the closet. I pushed the suits apart. There, in the gap, hanging on the drywall, was a diagram of the building showing the emergency exits. It was a typical old xeroxed diagram mounted in a frame. Stained and yellowed. I wondered why it was in the closet, where no one would see it. What was it hiding? My heart pounded in my chest.

I moved the poorly framed diagram. Just brushed it so it swung on its nail. Nothing.

My heart sank. This was going nowhere.

Then, just as I was about to turn away, I noticed a line in

the drywall. I took a closer look, wedging myself between the suits. It was a straight cut in the wall. I traced it with my fingers. It lined up with the diagram. The top line was covered by the closet shelf.

I worked at the edges of the square. The drywall came loose. It covered a dark hole in the wall. I could see from the bedroom light there was something inside. It was a portable safe like the ones sold at Office Depot. It used a key.

I pulled out the eighteen-inch-square safe. It was heavier than I had expected. I plopped it onto the bed. I hesitated as I held up the key I'd taken from the fish tank.

My first thought was *Why hide a safe* and *hide the key?* Then I remembered I was dealing with a slightly OCD FBI agent. It was his idea of intrigue.

There wasn't much in the safe. Some cash, a few papers. I moved them, then froze. My legs got a little shaky, so I sat again on the nicely made bed.

I looked back into the safe. Inside was a cell phone and a ring. I was pretty sure the cell phone was Emily's. It had a turquoise silicone case with a dolphin design. And I was certain the little ring with the green gemstone was Emily's. It was exactly as I remembered it, and how her mother had described it. Bobby's obsession with Emily must have screwed up any common sense and investigative training he had. Why would he keep any of this stuff? I just stared at it a moment longer.

Then I realized I had been hoping I was mistaken. I had wanted to find something that would exonerate Bobby. Or at least explain some of the things I had learned. All I had done was confirm what I had suspected.

Bobby Patel was a murderer.

CHAPTER 96

I WAS SHAKING as I rushed from the apartment. I sat in the Prius for a moment and texted a photo of the ring to Emily's sister. Within a minute she confirmed that it was Emily's ring. I told her I'd explain later.

I had been a fool. As I went over everything I had done in DC, I realized that most of the leads I had followed related to Rhea Wellmy-Steinberg had been given to me by Bobby Patel. He had been leading me around by the nose. He had been hoping I'd look at Rhea so hard, I'd never notice him. Sneaky and smart. It had almost worked.

I was pretty sure Bobby had kept Emily's ring and phone as mementos. He probably had her ID as well. This was all I needed for now.

I had to figure out how to prove a case legally. I had managed to do my scavenger hunt in his apartment because I had no official role. But if I wanted anyone to make a case on Bobby I'd have to find more. And do it legally. That was the trick. If we weren't going to follow laws, it would be easier to just track down Bobby and shoot him. Old-school justice. I was just about angry enough to consider it. There was no way I would let him get away with this.

I called Roberta Herring. She didn't pick up her cell. I was desperate enough to call her office. A secretary informed me that Roberta was completely out of touch today. She was testifying in front of some impromptu judicial panel in the Senate.

The secretary told me she knew I was Roberta's friend from the NYPD. She said Roberta had spoken highly of me. Then the secretary said, "The arrest of the Supreme Court justice's wife has sent everyone scurrying to make sure they weren't sitting on information that could've helped the investigation."

I had seen that on almost every newsworthy case I'd ever worked. No one ever cared anything about these cases until they hit the TV. Then everyone wanted to make sure they had no information that could've helped the cops investigating. I was glad not to be a part of that this time.

Now I had few options.

I was almost back in DC by the time I thought of an alternative to Roberta. Already my plan was starting to slide sideways. It was still early. I was confident something would break my way.

I made one call. I decided to stack all my chips and make a wager.

CHAPTER 97

EVEN WITH A firm plan, a lot could go wrong. That goes for any plan that involves humans. My biggest problem was controlling my emotions. I couldn't believe I'd fallen for Bobby's act. Now that I realized he was a killer, it would take all my self-control not to let that slip too early.

The weather was the best I'd experienced since coming to DC. Everyone was smiling as the sun shone in the sky and the temperature was a comfortable 70 degrees. If I hadn't been doing such serious work, I would've gladly been swept up in the good cheer.

I'd chosen the Lincoln Memorial for several reasons. The monument's solemn nature was almost calming, with Abraham Lincoln cast as a marble giant. The forty-four-foot columns all around the interior put into perspective the extent of Lincoln's contribution to history. At the same time, it made the viewer feel small. I'm not sure if that was the effect the designer had intended. I took a minute to read through the Gettysburg Address, etched into the wall. Then I turned and got ready to work.

I sat down on the top step of the descending stairs. There were about two dozen people milling around, several sitting on the ascending side of the stairs.

Everything seemed to be in place. I took a deep breath and tried to clear my head. Surprisingly, my fingers shook a little bit from nerves. I had Emily's phone in my hand. She had given a list of passwords to her sister in case of emergency. Thank God, because there was no way I would have gotten into this iPhone otherwise. I brought up Bobby's contact information. I imagined he was still at the FBI field office. I sent a simple text: Be at the Lincoln Memorial in twenty minutes or this phone and other evidence goes public. I'm sure we can work this out.

Almost immediately Emily's phone rang. Bobby was trying to reach me. I let it go to voicemail. I knew how this had to be playing out in his mind. He was going crazy trying to figure out who had just texted him. He also had to worry about how someone had gotten the phone.

That was one of the reasons I had given him such a short time frame. I didn't want him to be able to check his apartment or make any phone calls. By setting the meeting for twenty minutes out, I knew Bobby had to jump into his car immediately and race over here.

A text came across Emily's phone. It was Bobby asking, Who is this?

I texted him back: Nineteen minutes.

CHAPTER 98

I SPOTTED BOBBY hustling across the National Mall near the Lincoln Memorial Reflecting Pool about two minutes before his time was up. That meant he had hauled ass. His usual confidence was nowhere in sight as he quick-stepped toward the memorial.

He wasn't wearing a suit today. Just slacks and a nice dress shirt. I knew he had his gun concealed under his shirt somewhere.

I gave Bobby a little wave when he paused at the foot of the stairs, looked up, and noticed me. The look of shock on his face told me I was not one of the suspects he'd had in mind when he received the text. His head swiveled in both directions, looking to see if I had anyone helping me.

He stared at me in silence for a few seconds. Then he took each step deliberately until he plopped down on the stair next to me. He tried to recline and let his legs sprawl to another stair.

His effort to look casual came off as awkward. It exposed how freaked-out he was.

Bobby continued to act cool. The sweat on his forehead and the growing spots under his arms told me otherwise. He swiveled his head in every direction.

I said, "It's just us, Bobby. If there are any other cops around the memorial, they've got nothing to do with me."

Bobby said, "I checked over at the Office of the Inspector General and I know your girlfriend is testifying before the Senate all day. I believe that you're really on your own. What I can't believe is that you would break into my apartment."

"Really? That's the behavior that's over the line?"

"I don't know what else you've done."

"I guess we're in the same boat. I'm only sure about one murder you committed. You have any others?"

That got under his skin. He glared at me.

Bobby then forced a smile. "How are you going to explain where you found the phone? I can explain why I have it."

"Go ahead."

"I don't have to explain anything to you. I mean if someone asks me from the Bureau why I have it."

"So this is the game you're going to play? Just deny shit? Not very original. Neither is strangling a woman. Unfortunately, it's all too common for men to strangle women they know."

Bobby stayed silent. With his brooding expression, I was not sure if he was trying to figure out how to get away or how to eliminate me. Either way, it meant I had him for Emily's murder.

Bobby wasn't budging. I guess I had thought he might confess once I showed him the phone. I was waiting on the help I'd called for. So far, I had nothing.

Bobby said, "You're wasting my time, Detective Bennett." The way he had used the title *Detective* told me he planned to play hardball. "I've got a lot to do. I can't keep you company while you go senile. If you had enough, you'd turn it over to the FBI." That was all he was going to say. And it was enough. He was disrespecting me with efficient answers. I couldn't even bitch about it.

Then I felt my own phone vibrate. I pulled it out and looked at the text quickly. I did everything I could to keep the smile from my face. I memorized the text and slipped my phone back into my pocket.

I took a moment so it didn't seem like I was rushing. Then I casually looked over at Bobby and said, "I've got more than you might think. For instance, I know you bought that fancy Montblanc pen at a shop over in Arlington."

He couldn't keep his eyes from popping open a little. I managed to still suppress a smile.

"You paid for it with your Mastercard. The engraving took four days." I paused, then decided to go out on a limb. "But when you gave it to Emily, she didn't see it for what it was." I gave Bobby a chance to respond. He chose to remain a statue.

"She took it as a gift from a *friend*. But only a friend. That had to eat at you."

You didn't have to be a seasoned investigator to see how my analysis was hitting Bobby hard.

Now I was starting to worry that he would do something violent. No one wanted to see a gunfight outside the Lincoln Memorial.

Bobby just stared at me. But he wasn't getting up to leave. I was going to ride this out.

CHAPTER 99

BOBBY AND I assessed each other like boxers circling in the ring. Occasionally, that's how a challenging homicide interview can go. Often, homicide suspects think they're much smarter than they really are. They just assume they can talk circles around the detectives. In almost every case they are wrong.

This suspect was different. Not only was Bobby Patel extremely intelligent as well as educated; he'd also been with the FBI for over five years. He understood how interviews worked. This was a tough one.

I treated it like other interviews. I tried to get a feel for the "new" Bobby. Not the FBI agent who had been helping me but the suspect in a murder. Perspective is everything. It's rare that my perspective changes this much during an investigation.

Usually, I use some of the information I have but hold back key facts. I let the suspect fill in the gaps. That way no one can claim I led someone into confessing to something they didn't do.

Admittedly, most suspects aren't nearly as formidable as Bobby Patel. Besides being smart and well educated—although often one is not related to the other—Bobby was a black belt in judo. He was the total package as far as tough murder suspects go.

Then Bobby struck with the first verbal jab. He said, "If you have all this evidence, why not have your friend at the OIG just arrest me?"

I had been waiting for this one. And I was prepared. "Because I wanted to hear your side of the story." I sat still on the hard stairs, trying to project calm. The comment seemed to have struck a chord with Bobby. He stared at me but still didn't say anything.

I was counting on a guy like Bobby being so tightly wrapped that he wouldn't be able to hold in something as horrendous as a murder. Looking at him now, I felt like he might break.

"C'mon, Bobby. Let it out. You'll feel a hell of a lot better about it." It was a bullshit comment. It didn't really mean anything, but everyone says it. Even more surprising is the number of suspects who buy it.

Bobby said, "Cut the shit. I won't fall for any of your homicide detective tricks. You got nothing. And you know that no one will take you seriously. The FBI already thinks you're a meddlesome kook. You'll be laughed out of DC."

"That could be, Bobby. But someone will look at what I found out." I held up my phone with a photo of the DVD shard from the Whole Foods security office. "That's in your car. That DVD had you on video. I'm curious, what had you planned to do if the regular security system had been working? Would you have tried to trash the whole video system?"

Bobby was getting more agitated the longer we sat there chatting. His hands couldn't keep still as he scratched his ear, then wiped his eye. He also had a twitch in his cheek. He started scanning the National Mall. I knew that look. He was weighing his options and wondering if he should run.

I had one more idea. It was a risky choice. I said, "Right about now they should be executing the search warrant on your apartment in Alexandria."

That got Bobby to sit up straight. He stared at me. "You've been stalling me all this time? Just trying to keep me here? You asshole." He sprang to his feet.

I eased myself up, trying to keep from alarming Bobby. A group of schoolkids was close by. I didn't want to cause a scene.

Bobby reached toward his waistband. I said, "Hang on, Bobby. Don't do something stupid. Look around you."

That seemed to get through. He noticed the kids and moved his hand away. Then he kicked my right leg out from under me as he shoved me. I tumbled down onto the steps. It felt like someone hitting me on the hip and back with a steel rod.

I grunted in pain, then glanced over at the schoolkids. They were terrified. I scrambled to my feet. This was not the typical experience at the memorial.

I backed away, careful to not give Bobby a reason to pull his gun. I didn't care if we tumbled down the entire flight of marble stairs, as long as there was no shooting.

Bobby looked confused. Almost like he was lost. I tried to guide him away from the crowds. Everyone was staring at us anyway. I gently put my hand on Bobby's upper arm.

He moved like lightning. He trapped my hand on his arm. He twisted his body, and the world spun. I moved through the air like a meteorite, then struck the hard stone.

Fucking judo.

CHAPTER 100

AM I SERIOUSLY *injured? Will I be able to move?* These thoughts crossed my mind as I stared up at the ceiling of the Lincoln Memorial. I gasped, trying to replace the air that had just been knocked out of me. Slowly I sat up. The groan I let out at least let everyone know I was still alive. And seemed to startle the schoolkids.

Everyone around me was frantically dialing 911 on their cell phones. A woman herded the schoolkids away from me as if getting your ass kicked was contagious.

I spotted Bobby loping away from the memorial along one side of the reflecting pool. I managed to stand up, my legs a little shaky under me. I started down the stairs as quickly as I could. Pain shot through my hip like someone jabbing me with a knitting needle. I wobbled when I made it to the ground level and tried to run. I limped along, hoping I could get control of my battered legs. Finally I was able to pick up the pace, but it was still not exactly a sprint.

The mall wasn't too crowded. But I had to face the facts. I was hobbling after a younger man. That was stupid move number one. He was a black belt in judo. That was stupid move number two. And I couldn't call in a dozen uniformed cops to help me. Stupid move number three.

Somehow I closed the distance on Bobby. Mainly because he didn't bother to look behind him. He was confident he'd taken me out of action. I was pretty sure he was headed toward his car to get rid of the DVD shard. It may not have been the brightest move to show him the photo, but I'd had to get him talking.

I was almost on him. *Thank you, Mary Catherine, for making me ride bikes with you so often.* I managed to get a hand on his shoulder.

Bobby skidded to a stop. Once again, I was in the air without even knowing it. This time I hit the concrete path hard. I rolled to my left quickly. I had to do something to counter his judo skills. But what?

Somehow I managed again to stagger to my feet. Now my left leg had just gone numb. There was no one around us here. No one dialing 911 so the DC cops would swoop in and rescue me. I was woozy. How could I counter judo when I could hardly stand?

I turned to face Bobby, then suddenly had a strange sensation. In a split second he had stepped toward me and wrapped his hands around my throat. My air supply just stopped mid-breath. I saw stars immediately.

Damn was he strong.

The sunlight started to dim.

CHAPTER 101

I FLAILED AT Bobby's wrists. His hands were still locked on my throat. My training failed me. My brain was so scrambled I couldn't think back to all the ways I had been taught to get out of a chokehold. I wasn't having any meaningful effect on Bobby. I just panicked.

What was judo's weakness?

I desperately needed air. My oxygen debt was growing exponentially. I tried to make my brain work more efficiently. I tried to remember what I knew about judo. Then my mind jumped back to the pain I felt in my neck as Bobby's surprisingly powerful hands tightened their grip.

Judo was a sport. There were rules. No strikes. No kicks or punches allowed. Jesus Christ, that was it! Bobby might be following the rules, but it was up to me to break them.

I raised my right leg to strike Bobby in the thigh with my

knee. It was a solid blow. I felt his grip loosen slightly. I slammed his arm with a forearm strike. That broke the stranglehold.

I sucked in my first sweet lungful of air. Then another. I eased away from Bobby as I regained my senses.

Then Bobby tried to skirt past me. I shuffled to the side to block him. Every second I could breathe, I felt better. Stronger. Now I had the blueprint. I feinted with a right cross. When Bobby shifted his weight to block the punch, I kicked him hard. I aimed a kick at his groin but struck his hip. It was enough to knock him backward. I gulped more air and raised my fists. I realized I would enjoy smashing his nose into his face. I was ready for whatever came.

Bobby had other ideas. Apparently, I had already won the fight. I just didn't realize it. Bobby turned and sprinted north toward Constitution Avenue. He should've been a track star the way he could blast out of the blocks.

I grabbed another lungful of air and started to follow him. After two hard flips onto the ground, my body just didn't have much left. He had to be heading for his car. That's what I would do.

I crossed the wide, busy street at a full sprint. At least a full sprint for me. I dodged a delivery van, just catching the driver's raised middle finger out of the corner of my eye.

Bobby turned onto a side street. Once I fell in behind him, I could see his brown Taurus parked at the end of the block. There was no way I could let him drive away. Only God knew what he would do. There was even a chance he could disappear and never be found.

I felt panic rise in me. I didn't want to pull my pistol. But that's what it had come to. Even if I broke the law and shot out his tires. I'd rather explain that to a judge than let Bobby get away. Because when I looked up the street, Bobby was running faster and getting farther ahead of me. He still had to cross the street to get to his car.

I sighed as he started to change his angle and run into the street. He was only thirty yards from his car now.

Then a white Chevy Tahoe turned the corner. Fast. It caught Bobby solidly and sent him flying to bounce off a parked Toyota Corolla.

I kept running, then skidded to a stop near Bobby. He lay on the asphalt, moaning. The first thing I did was secure his pistol. I yanked it from his waistband and slid the Glock into my own belt.

The driver of the Tahoe approached us. I looked up at the grinning Detective Dave Swinson from the DC Metro Police Special Investigations unit. Perfect.

Swinson said, "I didn't mean to hit him quite so hard."

Bobby slowly moved to a sitting position. He shook his head. His eyes didn't look like they could focus as he tried to take in the scene in front of him. A couple of white pebbles from the road were stuck to his face and blood leaked out of his nose. There was a patch of road rash on his left cheek.

I kneeled down to get a better look at him.

Swinson said, "Is he okay?"

"Unfortunately, yes. Just shaken up a bit." I brushed the pebbles off Bobby's face. Then I patted him down quickly to make sure he didn't have any other weapons.

Swinson said, "Great job. Glad you told me to find his car and wait there."

I looked up at the detective. "I appreciate that. I'm impressed you found out where he bought the pen. The text you sent gave me some ammo to confuse him."

"Homicide investigation is a team sport. Glad we could help."

I could hear sirens in the distance. My body took that as a signal to collapse. I sat down hard on the street, my back resting on the front tire of the Toyota.

This wasn't a good day for anyone.

CHAPTER 102

BOBBY PATEL NOW sat on the curb between his car and Dave Swinson's city-issued Tahoe. We decided not to handcuff him. We let him gather his wits for a minute. We still thought he might make a meaningful statement. Swinson had already called off the patrol cars coming to the National Mall. We were alone.

Swinson leaned against the bumper of his Tahoe while I sat on the curb next to Bobby. Without meaning to, we had ended up in the perfect homicide interview formation. One person to ask questions. One to watch and act if the suspect got frisky. Swinson had already proven that he was prepared to take action.

For his part, Bobby looked like a broken man. His head hung down. His nose still dripped a little blood. The road rash on his face looked like it'd spread. I knew it was just the traumatized skin turning red.

Swinson got a call and looked at me. I wasn't sure what he was about to say. Then he spoke loud enough for Bobby to hear. He was giving someone information for an affidavit for a search warrant on Bobby's car and his apartment in Alexandria. It was the perfect setup to show Bobby he was done.

Bobby's panicked escape attempt had sealed it in my mind. Now Bobby knew it as well. There was nothing he could do. He sniffled and used a napkin I had given him to wipe the blood from his nose.

I didn't speak. I just sat there next to Bobby. Almost like I was a friend comforting him. But that's not how I felt. I was more distracted. My thoughts went back to Emily Parker. I couldn't help but wonder about everything she was going to miss in life. That didn't even take into account everyone who would miss her in their lives. This asshole sitting next to me had done more damage than he could ever imagine.

After a minute, Bobby murmured, "I screwed up. Big-time."

It took all my willpower, but I forced myself to pat him on the back like I cared how he felt. I just wanted him to keep talking. Swinson had heard him as well. He moved a little closer.

Bobby looked at me. "She called you. I saw it on her phone. You guys never connected. I wonder what she was going to say to you."

"I do too. I always will. I was in Ireland and thought I could get back to her." I didn't want to get into another subject. I shut my mouth and just waited for Bobby to talk. He finally decided it was time.

Bobby said, "I just got so frustrated. She dated a lot but wouldn't even consider me. I did everything. I even watched her neighbor's cat because she asked me to. I took assignments for her. I would've done anything for Emily."

I said, "Except leave her alone. The only thing she really needed you to do."

"I guess I'm screwed."

I said, "We all lost on this one, Bobby."

CHAPTER 103

ROBERTA HERRING FINISHED her testimony at the Senate early. She met me at Special Investigations' off-site office. The squad was busy working with the MPD homicide team to complete the search of Bobby's apartment before the media swarmed.

I was sitting behind a desk no one was using when Roberta walked up to me. She had sort of a silly grin on her face. "Why do you look so down? I knew you'd figure it out. I'm embarrassed to admit I never had a clue. Patel was such a diligent agent. It never occurred to me that he'd do something like this."

I said, "Isn't that what every neighbor says on the local news after a serial killer has been arrested?"

Roberta laughed. "Yeah, just about." She turned serious. She sat down on the desk, then looked around to make sure no one was close enough to hear us talk. "The whole story of how you found the phone in Bobby's apartment could be tricky if it ever goes to court."

"I don't know how to fix that."

Roberta shrugged. "We'll see what happens. I doubt anyone wants to expose the dirty secrets you discovered. Someone will offer Bobby a good deal. He'll take it. No one in DC will give you a second thought. Even if you did commit an outright burglary." Roberta looked around the room again, then turned back to me. "C'mon, Mike, what else is bothering you?"

It's hard to keep something from a friend, especially if that friend is an experienced investigator. I said, "I missed my train. I won't make it to Manhattan for Trent's ceremony with the mayor."

Roberta smiled. "Not being in the same room with the New York mayor is usually a good thing. He's so full of hot air it's a wonder Gracie Mansion doesn't float away."

I gave her a weak smile. She probably didn't realize what seeing the ceremony meant to me. I still didn't have the guts to call Mary Catherine and tell her I wouldn't be back until after nine.

Roberta smiled.

I had to say, "What?"

"I have an idea."

Thirty minutes later, Roberta dropped me off at a small fixed-base operation on the perimeter of Reagan National Airport. This was where the Department of Justice kept most of its air assets. Roberta had used her influence to delay a flight to New York on a government Gulfstream jet. She somehow got me on the passenger list. I was on board with two witnesses for a mob trial and three US marshals.

We stood in front of the small field-operations office at the airport to say our good-byes. I gave her a huge hug and a kiss good-bye. She'd done so much for me I couldn't even put it in words.

I waited with the small group of passengers to board the plane. The TV behind the courtesy counter was broadcasting the local news. The only story anyone was talking about was the arrest of Rhea Wellmy-Steinberg. I was surprised there hadn't even been any accusation of the charges being politically motivated. It seemed that a lot of people in DC knew about the Steinbergs' personal habits. I watched to the end, but there was no mention of Emily. I wondered if anyone might link Bobby's arrest with Baltimore's arrest of Rhea.

I sat next to a tall female deputy US marshal. She turned to me and asked, "You work for DOJ?"

"NYPD." That was enough to earn an entire trip without another word. I didn't really care.

I was going home.

CHAPTER **104**

AFTER THE DEPARTMENT of Justice plane landed at JFK Airport, I grabbed a cab and held up a fifty to the glass partition. "Get me to City Hall by 6:30 and this is yours on top of the fare." I looked at the license and the smiling face of the young Israeli driver. "Does that sound like a deal, Yossi?"

The young man with a mop of dark hair smiled. "That's easy. I feel bad taking your money."

I liked that kind of confidence. I wished my nerves were as steady as Yossi's confidence. The terror I felt on the ride would be worth it if we made it to City Hall alive. Yossi squeezed between a step van and a giant old-school Cadillac. I tried not to make a sound, but a yelp slipped out of me.

Yossi just chuckled. He skidded to a stop outside City Hall right on time. I'd have to run like Usain Bolt to make the ceremony. I gave Yossi an additional fifty to drop my bag at my apartment building. I had a feel for the young man and thought he was trustworthy enough. Just in case, I wrote my address on the back of one of my business cards. He glanced at the card, then looked up at me. "I guessed you were a newscaster, not a cop. I guarantee your bag will be there."

I dashed past some tourists taking photographs in front of City Hall. I was moving so fast I had to grab the gatepost to make my turn toward the front door. I checked my watch. I hoped the ceremony ran on the usual city schedule: about ten minutes late.

I was six minutes past the start time—yikes. I could feel my phone vibrate in my pocket. I knew it had to be Mary Catherine. I don't know if it was the ride or being late, but my stomach gurgled. This was more nerve-racking than most police work I did.

I burst through the front door of City Hall. The security guard's head popped up. Probably the first action he'd seen in months.

I said, "Ceremony with the mayor?"

The older African American man recognized a fellow father doing what he could to make a kid's event. He smiled and pointed down the hallway to the left. I nodded my thanks and raced away.

I could see the open doors to the reception room. I slipped inside, wondering how I'd find Mary Catherine and the gang. I don't know why I thought that would be a problem. They literally made up a quarter of the audience.

The younger kids gave me a hug as a mob. I kissed Mary Catherine, then focused on the podium. Eight kids stood in line with the mayor to one side. Trent was second from the right. He was dressed in his blue suit with a new, yellow tie. He looked remarkably snazzy.

I actually listened to the mayor for a change. He talked about kids from all over the city writing essays and these were the best. I snuck a glance at Jane. I was worried she still might be a little jealous of her brother. But when I looked over, she seemed okay.

Then the mayor said Trent's name. I was so thrilled, I felt a little dizzy. Trent beamed. I again looked over to Jane, and she was smiling and applauding like everyone else.

Life did have a way of working out. I realized my stomach issue had resolved itself.

This was going to be a night to remember.

CHAPTER 105

THE NEXT FEW days flew by. Harry Grissom came by the apartment and admitted he'd been told to put eyes on me in New York City. He was embarrassed. I was amused. Now it was all just a game.

Mary Catherine seemed withdrawn. I danced around the edges of asking her exactly what was wrong but did not get a clear answer. I chalked it up to having to deal with the kids by herself for so long. I gave her space.

Sunday, we attended mass at Holy Name. Everyone attended together. We took up an entire pew. Today Shawna and Seamus were unveiling their project.

Right as Father Calise finished conducting the service, he said, "We have a special surprise this morning. Father Seamus and his great-granddaughter Shawna have a presentation."

I found myself leaning forward in the seat, making sure I

could see the front of the congregation clearly. I couldn't believe how excited I was to find out what the secret project was.

Shawna nearly leapt from the pew. Seamus and an altar boy wheeled out a small cart covered by a cloth. I had to smile at how well rehearsed everything was.

Seamus yielded the floor to Shawna. She said in her loudest voice, "We'd like to thank Gigi Barborini and Paul Laska for taking the time to teach us the skills we needed to complete our project."

I glanced around quickly and realized I was not the only member of the church excited to see what they had made. I was completely intrigued. I had no idea what they could've created.

With a theatrical flair, Seamus pulled the cloth straight up in the air. He revealed a square-foot stained-glass piece. A whirl of color framed by black painted iron. There were five sections in the square with leading strips separating all the different-colored glass segments. It was perfect. It was beautiful.

Seamus said, "This will replace the window in the side entrance to the church. It's dedicated to my late granddaughter-in-law, Maeve Bennett."

The applause was instant and thunderous. Shawna was a star.

I got choked up. I couldn't say what affected me more, Shawna's art or the dedication to my wonderful late wife. I needed a minute to gather myself. Mary Catherine draped an arm across my shoulders. She handed me a tissue from her purse. I tried not to honk when I blew my nose.

After the service, we waited as a family while parishioners complimented Seamus and Shawna. I didn't think anyone could have as wide a smile as Shawna on this Sunday morning.

I could get used to seeing my kids honored.

CHAPTER 106

SUNDAY NIGHT, WE had a family meal. The boys insisted on doing all the cooking and the cleaning up. I was wary of a prank. Then I heard Ricky was in charge. That's how I knew it wouldn't go too badly.

We all sat at the long dining room table as the four boys walked out, each holding a platter of food. It was a great presentation. When the platters were set on the table, I saw there were hamburgers, hot dogs, potato chips, and homemade coleslaw. I knew the coleslaw was Ricky's contribution. It was a feast. Everyone seemed happy. No easy feat with thirteen people in New York City.

Later, Mary Catherine and I settled in bed with the news on our little TV. I had to watch a story about New York senator Lom Wellmy retiring immediately. The newscaster mentioned Wellmy's daughter's arrest for a homicide in Baltimore. The report said that Justice Steinberg had taken his wife's arrest hard and was in seclusion.

Mary Catherine turned to me in bed and said, "That was because of you. Is it satisfying?"

"Finding Emily's murderer was satisfying. This is just sort of amusing." I shut off the TV with the remote.

Mary Catherine fixed those lovely blue eyes on me. She said in a low voice, "Did you love her, Michael?"

I didn't have to think about my answer. I looked at Mary Catherine and said, "I love you." She didn't smile, but her eyes twinkled. I ran my hand across the smooth skin of her cheek. She was a work of art. Finally, I got around to asking what I wanted to ask. "Are you feeling okay? I tried not to be too intrusive. But you said you've been tired. You were nauseated a few times last week. Is there anything you want to tell me?"

Mary Catherine took a moment to gather her thoughts. I could tell there was something important she wanted to say. I kept my mouth shut and gave her my full attention.

Mary Catherine said, "I've been to see Dr. Jackson a couple of times recently."

My heart started to beat faster hearing that she had visited her ob-gyn.

Mary Catherine sat up in the bed. She turned and looked into my eyes. "Michael, I'm not pregnant. I know you've been thinking I am. I'm not. Dr. Jackson thinks it's unlikely I could ever get pregnant." Mary Catherine looked at me for my response.

I sat up and hugged her. She started to sniffle. I cooed, "It's okay, it's okay." I held her. After a moment, I added, "As long as you're healthy, that's all that matters."

Mary Catherine said, "I'm fine. Well, except for the ability to have a child." She tried to smile. Then she said, "Michael, cheer me up. Take my mind off it."

I tried to think what to say. Finally, I came up with "I wish we had something to take our minds off babies. Maybe something like, I don't know, ten kids."

She smiled. She sniffled and wiped a tear from her eye and then smiled again. "So you're okay with it?"

"Sweetheart, I have you. I'm okay with anything."

She kissed me.

I kissed her.

We fell asleep in each other's arms.

Have You Read Them All?

STEP ON A CRACK
(with Michael Ledwidge)

The most powerful people in the world have gathered for a funeral in New York City. They don't know it's a trap devised by a ruthless mastermind, and it's up to Michael Bennett to save every last hostage.

RUN FOR YOUR LIFE
(with Michael Ledwidge)

The Teacher is giving New York a lesson it will never forget, slaughtering the powerful and the arrogant. Michael Bennett discovers a vital pattern, but has only a few hours to save the city.

WORST CASE
(with Michael Ledwidge)

Children from wealthy families are being abducted. But the captor isn't demanding money. He's quizzing his hostages on the price others pay for their luxurious lives, and one wrong answer is fatal.

TICK TOCK
(with Michael Ledwidge)

New York is in chaos as a rash of horrifying copycat crimes tears through the city. Michael Bennett investigates, but not even he could predict the earth-shattering enormity of this killer's plan.

I, MICHAEL BENNETT
(with Michael Ledwidge)
Bennett arrests infamous South American crime lord Manuel Perrine. From jail, Perrine vows to rain terror down upon New York City – and to get revenge on Michael Bennett.

GONE
(with Michael Ledwidge)
Perrine is back and deadlier than ever. Bennett must make an impossible decision: stay and protect his family, or hunt down the man who is their biggest threat.

BURN
(with Michael Ledwidge)
A group of well-dressed men enter a condemned building. Later, a charred body is found. Michael Bennett is about to enter a secret underground world of terrifying depravity.

ALERT
(with Michael Ledwidge)
Two devastating catastrophes hit New York in quick succession, putting everyone on edge. Bennett is given the near impossible task of hunting down the shadowy terror group responsible.

BULLSEYE
(with Michael Ledwidge)
As the most powerful men on earth gather for a meeting of the UN, Bennett receives shocking intelligence that there will be an assassination attempt on the US president. Are the Russian government behind the plot?

HAUNTED
(with James O. Born)

Michael Bennett is ready for a vacation after a series of crises push him, and his family, to the brink. But when he gets pulled into a shocking case, Bennett is fighting to protect a town, the law, and the family that he loves.

AMBUSH
(with James O. Born)

When an anonymous tip proves to be a trap, Michael Bennett believes he personally is being targetted. And not just him, but his family too.

BLINDSIDE
(with James O. Born)

The mayor of New York has a daughter who's missing. Detective Michael Bennett has a son who's in prison. Can one father help the other?

THE RUSSIAN
(with James O. Born)

As Michael Bennett's wedding day approaches, a killer has a vow of his own to fulfil . . .

Discover the newest instalment in the Michael
Bennett series, coming July 2023

Read on for an exclusive extract . . .

CHAPTER 1

THE NYPD BOAT lurched and I almost slipped on the deck.

The waves made a monotonous slapping sound against the boat's hull, like an uneven drumbeat, as we cut through the choppy water. I sucked in a deep breath and could practically taste the Hudson River. The toxic odors of rotting fish and garbage didn't do anything to help the nausea I felt. I prayed it would pass.

One of the officers assigned to the boat tapped me on the shoulder. He grinned and offered me a piece of beef jerky.

"Very funny, asshole," Detective Terri Hernandez said as she snatched the jerky from the smirking cop and gave him a shove. "We're here to work. There's a woman's body out there." She turned to me. "You okay, Mike?"

"Never better. Fresh air, the sea. Who could ask for more?"

She smiled and said, "That's called karma for all the pranks you've played."

3

Terri was trying to distract me. That's why I like working with her. I was on edge, terrified that I'd recognize the body we were on our way to recover.

Suzanne Morton, a friend of my oldest daughter, Juliana, had gone missing three weeks ago. The last place anyone saw her was at a prestigious acting class in SoHo. Suzanne and my daughter had been in a few classes together in the past. The NYU sophomore kept a busy schedule but never missed an acting class. She had been a good influence around my house, encouraging my younger daughters to pursue their passions.

I'd spent hours with Suzanne's parents. I had first met them six months ago when we attended a short play both the girls were in. Since Suzanne's disappearance, they'd asked me over and over again what the NYPD was doing to find their daughter. I understood. If your child is missing, you want the whole world to stop and go look for them.

As a parent of ten kids, I always seem to have something to worry about. At least none of them was missing.

I didn't need to use my imagination to worry about what might have happened to Suzanne. I'd seen enough as a homicide detective. It felt like a knife in my abdomen every time I pictured the young woman, her light-brown hair framing a beautiful face that had deep dimples when she smiled.

I felt a change in the engine just as the pilot looked over her shoulder. She yelled in my direction, "Wind chop is really bad today! I'll get as close as I can."

I looked out over the whitecaps and spotted a figure floating in the water. A second boat, a Zodiac inflatable-hull outboard, discharged a diver. Recovery takes a lot of resources.

We idled alongside the body. Now that we were closer, I could see more clearly that the body was a woman, floating facedown in the water, with waves of long hair fanning out around her head. She was wearing a sparkly black cocktail dress that had attracted sea life. A fish nibbled at something in her hair.

Terri stepped behind me. "Is it her?"

Salt spray stung my face as I watched the grim procedure to recover the body. I shrugged. "Can't tell yet." I appreciated Terry's reassuring hand on my shoulder.

The female crime-scene tech on our boat pulled the winch line so the diver could attach it to the recovery basket. The wire basket was over six feet long, with sides tall enough to keep a person firmly inside. I was relieved to see the care they used. They didn't know about my possible connection to the victim. They were just professionals.

Against all sound judgment, I stepped closer for a better look.

The other crime-scene tech, a doughy guy in his mid-thirties, leaned over the edge of the boat. He'd been the first victim of the beef jerky prank. All it had taken was a quick whiff of the smelly, dried meat, and the tech had vomited over the side of the boat. But now he showed great concentration and focus, leaning so far out of the boat his face almost touched the water.

I heard a helicopter in the distance. When I looked up, I noticed it was a news helicopter. I hoped to God they didn't try to get too close and film the body coming onto the boat. I couldn't imagine a family ever seeing that on TV, but reporters continue to amaze me.

I heard one of the crime-scene techs say they were bringing the body on board. I took a deep breath and steadied myself.

CHAPTER 2

I WATCHED THE crime-scene technicians and police diver struggle in the choppy water. My stomach lurched as I stepped over to help. Forensic scientists and crime-scene investigators can be territorial. The crime-scene tech waved me off.

Then the male crime-scene tech slipped during a particularly rough wave. He grabbed the basket holding the body. It tipped. I tensed, expecting disaster.

The other tech sprang from the deck and managed to straighten the basket. At least temporarily. When the winch holding the basket swayed, the basket came forward onto the boat deck.

That's when it happened.

The body tumbled onto the deck of the patrol boat with a sickening thud. I kept my mouth shut. It was an accident, and conditions were dicey. It could've happened to anyone.

One of the basket's black straps fluttered in the wind as both crime-scene techs carefully picked up the body, turning her so that she faced up. We all stared at the victim for a moment as the female crime-scene tech kneeled and meticulously brushed wet strands of hair away from the woman's face.

It was not Juliana's friend. But whoever she was, this young woman had been stunning. Not just pretty or cute but an honest-to-God beauty. Long, gorgeous dark hair, a straight, petite nose, and high cheekbones. She hadn't been in the water long. She was fully clothed, and even still had her high heels strapped on. She looked like a peaceful angel lying on the deck of the boat.

Terri Hernandez leaned in close to me. She said in a low voice, "This is really similar to a body we found in the Bronx about two months ago. Both pretty, both in formal wear, and both discarded like an old fast-food container." She stepped past me and pointed at the body on the deck. "Looks like a puncture wound in the chest. It's small but noticeable." Terri turned and added, "See the red soles on those heels? This girl has really expensive taste. Those are Christian Louboutin stilettos, and the dress looks like a Gucci."

I just nodded. I always need a few minutes after recovering a body. I tried to picture the circumstances that led to the victim's death. There was something about being dumped in the water that felt extra evil. It's one of my nightmares. I said a quick, silent prayer for this poor woman.

At the moment, the only thing I could think of was catching whoever killed her.

The crime-scene techs took photo after photo from every angle.

The male crime-scene tech looked up from the body and said, "No ID of any kind. I'd put her age between nineteen and twenty-two. We'll try to get her fingerprints back at the lab. We'll see if she ever applied for a government job or has ever been arrested, but we might have a hard time figuring out who she is."

I shook my head. "Somebody's missing her. She'll match a missing person's report. We'll know in a day or two who she is." The thought of this girl dying alone caused a wave of sadness to pass over me.

I'd promised myself that if these kinds of feelings *didn't* come to me whenever I saw a body, I'd know it was time to retire.

CHAPTER 3

BY NOON, I was headed back to my office. Every time I walk through the doors of the Manhattan North Homicide unit, in an unmarked building on Broadway near 133rd Street, I am thrilled not to work anywhere near One Police Plaza.

I was hoping there would be more information waiting for me at my desk. I also intended to track down our criminal intelligence analyst to help me sift through the data from my newest death investigation.

I headed to the seventh floor, where my squad took the center of the space, with half a dozen small offices and interview rooms ringing it.

I slid behind my desk and took a moment to make a few entries in my notebook and just think about what to do next. Even though we've moved on from physical case files to an electronic system called ECMS, Enterprise Case Management System, I still trust my own handwritten notes.

Then I hustled to my boss's office. Harry Grissom's tall and lean frame fit well behind a desk, and I knew that sitting eased the discomfort he always felt. Harry favored his left side when he walked, the result of a knife wound that had severed his femoral artery when he was a young patrolman. He never complained, but it was clear from his gait that it was painful for him to walk too long.

I realized Harry was starting to show his age lately. The creases around his eyes were now cracks. The mustache that drooped below his mouth, contrary to NYPD grooming policies, was now almost completely gray. Recently, I'd heard whispers that the big shots at One Police Plaza wanted Harry to retire. I hoped it wasn't true. Work was all Harry knew. I worried that without the NYPD, Harry, with three ex-wives and no kids, might become one of the many suicides in the police ranks. It's an issue no one inside or outside police agencies wants to talk about. The pressure of the job can be intense. But the pressure of *losing* the job can be overwhelming.

Harry gave me a little wave and his version of a smile. "What do you got?"

I filled him in on the recovery from this morning, and told him about Terri Hernandez's mention of a similar victim. "I'd like to work with Terri on this and look at both homicides together. Just in case we're dealing with another serial killer, I don't want anything to put us behind the eight ball. For a change, I wouldn't mind being a step ahead of an asshole like this."

Harry gave me a nod. That meant to move full speed ahead. Other lieutenants might ask for memos or extra admin, but Harry's nod carried a lot of information. It told me to catch this killer any way I could. I almost ran from his office before things could be slowed down.

I looked toward the criminal intelligence analysts' room as I left Harry's office and felt my first relief of the day. Sitting by himself in the corner of his office was Walter Jackson, arguably the best analyst in the NYPD.

Without a doubt, Walter was the *biggest* analyst with the NYPD.

He stood six foot six and was every bit of three hundred pounds—the word *imposing* didn't completely capture the thirty-five-year-old African American. The big man's smile tended to lift everyone's spirits. Walter had always been interested in helping his community, but he didn't like some of the risks associated with being a police officer. He found he had a knack for piecing together information and solving puzzles when he studied English literature at Virginia, so when he saw a job announcement for criminal intelligence analyst, he thought he'd give it a try. Now he was a legend in the department.

I popped my head in the room. "Hey, Walter, I just caught a homicide and I've got a lot of information to put together. Any chance you're free?"

"I got plenty to do, but it's tough to turn down a new homicide. What do you need?" he asked.

I stared at him. He didn't say anything.

He returned my stare as he slowly smiled. "What is it?"

"That's one of the first times you've ever answered a question without a pun."

The big man laughed, his belly jiggling. "I bet my daughter, Janine, I could go a week without making a pun. I have to give her a dollar every time I slip up. Whether she hears it or not."

"What made her want to bet?"

"I asked her, when does a joke become a *dad* joke?" He paused, then added, "When the punch line becomes apparent."

I guess most dads share a little bit of the same sense of humor, but I couldn't help but groan at that one. I didn't tell him I'd use that pun almost as soon as I got home.

I gave Walter the recovery information I had and what I had learned from Terri Hernandez about her homicide in the Bronx. Walter didn't have to be told what needed to be done. He'd call the medical examiner's office to get the latest information, track down all the outside sources, like news stories, on the other homicide. Then he'd give it to me in a concise manner.

In short, it's people like Walter Jackson who make homicide detectives look efficient.

CHAPTER 4

I'D BEEN IN the office less than an hour, searching the ranks of missing persons, hoping to find a match for the girl we had pulled out of the Hudson, when a shadow fell across my desk like an eclipse. I turned to see the towering figure of Walter Jackson.

He eased down onto the hard, wooden chair across from my desk. Walter never sat down with force. He'd learned better, after a similar city-purchased chair had once crumpled under his weight. Now he instinctively tested each chair.

He gently placed a photo on my desk. It was clearly a recent picture of the beautiful victim from this morning. It hurt my heart a little to see her smiling in the photo. I said, "That was fast."

"Me and Fotomat promise to develop photos in less than an hour."

"Jesus, Walter, Fotomat? You're not that old. How do you even remember them?"

"You're not much older than me and you remember them." He looked at the photo. "I got lucky. The ME's office picked up immediately. They have a fingerprint scanner connected directly to the FBI. Turns out the girl had once applied to work at a preschool in SoHo. We were able to match her fingerprints to that application.

"Her name is Estella Abreu. Nursing student at Pace. Lived in East Harlem with her family on 116th Street." He bent his head for a silent prayer. Walter did that any time he talked about a recent homicide victim. A common practice around people who deal with tragedy every day.

"Good work, Walter."

"Autopsy is scheduled for tonight. Aurora Jones is the assistant medical examiner on duty."

I was glad to hear it. Aurora was a hell of a coroner. I nodded and looked at Walter. "That's outstanding. Can you see if there're any connections between this victim and the one from the Bronx? When you have more information, we'll compare them."

Walter didn't waste a second. "The girl in the Bronx, Emma Schrade, was a student at Juilliard. There is one connection right there. Both were students. Emma was a soprano." He tossed an envelope onto my desk.

I opened it to see a bright-eyed blonde with a spectacular smile. "Where did these come from?"

"I just pulled them off the internet. I printed them so you could take them on interviews. I saved the original photo in ECMS."

"Walter, just when I think you're out of surprises, you pull one more out of the hat. This is impressive for just a few minutes."

"I've got two daughters. You think I'm not motivated when I see a photo of a girl who's been murdered? I don't understand how you guys ever sleep at night. I'd be consumed with all the leads that come into a case like this. How do you handle it with your ten kids?"

"It's definitely a balancing act. Between sports, homework, and just trying to spend some time with them, this is a tough job."

Walter shook his head. "I don't know how you do it, Mike. With your crazy-ass cases and all those kids, how do you find time in the day?"

"It's all about being efficient and keeping moving like a shark. I'm afraid if I ever stand still, it'll kill me. Believe it or not, I also start coaching my daughter Fiona's basketball team this week."

"All school officials see when they look at me is a potential football coach," Walter said. "No one can believe it when I tell them I've never even seen a football game all the way from beginning to end." He sighed. "I don't know that I'd give up my steady daytime hours and comfortable desk for your job. I'd already be burned out and barely able to talk to my family."

"Walter, I know your family. It doesn't matter if you talk to them or not, they'd be talking to you." We both laughed because we both understood what it meant to be true family men.

"I know what you mean. Questions at work, questions at

home. Sometimes you want someone to answer *your* damn questions."

I nodded. "Elementary school math and science can baffle me."

Walter paused. "You mean like what weighs more, a gallon of water or a gallon of liquefied butane?"

"They weigh the same, right?"

Walter grinned. "No, butane is lighter fluid."

I groaned and said, "You owe your daughter another dollar."

"Totally worth it."

CHAPTER 5

I STUDIED THE information Walter Jackson had come up with on both victims. It was during times like this, slouched at my desk, that I appreciated the padded chair I'd bought for myself. The city didn't care if hours at my desk hurt my back.

As usual, Walter Jackson's packet on my homicide victim was outstanding. The right criminal intelligence analyst makes any case easier. Walter always sticks in little bits of information other analysts might ignore, putting in data on siblings and old addresses, giving investigators more options to pursue when starting out on a case.

Sometimes, as a homicide detective, you've got to re-create the victim's world in your head. You've got to be able to live their life and see the world through their eyes, at least briefly.

I was deep into Emma's and Estella's worlds and was startled when my phone rang. The kids had installed a new ringtone, the start of the piano solo from Eric Clapton's original "Layla." As soon as I heard it, I remembered that my wife, Mary Catherine, was going to call me after her doctor's appointment.

The first words out of my mouth were "How'd it go?"

Instead of a concise answer, I heard a series of shrieks and laughing in the background.

Using my razor-sharp detective skills, I made an assessment and said, "You have the kids with you?"

"Only sixty percent of them. We're on our way to buy some school clothes."

"I thought you were going to call as soon as you were done at the doctor's office."

"Things got crazy and I was running late."

I heard my youngest child, Chrissy, whine that she wanted to talk to me. That started her sisters Fiona and Shawna doing the same thing. I could barely hear Mary Catherine as she tried to explain things in code.

"Michael, I know I said I wanted to go to this first appointment on my own, but there was a lot to absorb. It was almost like the…" She searched for another word. "The cashier was trying to talk me out of any purchase."

I was careful with my reply. I said, "To be clear, the *doctor* tried to talk you out of *fertility treatment*."

"I have no idea why crime is rising with brilliant detectives like you running around."

I snorted a laugh. I didn't want her to think I was trying to influence her one way or the other about her efforts to get pregnant. Finally, I came up with "How do *you* feel about it?"

"I really don't know. I think I'd like you ... to come next time."

I knew her pause was a last-second change from *I'd like you at the next doctor's appointment.*

All I said was "Anything you want."

"I think about how great our life is now in a home filled with children." Mary Catherine paused to yell at the kids. "Everyone quiet for two minutes!"

I heard Trent sneak in an "Or what?"

The silence over the phone was terrifying. I knew those kids were facing the toughest of Irish glares. I felt sorry for them.

She came back on the line and her voice betrayed no hint of anger. Mary Catherine said, "I look at it two different ways. I think how happy another"—there was a pause—"*visitor* would be in our house. I also think we have the perfect balance now."

"No matter what, we can't lose. We have a great life, and a baby would make it better."

Mary Catherine said, "I thought irrepressible optimism was supposed to be my thing."

We both laughed as she broke the tension. We chatted for a few moments about the rest of our day. Then I built up the nerve to tell her, "Listen, I caught a homicide earlier today. I'll probably be home late." A homicide detective's spouse hears this phrase dozens of times a year. But it felt harder to say, knowing she was having a rough day.

There was silence for a few moments on the other end of the line. Then Mary Catherine haltingly asked, "I know you've been looking for Juliana's missing friend, Suzanne..."

"No, it wasn't Suzanne. Suzanne's father left another message for me this morning. I've been over to Missing Persons at One Police Plaza several times, hoping to find out something. So far there's nothing on her. But Suzanne wasn't the girl we fished out of the Hudson."

"Oh, my Lord. Someone dumped a body in the river? That's horrible."

I try not to bring home the terrible things I see on my job. I guess I have achieved my goal because Mary Catherine was still reeling from the few details I had told her. I never want my family to become numb to the horrors that happen. Just like I don't want to lose sight of what each homicide means, especially when the victim is young. Somewhere a family had lost a child. Every homicide victim means potential that won't be reached. I know in my heart someone feels the loss every time a person is murdered.

Mary Catherine said, "Don't worry about a thing, Michael. I have a plan for the afternoon that includes helping the twins with a project, then showing Ricky how I make my Irish stew."

Her kind understanding—especially when she said things with that light Irish accent—made me want to rush home that much faster.

CHAPTER 6

TERRI HERNANDEZ MET me in East Harlem near where Estella Abreu, the young woman we'd pulled out of the Hudson, had lived. I caught Terri up on everything I'd learned about our victim.

"The only address listed for her is this one, with her parents, on 116th Street. A patrol sergeant made notification almost as soon as we knew who she was."

We were about to do one of the most challenging things all homicide detectives do: interview the family of a homicide victim. You never know what you're going to find. A family in denial. A family grieving so deeply they can't focus. A family so shattered by the loss of the child they don't know how to cope. There's a wide array of responses to losing a family member to homicide, and none of them are positive.

"You know I did some work not too far from here. Did a

year in Narcotics that, for a time, had me coordinating with officers at the Two-Three," Terri said.

"Is the neighborhood better or worse than back then?"

"Same. Still tough. Right over there is where a convenience-store robber shot at me."

"What happened to the shooter?"

"He ran and ended up shooting a cabdriver. Then he took the cab and went on a high-speed chase. The New Rochelle cops finally got him with Stop Sticks. He was booked, but since he didn't hit me and the cabdriver survived, he got time served and two years' probation."

I said, "If the shooter had hit you, the judge would've given him another month or two for sure."

"I don't think people realize how close most cops are to just stepping away."

"I hear ya. All we can do in the meantime is our best. Maybe if we did a better job, this neighborhood wouldn't be so rough."

Terri pointed down the street. "Over where those guys are selling dope was the site of my biggest fistfight. Place looks about the same. For a girl to get out of here and go to nursing school is really something. Her parents have to be special." She shook her head and added, "And this is their reward? Makes you wonder why we all try so hard. Shit happens no matter what."

All I could do was nod. I'd been thinking about this most of the afternoon. This beautiful young woman, studying to be a nurse at Pace University, and suddenly everything was taken from her. It made me sad, but it also made me angry.

CHAPTER 7

WE PAUSED OUTSIDE the building, a five-story apartment complex a few blocks from the East River. It was quiet on the street this time in the early evening. A few people were coming home from work. There were no kids playing outside. That said all that needed to be said about the neighborhood.

A man standing by the steps saw us pull up and immediately called someone to let them know the cops were here.

Terri said, "Relax, we're not here for you or any of your petty crimes."

The man looked insulted and relieved at the same time.

We climbed up two flights of stairs to the Abreu family's three-bedroom apartment.

As we walked, Terri asked, "Any indication why Estella was so dressed up, or where she was going? Some kind of university function?"

"No. Nothing like that. Still checking."

I took a deep breath to prepare myself for what we were about to do. The apartment door was open, and we could hear people talking inside. I knocked lightly, hoping someone would notice me at the open door. I'd seen scenes like this play out too many times. Still, there was something positive in seeing people here, comforting grieving parents.

I spotted a couple I assumed to be the Abreus together on a small love seat: a short, pudgy man wearing a work shirt with the name RAUL stenciled across his left breast, sitting with his arm around a small woman dabbing her eyes with a handkerchief. She had the same long dark hair as Estella, and I could see a strong resemblance.

One wall looked like a shrine to Estella, with photos from her First Communion and soccer trophies all set up on a library table in the corner of the room. An elderly woman who I thought might be Estella's grandmother silently arranged more photos on the table.

A young man came to the open door and said, "May I help you?"

I leaned in close and told him who we were and why we were here. He appreciated the quiet introduction. He motioned us inside, then said to the couple on the love seat, "Tio, I think you need to talk to these people."

A few minutes later, we were in a bedroom with Mr. and Mrs. Abreu, sitting on a bed covered by a thick, vibrantly colored comforter printed with birds nesting in trees. We'd waited for Mrs. Abreu to compose herself in the bathroom. It looked like she could've used a couple more minutes.

We started slowly. Grieving parents don't usually come up

with the details that can really help in an investigation right away. We chatted about their daughter's life. That is always the best route to information.

Mrs. Abreu spoke with a thick Spanish accent. "My Estella was not just pretty, she was *beautiful*. Since the day she came into this world. Smart as a whip too. She was also nearsighted, and she started wearing glasses at six. She always chose stylish frames, but she tried to not wear them for pictures. Without them she was almost blind. She could wear contacts for a short while."

Mr. Abreu kept nodding. "Estella is sweet too." He froze. Then eked out, "I mean she *was*." Then he started to cry.

We went back to short questions about friends, interests, and relationships.

After a few minutes of simple questions, Terri Hernandez asked Mrs. Abreu, "Do you have any idea where Estella was going last night? She was dressed up like she was going out on the town."

The grieving woman shook her head. After blowing her nose into the handkerchief, she looked up and said, "When Estella went out yesterday evening, she was dressed in casual clothes. I don't know anything about being dressed up."

Terri politely asked if she could see Estella's bedroom and closet. I followed along as Mrs. Abreu led us to the third bedroom. All eyes followed us as we walked through the crowded living room. There was no question who we were or why we were here. These people expected results.

I watched silently as Mrs. Abreu showed Terri Hernandez her daughter's room and closet.

After rooting around for a minute, Terri pulled a shopping

bag out of the closet. She looked to Mrs. Abreu for approval. The middle-aged woman nodded, and Terri opened the bag. Inside was another bag, which held a long, flowing designer gown. She stood up and held the dress almost to her chin so it just barely cleared the floor. It was a dark green and looked like what someone would wear on a red carpet at the Oscars. It would make anyone look elegant. Especially someone like Estella.

Terri said, "When did Estella wear this?"

Mrs. Abreu took a tentative step forward. She reached out and felt the material between her thumb and forefinger. She focused on the dress for several seconds, then turned to Terri. "I have never seen this."

Terri took some photos of the dress, then carefully folded it and put it back in the bag. She left it in the corner of the closet.

Estella's mother had a vacant stare. It was like we weren't even in the room with her. Without hesitation, Terri wrapped her arms around Mrs. Abreu. The woman started to sob.

We stood in silence for minutes while Mrs. Abreu let out the emotion of the worst day she was ever going to have. Terri continued to hug her. When Mrs. Abreu recovered, we headed back into the main room, where her family had gathered. Everyone looked at us to make an announcement. Instead, I awkwardly eased toward the front door. Mr. Abreu acted as my escort as people parted to let us exit.

I left my card and told them we might have more questions and let them know it was okay to call me anytime.

Mr. Abreu stepped out, grabbed my arm. He said in a low, shaky voice, "Tell me, Detective. Who could do something like this to a beautiful girl like Estella?"

"I don't know, sir. But you can bet I'll do my best to find out."

Also By James Patterson

ALEX CROSS NOVELS

Along Came a Spider • Kiss the Girls • Jack and Jill • Cat and Mouse • Pop Goes the Weasel • Roses are Red • Violets are Blue • Four Blind Mice • The Big Bad Wolf • London Bridges • Mary, Mary • Cross • Double Cross • Cross Country • Alex Cross's Trial (*with Richard DiLallo*) • I, Alex Cross • Cross Fire • Kill Alex Cross • Merry Christmas, Alex Cross • Alex Cross, Run • Cross My Heart • Hope to Die • Cross Justice • Cross the Line • The People vs. Alex Cross • Target: Alex Cross • Criss Cross • Deadly Cross • Fear No Evil • Triple Cross

THE WOMEN'S MURDER CLUB SERIES

1st to Die (*with Andrew Gross*) • 2nd Chance (*with Andrew Gross*) • 3rd Degree (*with Andrew Gross*) • 4th of July (*with Maxine Paetro*) • The 5th Horseman (*with Maxine Paetro*) • The 6th Target (*with Maxine Paetro*) • 7th Heaven (*with Maxine Paetro*) • 8th Confession (*with Maxine Paetro*) • 9th Judgement (*with Maxine Paetro*) • 10th Anniversary (*with Maxine Paetro*) • 11th Hour (*with Maxine Paetro*) • 12th of Never (*with Maxine Paetro*) • Unlucky 13 (*with Maxine Paetro*) • 14th Deadly Sin (*with Maxine Paetro*) • 15th Affair (*with Maxine Paetro*) • 16th Seduction (*with Maxine Paetro*) • 17th Suspect (*with Maxine Paetro*) • 18th Abduction (*with Maxine Paetro*) • 19th Christmas (*with Maxine Paetro*) • 20th Victim (*with Maxine Paetro*) • 21st Birthday (*with Maxine Paetro*) • 22 Seconds (*with Maxine Paetro*)

DETECTIVE MICHAEL BENNETT SERIES

Step on a Crack (*with Michael Ledwidge*) • Run for Your Life (*with Michael Ledwidge*) • Worst Case (*with Michael Ledwidge*) • Tick Tock (*with Michael Ledwidge*) • I, Michael Bennett (*with Michael Ledwidge*) • Gone (*with Michael Ledwidge*) • Burn (*with Michael Ledwidge*) • Alert (*with Michael Ledwidge*) • Bullseye (*with Michael Ledwidge*) • Haunted (*with James O. Born*) • Ambush (*with James O. Born*) • Blindside (*with James O. Born*) • The Russian (*with James O. Born*) • Shattered (*with James O. Born*)

PRIVATE NOVELS

Private (*with Maxine Paetro*) • Private London (*with Mark Pearson*) •
Private Games (*with Mark Sullivan*) • Private: No. 1 Suspect (*with
Maxine Paetro*) • Private Berlin (*with Mark Sullivan*) • Private Down
Under (*with Michael White*) • Private L.A. (*with Mark Sullivan*) •
Private India (*with Ashwin Sanghi*) • Private Vegas (*with Maxine
Paetro*) • Private Sydney (*with Kathryn Fox*) • Private Paris (*with
Mark Sullivan*) • The Games (*with Mark Sullivan*) • Private
Delhi (*with Ashwin Sanghi*) • Private Princess (*with Rees Jones*) •
Private Moscow (*with Adam Hamdy*) • Private Rogue (*with
Adam Hamdy*) • Private Beijing (*with Adam Hamdy*)

NYPD RED SERIES

NYPD Red (*with Marshall Karp*) • NYPD Red 2 (*with Marshall Karp*)
• NYPD Red 3 (*with Marshall Karp*) • NYPD Red 4 (*with Marshall
Karp*) • NYPD Red 5 (*with Marshall Karp*) • NYPD Red 6
(*with Marshall Karp*)

DETECTIVE HARRIET BLUE SERIES

Never Never (*with Candice Fox*) • Fifty Fifty (*with Candice Fox*) •
Liar Liar (*with Candice Fox*) • Hush Hush (*with Candice Fox*)

INSTINCT SERIES

Instinct (*with Howard Roughan, previously published as*
Murder Games) • Killer Instinct (*with Howard Roughan*) •
Steal (*with Howard Roughan*)

THE BLACK BOOK SERIES

The Black Book (*with David Ellis*) • The Red Book
(*with David Ellis*) • Escape (*with David Ellis*)

STAND-ALONE THRILLERS

The Thomas Berryman Number • Hide and Seek • Black Market •
The Midnight Club • Sail (*with Howard Roughan*) • Swimsuit (*with
Maxine Paetro*) • Don't Blink (*with Howard Roughan*) • Postcard

Killers (*with Liza Marklund*) • Toys (*with Neil McMahon*) • Now You See Her (*with Michael Ledwidge*) • Kill Me If You Can (*with Marshall Karp*) • Guilty Wives (*with David Ellis*) • Zoo (*with Michael Ledwidge*) • Second Honeymoon (*with Howard Roughan*) • Mistress (*with David Ellis*) • Invisible (*with David Ellis*) • Truth or Die (*with Howard Roughan*) • Murder House (*with David Ellis*) • The Store (*with Richard DiLallo*) • Texas Ranger (*with Andrew Bourelle*) • The President is Missing (*with Bill Clinton*) • Revenge (*with Andrew Holmes*) • Juror No. 3 (*with Nancy Allen*) • The First Lady (*with Brendan DuBois*) • The Chef (*with Max DiLallo*) • Out of Sight (*with Brendan DuBois*) • Unsolved (*with David Ellis*) • The Inn (*with Candice Fox*) • Lost (*with James O. Born*) • Texas Outlaw (*with Andrew Bourelle*) • The Summer House (*with Brendan DuBois*) • 1st Case (*with Chris Tebbetts*) • Cajun Justice (*with Tucker Axum*)• The Midwife Murders (*with Richard DiLallo*) • The Coast-to-Coast Murders (*with J.D. Barker*) • Three Women Disappear (*with Shan Serafin*) • The President's Daughter (*with Bill Clinton*) • The Shadow (*with Brian Sitts*) • The Noise (*with J.D. Barker*) • 2 Sisters Detective Agency (*with Candice Fox*) • Jailhouse Lawyer (*with Nancy Allen*) • The Horsewoman (*with Mike Lupica*) • Run Rose Run (*with Dolly Parton*) • Death of the Black Widow (*with J.D. Barker*) • The Ninth Month (*with Richard DiLallo*) • Blowback (*with Brendan DuBois*) • The Twelve Topsy-Turvy, Very Messy Days of Christmas (*with Tad Safran*) • The Perfect Assassin (*with Brian Sitts*)

NON-FICTION

Torn Apart (*with Hal and Cory Friedman*) • The Murder of King Tut (*with Martin Dugard*) • All-American Murder (*with Alex Abramovich and Mike Harvkey*) • The Kennedy Curse (*with Cynthia Fagen*) • The Last Days of John Lennon (*with Casey Sherman and Dave Wedge*) • Walk in My Combat Boots (*with Matt Eversmann and Chris Mooney*) • ER Nurses: True stories from the frontline (*with Matt Eversmann*) • James Patterson by James Patterson: The Stories of My Life • Diana, William and Harry (*with Chris Mooney*)

MURDER IS FOREVER TRUE CRIME

Murder, Interrupted (*with Alex Abramovich and Christopher Charles*) • Home Sweet Murder (*with Andrew Bourelle and Scott Slaven*) •

Murder Beyond the Grave (*with Andrew Bourelle and Christopher Charles*) • Murder Thy Neighbour (*with Andrew Bourelle and Max DiLallo*) • Murder of Innocence (*with Max DiLallo and Andrew Bourelle*) • Till Murder Do Us Part (*with Andrew Bourelle and Max DiLallo*)

COLLECTIONS

Triple Threat (*with Max DiLallo and Andrew Bourelle*) • Kill or Be Killed (*with Maxine Paetro, Rees Jones, Shan Serafin and Emily Raymond*) • The Moores are Missing (*with Loren D. Estleman, Sam Hawken and Ed Chatterton*) • The Family Lawyer (*with Robert Rotstein, Christopher Charles and Rachel Howzell Hall*) • Murder in Paradise (*with Doug Allyn, Connor Hyde and Duane Swierczynski*) • The House Next Door (*with Susan DiLallo, Max DiLallo and Brendan DuBois*) • 13-Minute Murder (*with Shan Serafin, Christopher Farnsworth and Scott Slaven*) • The River Murders (*with James O. Born*) • The Palm Beach Murders (*with James O. Born, Duane Swierczynski and Tim Arnold*) • Paris Detective

For more information about James Patterson's novels, visit www.penguin.co.uk.